I0784480

SEVEN LITTLE KISSES

By,
Samantha Ferrand

Praise for
Seven Little Kisses

"Seven Little Kisses is a collection of forgotten diary entries plucked from my subconscious. Samaya's character growth is at once relatable, eye-opening and utterly gut-wrenching. Somehow, Ferrand crafts a coming-of-age story that all women have lived and endured and survived in one sense or another. The anecdotes are so nostalgic they're almost tangible, the throes of adolescence painfully familiar. Yet, somehow, Ferrand has stripped the veneer of our combined youth experiences and made them new, clearer, more decipherable. Ferrand takes your hand, points to the page and says: "look at it from up here. It's clearer when you're standing outside of it, looking in." Seven Little Kisses is a masterful story of growth, of self-discovery, of survival, and of the great enduring spirit of strong women."

— Stacey McEwan, author of *Ledge* and *Chasm*

"Samantha Ferrands writing transports you to a world about youth, love and fun while also delivering on heart wrenching feelings. If you loved movies like *Under The Tuscan Sun* or *P.S I Love You* then Seven Little kisses is for you."

— Amber V. Nicole, author of *The Book of Azrael*

"Seven little kisses is a delight of tender hearted moments, warm memories, and hard ones. It captures you from the first page and keeps you safely tucked close with a relatable commentary on girlhood, a tender romance, and how our experiences become pieces of who we are."

— Hannah Nicole Maehrer, author of *The Assistant to the Villain*

Copyright © 2024 by Samantha Ferrand

All rights reserved. This book or any portion thereof may not be reproduced or used in any manner whatsoever without the express written permission of the publisher except for the use of brief quotations in a book review.

<u>Content Warning</u>

Sexual Assault
Drug Abuse
Religion

For my mother, my namesake, and my muse.
I pity anyone who doesn't have the chance to stand in your light.
Thank you for believing in me when I didn't believe in myself.
Thank you for being the parent who stayed.

THE FIRST KISS

I

Mami woke me up that morning perched upon my half of our shared pullout bed with the news that Mr. Haas and his son, Isaac, had invited us out on another playdate. Mami accepted on my behalf.

Mami was excited. I was not.

I did not like Isaac. I did not like how loud he was in class, the bits of cookies that fell out the sides of his mouth when he ate, or the company he kept, running about the kindergarten playground as if they owned the land while I sat inside, playing with dolls alone. I knew I didn't need an invitation to join the rest of my classmates, but I felt unwelcome.

I sat on the sofa watching reruns of *Sex and the City* while Mami prepped for our date. The bathroom was a disaster of colorful powder, lipstick, and perfume I wasn't allowed to play with yet. I prayed the scent covered every inch of me; I needed its strength to get through the day ahead.

"Samaya, ¿dime la verdad?" she asked, shoulders lifting with nervous breaths as she blocked my view of Carrie running back to Mr. Big for the umpteenth time. Two hangers dangled in her hands. "Which blouse?"

Both options were slinky numbers leaving little to the imagination, but one was black and the other pink. I chose the latter as it looked like something Carrie Bradshaw might wear, and Mami always felt like a Carrie to me.

I hated Florida the moment we stepped off the plane from Peru. I hated the heat, the iguanas, the suffocating humidity, the kids who mocked my accent, and the way none of them had watched *Sex in the City*. I loved our apartment, our fortress, but Mami insisted on filling our moat with cement, lowering the drawbridge, and dragging me out to *play* with Isaac Haas.

Isaac moved to Florida the week after I did. He had a funny accent like me. But he didn't blend; he made waves, and the children praised him for being *unique*. I was just *different*. I hated how easily he swam through life while I only managed to tread. Mami pinned my hair up in butterfly clips to sweeten my sour mood. I didn't say a word the entire drive to the park.

"If you keep scrunching your face like that, it's going to freeze," she joked.

I held her hand tight as we walked over to meet the boys. I had no experience playing with kids my age; we never stayed put long enough for me to make friends. The idea of embarrassing Mami left a pit in my stomach, roots crawling up my neck, threatening to spew bile. I mimicked Mami, strutting across the parking lot with my shoulders pulled back and hips swinging wildly.

"Rebeca!" Mr. Willem Haas called out to Mami from across the parking lot. He was dressed sharply in a simple pair of jeans and a cream-colored blazer. He smiled at Mami, greeting her with a kiss on each cheek and a bouquet of wildflowers. Mami blushed and then he pulled one flower loose from the bouquet and presented it to me on a bent knee.

"Thank you for befriending my son, Samaya," his accent came from Poland, or Germany, or Denmark, or—

"Mr. Haas is from the Netherlands, *Tesoro*," Mami played with my hair, twirling it around her finger as I pressed tight to her hip. "He moved to the United States just like we did."

"But I've never had the opportunity to visit Peru," he smiled, still crouched beside me, but eyes focused upward at Mami. "You'll have to show me sometime."

I took the flower from his outstretched hand, twisting the stem between chipped, glitter-polished nails the size of corn kernels. It was a daisy. I liked daisies.

Isaac barely acknowledged that I'd stepped foot onto the playground. He hooted and hollered in a typical fashion. His slobbering lips spat raspberries into the wind like a jet propeller. Mami patted my back as she drifted toward a bench just on the outskirts of the sand pit. Willem's arm wrapped around the back of her seat, open and loose. Mami smoked a cigarette, shoulder digging into his while they leaned close to chat. I didn't know why, but it made me uneasy to see her like that.

I was three years old when she woke me up late one night, perched on my bed, with her finger held over my lips and our bags packed by her feet. We tip-toed through the house in our pajamas, slipped the car keys out of Papi's coat pocket, and drove off without the radio on. Mami wouldn't stop crying, but I wasn't sad.

The only memories I had of Papi were of him crying or yelling. Both of which he did too much of. He used to come by every week, and then it dwindled to every few months, and then the years faded into vacant birthday cards and clipped phone calls until there was no trace of him at all. But it was okay. I preferred it when he stayed away.

I sat on the swing set, palms wrapped around the rusted chains as I stared at the sand miles beneath my feet. I picked at the daisy, repeating words I saw a million times in movies. "He loves me, he loves me not…" I muttered.

It calmed my nerves to daydream about love. How nice it would be for someone to push me on the swings, arms kicking and hair blowing, just like in the movies. My boyfriend would be quiet and gentle. He'd reserve his tears for war wounds or confessions of the heart. Until then, I focused on the half-naked daisy and the love of plucking something beautiful apart until it was nothing. "He loves me…"

Flying in at the speed of light, arms flailing at his sides, Isaac knocked me out of the swing. I screamed for help before I even hit the dirt.

"Mami!" I wailed, dusting sand off my now dirty red corduroy skirt with a *Minnie Mouse* patch on the pocket now smeared in dirt. It was my favorite, and he'd wrecked it. I righted myself until the world settled while the little monster ran off toward the jungle gym, his mud-stained sneakers leaving tracks in his wake.

It took a second longer than it should have for Mami to reach me. She fluttered across the playground in kitten heels, pulling pieces of sand from the spots they shouldn't be. She laughed at the angry flush on my cheeks.

"Shh," Mami rubbed soothing circles into my back, pulling me close for a hug. *"Cálmate, Tesoro. No grites".*

"He pushed me!" I simmered, but my voice came out more

desperate than angry. I leaned into her embrace, breathing in her perfume, but my pulse wouldn't calm.

"Everything alright?" Willem's voice permeated my ears, but I didn't want to listen. "Sorry, sweetheart, Isaac doesn't know how to treat ladies yet."

"Can we have a moment?" Mami turned up toward him, a softness in her smile, but her tone was sharp. *I will speak to my daughter, not you.*

"You said you would watch me!" I cried, tearless sobs wracking through my chest.

"Well, now I am. Happy?" Mami snapped. My bottom lip wobbled; I stared at my sandy skirt, waiting for the shame to pass. Mami lifted my chin, eyes boring into mine as she planted seeds that would take a lifetime to weed out.

"How am I supposed to play if he keeps pushing me around?" I whispered.

"Mi Tesoro," she purred, smiling sweetly. "Don't you know boys only pick on you when they like you?"

She said it in English. She said it with confidence. She said it so that I wouldn't forget it.

"Por favor," she pleaded, wiping at the creases in her satin skirt. "Play nice." The adults walked back to their island bench while I stood frozen.

Isaac was only picking on me because he liked me.

The thought made my cheeks flush bright pink. I didn't want him to like me. He sat at the top of the monkey bars, staring down at me with a smile so wide I saw the gaps in his teeth. He pounded on his chest like a gorilla.

"Stop liking me!" I yelled, fists clenched at my sides, unaware that I had just smashed the naked daisy into oblivion. I turned over my shoulder, chin held high, ready to point my finger at his ridiculous display when I saw it happen. "Mam—"

Willem brushed a strand of hair off Mami's cheek. She let him, leaning closer as he kissed her. A weird, bitter feeling bubbled in my stomach, but the bile remained at bay. My eyes burned, and I let the tears cascade over my face.

"Hey," Isaac called out to me, dangling upside down off the bars.

Isaac and his father shared very few similarities in appearance. Where Willem had blonde hair and sun-chapped skin, Isaac had skin of umber with thick brown hair. Isaac had eyes like an owl only sweeter. Less knowing and more curious. I didn't mean to compliment him, but it was true. I stood at the base of the monkey bars, trying not to think about what would happen if I fell. Those owl eyes watched me settle onto the bars, a thin smile spreading across his cheeks. "It's okay. I was scared, too."

I sniffed, wiping my nose. "I want to go home."

He reached his hand out to me, and I was foolish enough to accept it. The moment I grasped his palm, shoes slipping off the bottom bars, Isaac let go of my grip, and I slammed into the unforgiving earth.

The sky above me was baby blue, with thick, fluffy clouds that reminded me of Isaac's hair. Everything in my vision spun, but I could hear Mami screaming my name somewhere far away. I hugged my throbbing knee tight to my chest, wailing at the pain, with my eyes shut tight.

"Samaya!" Mami screamed, scooping me into her arms and searching for signs of injuries. All she could find was a red splotch on my once-fresh white T-shirt where the gash on my knee had pressed too close. Mami lost all her softness and, in perfect English, called up at Isaac. "Isaac, get down here right now!"

I recoiled at the reproach in Willem's voice as he joined the chaos. Isaac rushed down the bars, shrinking behind his father's legs, but he never took his eyes off me.

"Hey, don't talk to my kid like that," Willem warned, jaw locking into place as his hands found purpose at his hips.

"Your *kid* just pushed my daughter."

"I see that, and I am sorry. But it's not your place to reprimand *my* son, Rebeca."

"Not *my* place? *¿Estás loco? Mira,* if you're not going to discipline him—"

"I'll deal with it," Willem cut her off with a dismissive wave. Mami scoffed. "Don't talk to me as if I'm a bad parent—"

Isaac approached me, leaving our parents to argue in the background. He crouched down and gently moved my hand away from my bloody knee. He bunched up the side of his jersey and dabbed at the blood, wiping the wound clean. Then, he kissed my knee, soft as a winter wind, wishing it better.

"I'm sorry," he murmured, eyes not meeting mine. "My hand

slipped."

"That's a girl!" Mami screeched, "Why doesn't he know how to treat a girl?"

"He knows how to treat a girl. He's just a child. He made a mistake."

Isaac smiled at me, and for some reason, I stopped crying.

Mami chain-smoked cigarettes on the way home, rambling promises with a determined look in her eyes. "I will never put you in a situation like that again. Do you hear me? *Nunca,*" she promised, and she meant it, but I was too lost in my thoughts to listen.

"Mami?" I asked, and she jumped at the chance to break the silence.

"*¿Si bebe?*"

"When did you fall in love with Papi?"

She took a drag of her cigarette while she mulled it over. "Immediately."

"When did you stop loving him?"

This time, she laughed, but there was no humor in it. She whistled, shaking her head while biting her bottom lip to keep from trembling.

"I didn't," was all she said, her words as breathy as the cigarette smoke filling her lungs.

"Why doesn't he visit us anymore?"

"I don't know," she snapped, blowing white smoke out the window. "I wonder the same."

"It's okay," I turned back toward the window. "Papi cried too much."

That caught her attention. She turned toward me as we came to a creeping halt at the stop sign. We were only five minutes away from the apartment, yet home felt like miles away.

"Samaya Ximena," Mami enunciated each letter of my name. I turned to look at her as she ashed the cigarette out the window, her eyes burning into mine. "*Never* trust a man who cries but won't change."

"Where's Isaac's mami?"

"I don't know." Mami shrugged. "They're getting a divorce. They don't live together anymore."

"Why doesn't Isaac live with her?"

"Because Willem is fighting to keep him," she said.

"Why didn't Papi fight to keep me?"

She didn't have an answer.

Isaac's Mami eventually won custody, and he moved away shortly after. We never spoke about that day in the park, and I never expected to see Isaac Haas, his gap teeth, or owl-bright eyes ever again. But life never plays out the way we expect.

THE SECOND KISS

I

"Samaya?"

Crap, I sighed, tucking my shoes up onto the closed toilet seat. "Just a minute, Mrs. Turner. I'm not, um, I'm not feeling well." The bathroom door creaked open, and I blushed at the sound of my gym teacher shuffling closer toward the stall I was hiding in.

I pulled my backpack off the floor and hugged my knees to my chest, curling into a ball. Maybe if I stayed quiet, she'd just go away. Or maybe I missed lunch block long enough for the teachers to worry about my stomach issues. Mrs. Turner stopped in front of the partition, shoes peeking through the gap at the bottom as if she could see me right through the door.

"That's funny, honey, because you seemed fine during gym class." Her southern voice crackled through each word with the kind of perception decades of teaching gave women like Mrs. Turner.

"I ate something funny," I countered.

"You ate something funny every day for the past week?"

She waited for a rebuttal, but I had none. "Honey, would you feel comfortable opening the door?"

I took a deep breath and undid the latch.

Mrs. Turner winced as she leaned against the partition. She was tall with gray eyes, gnarled hands that hurt when she jotted down notes, and a soft-tempered voice that barely carried across a court.

"It's not easy being the new kid," she said.

I rubbed the sleeve of my fleece jacket over the sweat piling up on my forehead. I shook my head but kept my eyes glued to the linoleum floor. No, it was not easy being the new kid. It seemed like everyone at St. Anthony's Catholic School foraged alliances back in kindergarten, and only war could disrupt them. Transferring from public to private school halfway through seventh grade only gave the others something to gawk at, not befriend.

"Honey, how long have you been eating lunch in the bathroom?" she asked.

All week, I thought. I hid my lunch box deep within my backpack. "I just ate something funny."

"Okay," she nodded with a slight disapproving shake of her chin. "Come with me. You need a nudge."

"No, thank you," I mumbled, but Mrs. Turner was already hauling me up and out of the girls' room with my backpack resting on her veiny arm.

She nudged me through the lunch hall, passing tables of laughing pre-teens in matching plaid skirts and ties, fighting over homework, and tying ribbons in their hair in the hopes a boy would rush over to tug on. I shrank further into my jacket, tugging the fabric past my bum, and prayed we would avoid the boys who found it funny to ask me about my cup size.

We did not.

Mrs. Turner nudged me into a single empty seat smack dab between the two groups of students I tried to avoid at every corner. The Beautiful People and the boys who drooled over them. I fought the urge to stomp on Mrs. Turner's shoes as she placed my backpack on the back of an empty plastic chair. I would rather get suspended for assaulting a teacher than sit with Katie DeMarco.

"Girls, this is Samaya Ximena," she pronounced the *X* with an exaggerated *H*, which she probably did to be culturally respectful, but just sounded like she was hissing at them. The eight girls stared back at us with vacant smiles and pursed lips, politely waiting to return to their conversation.

"She's our new transfer student for the seventh-grade class. Perhaps y'all can take her under your wing?"

"They don't need—" I stammered, but I was the only one in the equation no one acknowledged.

"Of course, Mrs. Turner," Katie smiled, hands folded neatly on the table. "So nice of you to think of us."

"Excellent! Have fun, girls." She patted me on the back, pulling out the chair for me to sit. The second Mrs. Turner left, the inquisition began.

"Why'd you transfer so late in the year?" Katie asked, her blonde hair pushed back behind her ears with hair gel and blue barrettes.

"My mom got a promotion," I smiled, pulling my lunchbox out of my backpack. It was the same *Hello Kitty* lunch pail I had since pre-school. I tried to cover the tell-tale drawing with my hand as I cracked open the lid. "I was on the waitlist, but a spot opened up—"

"That's cool," a brunette from my algebra class chimed in. "What does she do?"

"She works at a hotel on the pier—"

"She's a maid," Katie answered for me, taking a small fork full of her baked potato without meeting my gaze. "My mom met your mom in the spa, working as the maid."

"She was, but now she's the head of housekeeping—"

I tried to speak again, but the girls' changed directions with the ease and destruction of a tropical storm. The attention they gave me was now directed toward the center of the table, each of them whispering fervently in pig Latin, giggling as they realized I couldn't understand a word.

The moment we could afford it, Mami enrolled me in a private school on a scholarship. I liked the comforting stench of cigarette smoke wafting off our elderly Social Studies teacher's blazer and how it reminded me of home. I liked how we didn't just *talk* about *Romeo & Juliet* but performed it in class. I loved my teachers, but I hated the students.

The Beautiful People rolled their skirts above the knee with shimmering hair in shades of sunlight draped over thin limbs and flat stomachs. They gossiped with each other about which boys they found attractive and the stupid *Romeo & Juliet* presentation. I hated the way I stared at the other girls in the locker room, as if I could have transfigured my body to mirror their perfection. I prayed to the back of my locker they would ignore the soft flesh of my stomach as I changed into gym shorts that were a little too snug. That the girls would not see the tags of my Soffes, proving I was three times their size. I prayed my frizzy brown hair would magically soften or that they would at least stop commenting on how to fix it. How to flat iron my hair, what shampoo to avoid, or how to shave it all off and start fresh. The Beautiful People loved to remind me I wasn't beautiful.

I bit into a cracker just as a tiny piece of crumbled-up napkin plopped onto the table beside me. The girls giggled behind their palms, falling into each other as they stared above my head at the table of boys at my back. I did not want to turn around, but I knew I had to. It was not the first time they played this game, and it would not be the first time they saw me cry about it.

I reached a trembling hand onto my scalp and felt around for the pieces of paper I knew I would find. Their favorite game was to crumble ripped-up pieces of paper to see if it would stick in the frizz of my curls. Another fell beside me as the laughing increased, gaining more attention from nearby tables. Behind me sat a group of stoner boys with untucked shirts and ties hanging loosely around their throats. I turned too fast and accidentally took a paper ball to the forehead. The Beautiful People loved that, and the boys found their approval through throaty laughter. All but one, their leader Q, who was too busy chatting up a girl at the next table over to notice my ridicule and torment.

My eyes closed with a sigh as I gathered up my belongings before the tears spilled over. My knuckles went white, curling my fingernails deep into my palm. I refused to cry as I swatted the pieces of paper from my hair. I turned back around, facing my forgotten lunch, just as a boy shouted out, "What's your cup size?"

As I stood up, Katie leaned in close, a smile curving across her cheek, the kind reserved for puppies at the adoption center and not thirteen-year-old girls.

"You know, my neighbor had hair like yours once," Katie DeMarco levied over the table at me, hands folded in front of her and a soft smile curling at the edges of her rosy cheeks.

I looked up at her from furrowed brows, not realizing until then that I was slouching. I straightened and took the full weight of her examination with a raised chin.

"Oh?" I answered, unconsciously twirling my curls around one finger like Mami was prone to doing.

"Mhm," she nodded, fast and chipper. "But then she went through chemo, and it all fell out. She wears scarves now. *Super* pretty. You could do the same."

"Or just shave it," the brunette chimed in between sips of water.

"Yeah," Katie smiled, tilting her chin to the side as if waiting for me to clap back. But I did not. "That way, it'll all fall out, and you wouldn't have to worry about it anymore."

Katie DeMarco spoke as if she was offering me a gift. And if I ever got mad or fought back, they would cower in confusion, leaving me to look like the monster that raised her voice.

It was much easier to zip up my belongings and leave.

How stupid I felt whispering, "Thank you," as if we were old friends sharing beauty secrets.

II

I pushed through the double doors of the cafeteria and didn't stop running until I made it to the library. The first graders were usually resting on cots for naptime at that hour, which made it the perfect spot to read and cry without being noticed. I had become a regular. I learned to keep a copy of whatever book I was reading tucked away safely at the bottom of my backpack. While the little ones occupied the main carpet area, I went around the back of the stacks to the rectangular wooden tables lining the walls. I waved hello to the librarian, rearranging books in the history section as she motioned for me to '*keep it down*'. But someone was sitting in my spot.

The girl wore chunky over-the-ear headphones that matched the thick wool socks scrunched up by her ankles. I couldn't see her face buried behind the copy of *Twilight* by Stephanie Meyer, but I admired the glossy nature of her pitch-black bob and the rosary that poked through her blazer. It matched the one I wore beneath my button-up, and I just knew she'd bought it at *Hot Topic*. I stared down at her, trying to decide whether I should leave or continue to stand there like an idiot.

"I like your necklace," I said, coughing out my words like speaking was an accident. She peered at me, gave me a once over, and decided I was worth putting her book down for.

"Is that your first time reading *Breaking Dawn?*" She asked. Her shoulders shot forward as if she wanted to take the book from my hands and check the binding herself for evidence. I smiled.

"No, like… my fifth. I am going to see the movie this weekend with my Ma—" I blushed at the sound of my words, questioning if it was shameful for a thirteen-year-old to still hang out with her Mami.

I cleared my throat, "I'm doing a reread before the movie."

A shadow crossed over the girl's black, crescent eyes. "With your mom? That's cool. I'm Lila," she offered a hand up at me, her nails painted black with blue stars. I wondered if she'd ever let me borrow the polish.

"I know," I nodded, shaking her hand. "I mean—"

"I know what you mean. There are, like, thirty kids in our year. It's easy to connect their names and faces. Samaya. Why did you stop saying, Mom?"

"Oh," I huffed a laugh. "Well, because *Mami* sounds like mommy, which sounds kind of stupid in English, and I didn't want you to think I was…"

"I call my mom Omma. It's Korean. If I could, I would probably see *Twilight* with her too." She slid her headphones off her ears and laid back on the bean bag. "But she thinks vampires are the mark of the devil, so… yeah."

"I'm sorry," I muttered, worried I'd shoved my foot in my mouth. I almost walked away because I could tell the conversation was over and because Lila Park had a bit of a reputation around school. But I didn't want to. "Have you read the leaked *Midnight Sun* chapters?" I asked, and this time, she closed the book and gave me her undivided attention.

"You found them?" She asked.

I nodded, and she smiled like a cat sizing up a mouse.

"Oh, yeah! I couldn't sleep until I did."

"You can sit if you want." She scooched over on the bean bag for emphasis, making room for me to squeeze next to her.

I held my breath, arms tucked tight to my sides as I pressed close beside her. She returned to her book, clutching the spine with long fingers that curved around the pages like an old friend. I breathed out, easing into the cushions just as she launched out of nowhere, pretending to bite me like a vampire but stopping herself a centimeter away from my shoulder. I yelped, knocking myself out of the bean bag. She laughed so loud the librarians hissed. But the sound of her laughter undid the tension in my spine, and I couldn't help but laugh just as viciously.

"I'm sorry," she chuckled, leaning a hand forward to pull me back up. "That was weird." I took her hand, smiling ear to ear. It was weird, but it was the kind of weird thing I'd been dreaming of finding all my life.

I heard the name *Lila Park* whispered down every hallway around campus. To claim she was not beautiful would be a point of jealousy. She could have easily dethroned Katie DeMarco if she hung around campus long enough to try. It was true that Lila came from money and that her mother had been battling cancer for the better part of the past year. But the main points of focus on Lila's life were her many sightings at high school parties, smoking weed with boys behind closed doors, and the distorted recounts of what went on when the doorknob locked.

"You should sign up for the reading program," she said, gesturing to the sleeping first graders. "It gets you out of lunch for the first half, and then you're free to do whatever. Plus, it makes you look like the kind of person who reads to seven-year-olds for fun. Even if it is to get away from Katie and them."

"You're not friends?"

"She's Satan's seed. It's okay; she's my neighbor. I know for a fact that she hatched like that. She used to hang around my older brother, Lucas, all the time because she had this like, crazy big crush on him. Which was already weird, but then they kissed once, and she never went away. Literally. Her parents moved in when the Dutch family moved out. Carrot?" She offered me a stick from her backpack, and I accepted to be polite, but I didn't eat it.

"You lived next to Isaac?" I tried to keep my voice level, disinterested, but I'd be lying if I said I didn't think about that boy from time to time.

"Yeah, like a long time ago." She nodded. "Why? Were you two friends?"

"Sort of. Kind of." I muttered, flipping through pages in my book.

Lila smiled at my profile, biting the inside of her cheek. "Hm. I love sort of, kind of, friends. They're the most fun."

"Were... you... friends?"

"When we were babies? God, no," Lila cackled, leaning back onto the bean bag. A rough whispered, *shh,* came from the librarian in response. Lila hid her face in my shoulder as if that would save her from the older woman's wrath. "Not really. We're Facebook friends, but that's all. But his dad did leave us all their old DVDs. That was nice."

"You have Facebook?"

"You don't?"

"Why the hell would I need Facebook?"

"To stalk your sort of friend, Maya," she giggled, and I couldn't help but do the same.

Maya, I let the name mull about in my mind. It was the first time anyone had ever given me a nickname, and though it was new, it felt like I'd held the moniker my entire life.

I got the impression that if Lila took a deep breath, I'd find the need to breathe along with her. If she held her breath, I'd get comfortable with drowning. Such was her gravitational pull.

The school bell rang, and the sounds of first graders startling awake from their naps filled the air. Classrooms opened, students ran about the halls, and Lila Park busied herself with her backpack when I was just starting to feel comfortable in her presence.

"Hey, are you—" I started.

"Wanna hang out after school?" She finished, and that pattern became the foundation of our friendship. "You can show me *Midnight Sun,* and maybe I can find the DVDs from your sort of, *kind of,* friend. You know… if you care."

I blushed, hiding my face behind my loose hair. "It's not important—"

"Can we go to your house?"

"Of course," I smiled, filled to the brim with excitement at the fact that I organically planned a hangout with Lila Park. "My mom can pick us up!"

She hooked her elbow through mine and hauled me out of the library. Her skin brushed against mine like my favorite sweater, keeping me safe in the warmth of her company. She was a stranger, and yet I felt so comfortable falling into step beside her. She wore perfume with hints of sandalwood and peony, and her lips were coated in shiny pink lip gloss we weren't allowed to wear at Saint Anthony's. She smiled when she walked, her lips permanently turned upward with the joyous possibility of what lay before her. I could feel the eyes trained on her as we passed down the hallway, but her focus was all on me.

"And if you want, you can use my account to do some… light stalking," she winked at me, and I covered my gaping mouth with the back of my hand. "Only if you want."

"No, it's not like a big deal or anything. He was barely my friend. We weren't friends. At all. It's not a big deal. I don't even think about him. You just mentioned the Dutch family, and I thought, oh, wow, what are the odds—"

"Dude. Breathe," she laughed, wrapping her arm around my neck. "It's a crush. They're supposed to be fun!"

"Lila!" A girl wearing a pink headband waved over to Lila with a note in her hand and a worried look in her eyes.

"Oh, no, keep walking," she urged me on, practically skipping toward the parent pickup. There was no reason to hurry; Mami was always half an hour late when coming from work.

"Why? What's that about?" I asked, checking over my shoulder to see the girl's disheartened face as we blatantly ignored her.

Lila sighed, "It's nothing. Sarah Beth wants me to pass a note to this guy I'm friends with again, and it's getting sad."

"I thought crushes are supposed to be fun," I cringed, laughing to cover up the blush creeping up my cheek.

"No, no. Don't internalize that. *You* have a crush; *she* is chasing after a boy that does not want her. There's a difference. Does she look like she's having fun?"

No, I thought, *she did not.*

III

LILA PARK BECAME A fixture at our house. By Saturday, Mami chatted with Mr. Park so often about dietary restrictions, curfews, and week-night sleepovers that she kept his number saved in her contacts under *Lila's Appa.* We were meant to spend the night in. Smores were baking in the oven, flooding the home with rich chocolatey goodness. Mami rustled about in the kitchen, assembling goodies for us to savor as we worked our way through the box of DVDs Lila had brought over earlier in the week. The Haas' had eclectic tastes ranging from Disney cartoons to foreign films Mami wouldn't allow us to watch without her supervision. I liked those the most.

"You can keep them," Lila offered. I greedily accepted.

Lila scrolled through the leaked chapters of *Twilight* while I lounged out on my bed rereading *New Moon*, patiently waiting for her reactions.

"Oh, my God," Lila gasped, fingers clasped across her lips to keep her voice down. Her eyes glued to the screen as if she were living the words in real-time, "so, she was in danger from the moment he rolled into school?"

I slammed the book shut between my hands, not worried about los-ing my place. I had too many annotations throughout the binding for that to happen. "Exactly! He wasn't trying to be cruel when he left—"

"But it *was,* Maya," she called out to me, "I mean it makes sense now after watching it, but it was so hurtful! Pathetic! She just sat there for months!"

"He was trying to protect her from himself!" I screamed, and that made Lila roll her eyes.

Lila swiveled back to me, clearly heated. "Jacob protected her."

"Oh, puh-lease, Lila. He was a creepy pedophile who stalked her!" I slammed back onto the pillows. She gaped at me, waiting until I realized how hypocritical I sounded. I rolled my eyes, biting back laughter. "It was different when Edward did it!"

She swiveled back to the screen. "Whatever helps you sleep at night."

A moment passed, and we turned back to each other with mischievous smirks. "Edward would help me sleep at night," we said in unison, bursting into laughter.

Mami pushed open the door carrying two glasses of soda, one ginger ale and the other coke, a fruit tray, and a wide-eyed grin etched across her face. It was Saturday night, and Lila Park was hanging out at our house for the fifth time that week. It was hard to imagine weekends before her, and I never wanted to again. There was laughter in our home that did not come from the two of us, thick as thieves hidden away in our fortress.

How often had Mami worried about me cooped up alone in my room? I stopped counting all the times I came home from public school crying because some boy on the bus called me names. To us, Lila Park was a God send. If it were up to Mami, we would trade my bed for bunk beds and invite Lila to move in.

"¿Cuáles son los planes para esta noche?" Mami flopped onto the bed beside me, a casual arm draped beneath her head as she entered our pre-teen world.

"We're having a read-a-thon," I said, munching on a grape.

"¿Que?"

"Lila's reading one book, I'm reading the other, and then when we're done, we're going to read the sequel together at the same time." Lila was too fixated on the computer screen to register Mami's vacant expression. I did a double take, confused by the borderline glare she sent my way.

"Ay, no. Samaya, come on! *Es une sábado.* You need fresh air. *No fuerces a tu amiga a leer."* She whispered as if reading were a hate crime.

"I'm not forcing her!" I whined, arms crossed, full of reproach. She opened her mouth to argue further but was cut off by the sound of Lila's voice.

"We could go see *Twilight.*"

"But we already saw it last night," I shook my head, eyes falling toward the ticket stubs I kept displayed on my nightstand.

Lila's eyebrows creased, "And you wouldn't wanna see it again?"

I attempted to form words but found none. I hated how Lila locked eyes with me, but I hated it even more when I broke away first.

"Beautiful!" Mami hopped off the bed, adjusting her blouse until the creases loosened. "I'm going to go fix my hair and we can make it out of here in ten."

"But—"

"*¡Samaya, cepilla tu cabello!*" She instructed before running down the hall to her bedroom.

"I already brushed my hair!" I hollered back, but it didn't matter. I caught a glimpse of myself in the reflection of the full-length mirror hanging off the back of the door. Baby hair haloed my face in a frizzy mess. I tried to smooth them down with the sweat of my palms to no avail. I discarded the book to reason with the back of Lila's head. "Dude, what's going on?"

"How likely is it that we can ditch your mom at the theater?" Lila asked, still focused on the screen. Her fingers floated over the keyboard at rapid speed.

"Very unlikely, and why?"

"Because Bryce and them want to meet up with us."

"No, Lila. Your sort of boyfriend doesn't want to meet up with us. He wants to see you."

"Really? So, why'd they ask if you were coming?"

"Bullshit," I snorted, but there it was, clear as day. My name written across the screen. I was too scared to scan through the chat. My cheeks grew hot, and all I wanted to do was climb back into bed, put on a movie, and call it a night. But it was only seven o'clock, and Lila looked excited. She looked determined, and I didn't know how to tell her it felt like a bad idea.

"What's wrong?" Lila asked, chin resting on her fist as I stared at the posters on my walls.

"Nothing, I just thought we were hanging out."

"We are. Why can't we hang out with them?"

"Because they're not my friends," I shook my head, fisting my hands into the pockets of my sweatpants.

"Samaya, you don't have friends."

The honesty of the comment made me sigh out a high-pitched whistle.

She backtracked, hands held up in defense. "You're new. How are you going to make friends if you don't try?"

"You told me they're all shit and not worth the try," I spat, sitting on my bed with my knees pulled tight to my chest. I felt dizzy and sipped ginger ale like a hospital IV.

"The guys are a vibe. Promise." She turned back to the computer at the sound of a *ping*.

"How? How are they a vibe?"

Lila giggled at some one-word acronym I didn't understand. The truth of the matter was that while I developed early in life, Lila did not. She had a thin frame, thick skin, and came alive under introspection. It was almost as if she grew lovelier the more you had to think about it. The only time those guys paid attention to me was to ask about my cup size. Later in life, I'd realize those boys were sexually harassing me, but they never would.

"They're just pieces of shit," Lila rolled her eyes, shaking her head at the silliness of men. "Totally harmless. You just need to ignore them, and they'll stop."

"Lila—"

"Don't make me go alone," she pouted, lip playfully trembling like a wounded puppy. "I'll miss you too much."

"Don't go!" I flopped back onto the bed and picked up my book.

"Fine, then I'll just tell Q you're not coming." Lila knew how to pique my interest.

"Q did *not* ask about me, Lila. That is a bold lie."

"Oh, really? Read it. Come here. Don't be shy. Look, he asked Bryce to ask me if you were coming."

Hook. Line. Sinker.

"I've never spoken to him," I said.

She scoffed, already getting up to scavenge through my closet. "You don't need to speak to him. You're pretty, and he clearly noticed."

"You think I'm pretty?" I whispered, my cheeks flushing with heat.

Lila turned to me with soft eyes and a crooked expression, "Don't you?"

"*Chicas,* five minutes!" Mami called out to us from down the hall, and my throat closed shut at the ticking clock forming at the back of my head. I tried to think of reasons to end the night early but found none.

"Let me guess, you're not allowed to go without me," I reasoned.

Lila threw a couple tops onto my bed, nodding along. "True, but I could sneak out and say I slept over. But I'm not, because I want you to come."

"I'm not allowed to date," I muttered, staring at the cover of my *Taylor Swift* debut album CD, wondering if this was how she felt right before hanging out with Drew for the first time.

"Whoa, it's not a date."

"But Bryce is your boyfriend—"

"Sort of," she corrected, checking out her denim mini skirt and Abercrombie t-shirt in the full-length mirror. I looked down at my body, wondering if I should change. "He's sort of my boyfriend, so let's not make that mistake in front of him."

"But—"

"Dude, what?" She snapped.

I stammered, looking up at her with shame. "I don't want to look stupid."

Lila shoved skinny jeans and a button-up into my clenched hands. "Put this on. Give me your hairbrush. And chill."

"What are you looking for?" I asked as she opened every drawer of my desk.

"Gel."

"It's in the bathroom," I pointed down the hall, but Lila smiled, turning back to me like a little league coach.

"You're meeting up with friends. Friends who invited you to hang out. If you think you sound stupid, don't talk, and keep breathing. But you don't, they do. Just laugh, breathe, and I promise you'll have a good time."

I didn't like the idea of rejecting the first opportunity I had for something different. What if it never came back around? What if I resigned myself to a million nights in, reading *Twilight* for the mil-lionth time, and what if there were no friends to sit at my computer gushing over vampires with me?

"Two conditions. One, don't ditch me. Please."

"Maya," she sighed, perfectly at ease in her body. "It's a movie theater. Where would I even go?"

"Promise," I commanded, sticking out my pinky for emphasis. She accepted immediately.

"I promise, what's the second condition?"

"Mami can't find out."

IV

Lila fussed over my hair for a solid ten minutes, fixing me with a tight, gelled-back ponytail that could take an eye out. We blasted Juanes the entire drive over to the movie theater. Mami and I sang *fotographia* so often that even Lila, who could barely speak Korean with her own parents, knew all the lyrics.

The night peaked there.

I reached for the volume the second we pulled up outside the theater and turned it all the way down. I had a speech planned and knew exactly when to broach the change of plans with Mami. But every time I opened my mouth, no words came out. I meant to tell her in the kitchen but shoved smores in my mouth instead. I meant to say something in the car, but the music was too good to overpower with bad news.

I'm growing up, I'd tell her, *and it's time for me to go out alone.*
She'd understand.
It would be calm, rational, and mature.

But, alas, she did not pull up to the curb as planned because there was no line wrapped around the building this evening like there was for the *Twilight* midnight premiere. Mami pulled right into a parking spot in the front row, too fast for me to collect my bearings, and my throat constricted the moment she unbuckled her seat belt.

"What are you doing?" I spat out, eyes wide and cheeks flushed.

Mami looked understandably taken aback. She hated conflict, most of all with me. "I'm going to go buy the tickets," she said, and I could see the irritation hidden behind her ear-to-ear smile.

"Um, thank you," I swallowed, trying to navigate how to decline her company in a way that wouldn't hurt her or make her suspicious.

"But I… can… do that."

The silence that followed felt so foreign it sent a chill down my spine. The wrinkles along her eyebrows furrowed in either confusion, hurt, or a mixture of the two. I cleared my throat. *Run,* the voice inside my head commanded, *this is a trap.* But I wanted tonight to happen. I wanted all of it.

Mami turned toward Lila in the back seat with a sweet curve of her lips. "Lila, why don't you go ahead and save our spot in line?" She asked, and Lila wasted no time complying. I started to unbuckle my seat belt, but the full power of Rebeca Ximena's voice parked me dead in my seat. "Samaya Renee Ximena. *¿Qué pasa, Tesoro?* Why are you acting like this?"

I stared out past the windshield wondering where the guys might be lurking, and if they could see me now, scolded like a mouse caught in the kitchen.

"Samaya," she ordered.

"I want to see a movie with my friends," I grumbled, slumping down in my seat as if I could evaporate into the humidity. *Lila's friends,* being the unspoken meaning.

"*Pues,* so do I."

"Well, we can rent one together tomorrow night."

Mami nodded, gripping the steering wheel and trying to swallow the fact that I was no longer the little girl plastered to her thigh, begging not to get dropped off at school. I was a blood-sucking, soulless teenager, breaking her heart. "How do you plan on paying for the tickets?" In answer, I pulled out a birthday card from a couple of years back with money stuffed inside. She just laughed, pinching the bridge of her nose. "No, Samaya, save your money."

"I don't need your money. I got it," I grumbled.

"Oh, don't worry. When you make it in life, you can buy me my Louis or Gucci—"

"So, what? You're upset with me because I don't want to take your money?"

There was this hideous tone coating all my words, but I couldn't stop it.

"*Oye, ¿Qué pasa?*" Mami's voice was a step away from anger. "What's gotten into you?"

"Nothing," I spat. "It's just hot."

"So, take off your jacket."

"I don't want to," I hissed, teeth grinding. My eyes focused everywhere but hers.

"Samaya, you will feel better with it off. Or do you want to complain? *Solo para que sepas,* my mother never let me go out alone. Especially not at thirteen. She didn't even let me cross the street without one of my friends holding my hand!" Mami laughed, but there was none of the usual mirth between us. She hated being cross with me. She hated raising her voice or saying no, but she also cared for me. Sometimes, caring came in the form of denial. I never thought I would resent her for it.

"Yeah, but you got expelled for hosing down your principal because she wouldn't let you hop on a bus with your friends on a class field trip. So, I think the standard of security can be a little different."

She sat there in silence. She did not raise her voice. What she did was far scarier. She closed her eyes, chewed on the inside of her cheek, and exhaled a deep breath as if she wanted to throttle me. But she did not. That was Papi's form of conflict resolution, not hers.

"Mírame," she ordered, and so I did. I turned in my seat, actively trying not to flinch at the suspicion in her hazel eyes. "Are you meeting boys?"

She said it in English. She said it coated in disappointment. She said it so that I had the opportunity to correct it.

I lied through my teeth.

"What?" I shrieked, my hands flying in different directions as if evading an attack. "Mami, what are you talking about?"

She nodded, smile gone and eyes cold. "Then why are you sweating?"

"Because it's humid," I yelled. But Mami's voice remained calm.

"Then take off your jacket—"

"I don't want to take it off. I like my jacket. I feel comfortable in my jacket, and I don't like how I look without it so please, stop!" I was yelling, and I knew I was being mean. I could feel the tears burning at the back of my eyes, and I wanted nothing more than to choke them down. "I'm not like you. People don't notice me when I talk. They ignore me. Years from now, no one is going to pull out their yearbook and say, 'Oh, wow, you were so pretty! You must have been so cool with so many friends!' They'll ask me where the hell are all my photos in the yearbook. Please. Can't you understand that?"

Can't you spot armor when it's sitting right in front of you?

"Samaya, you are my daughter," she said. "You look exactly like me."

I shook my head. "No, I don't."

Every night, I laid awake praying that I'd grow into my nose, my body, and look more like Mami. Every morning, I woke up, looked in the mirror, and realized that the face staring back at me would never look like Rebeca Ximena. I looked just like Papi. Mami knew it was true, and she didn't press the detour further. But she did put the fear of God in me.

She leaned forward. "All you have in life is your reputation. Once it's gone—," Mami snapped her fingers. The noise made me jerk uncomfortably in my seat. "You're done."

Mami slipped a crisp twenty-dollar bill from her purse and handed it over to me. "I'm trusting you." She pulled me close and pressed a kiss to my forehead. I didn't pull away.

After a moment of silence, I took the money and whispered, "Thank you," as I hopped out of the car. The air felt better once I closed the door behind me.

"I'll be waiting over at the ice cream shop when you're done, okay?" She called to me through the passenger window, and I nodded. "*¿Y Samaya?* When someone yells, it's because they know they're wrong. You understand?"

"Yes, Mami," I said, hands digging into my pant pockets.

"Okay. Now, go buy some popcorn and have fun," Mami smiled. I did the same.

After she left, I toyed with the idea of unzipping my jacket just to get a bit of air. But then I heard my name. Lila was waiting in line, watching from afar for Mami's car to disappear from the parking lot. Once it did, she immediately ran out of line, motioning for me to follow her. She was already halfway toward the back alley of the theater when I caught up to her.

V

Lila defined ditching me as disappearing without a trace. I knew exactly where she was; therefore, Lila had not ditched me. She merely walked ahead of me to join the group. But my legs were lead weights, and I couldn't figure out how fast was *too* fast to run through the back alley of the movie theater.

I needed to face them. I needed to stop feeling small in the face of their opinions. I needed to stop hiding behind a cement wall, waiting for a disgruntled employee in a colorful vest, flashlight in hand, to come around and break up the party.

No one came. No one cared.

Those boys carried themselves through life as if they were untouchable, and so they became untouchable. Laughter buzzed in my ears. I made a silent prayer to the sunset, dipping below the strip mall next door so that the thick stench of weed wouldn't leave a trace on my clothes. I refused to be the person who spent the night with their back against a wall.

Their names were Bryce, Keenan, and Q.

They laughed over a joke I did not understand, but I smiled as if I did. All three boys wore different variations of the same outfit: skinny jeans, bloodshot eyes, and black oversized zip-up jackets with a bit of their individual personality peeking through the artwork embedded on the back. Q was the first to make eye contact with me at the edges of the group, but Keenan was the one who said hello.

"Lila! Your friend showed," Keenan bounced in his shoes like a golden retriever, baby blue eyes crinkling as he took a lighter from Q's outstretched hands. The artwork on his back belonged to my favorite anime, but instead of pointing it out, I shrugged and said, "Hey."

Bryce was the tallest of the group, but you couldn't tell from the way he hunched over Lila, slobbering all over her as if she were his favorite bone. I had not interacted with him much at Saint Anthony's, but what I gathered was he had a severe dependency on Adderall, clearly didn't own a belt from the way his pants hung off his hips, and had a desperate need to touch Lila, wherever and whenever. She pulled away long enough to link arms with me, making me a permanent fixture in the circle.

"You smoke?" Q asked, scooping the tobacco out of a Black & Mild cigarillo.

Q was infamous for disrupting class by asking ridiculous questions.

"Where does Africa get its name?" He asked the gym coach.

"Can you explain photosynthesis?" He asked the art teacher.

"What are the birds-and-the bees?" He asked the priest, leaving the old man blue in the face.

I hated to admit it, but I woke up looking forward to science class every morning. I daydreamed about him catching me laughing at his jokes, and he'd think I was cool enough to talk to. Maybe befriend. Then, one day, he'd wake up thinking of me, too. Q was a celebrity in our world, and I was a fan. He wasn't conventionally attractive or even had similar interests to me. I liked him because he didn't like me. He didn't like anybody. But in the alley, he smiled at me.

When he finished wrapping the blunt, he licked the edges clean and offered it to me between two fingers. It took me a moment to realize he was offering it to me to smoke and not just appraise.

I shook my head. "Oh... uh, no. I don't do weed. But I'm like, down with... the culture of it," I pantomimed the word 'culture' with a hand wave. *What the hell was I doing?*

Q slipped the blunt between his lips, his cheeks curving into a smile as he leaned into the premature spark of Keenan's lime green lighter. "The fuck?" Bryce half coughed. I wanted to throw up the moment they started laughing, but I kept it together.

Lila immediately swatted at him to "back off."

"You don't 'do' weed. You smoke it," Q clarified.

"Okay," I shrugged.

"You don't fuck it or inject it into your bloodstream. You can't 'do' it." He laughed, pleased with his quip, as he passed the blunt to Bryce, who inhaled hard and blew the excess smoke directly into Lila's open mouth.

"It's called shotgunning," she explained with a twisted smile, droopy eyelids, and a flick of her wrist as if it were no big deal.

"Sure," I nodded. "Well… I don't, and I won't. So, I think I'm okay with semantics. We're going to miss the trailers—"

"Are you in my homeroom class? You look so familiar," Q asked, smoke billowing out of his lips. I snorted a laugh, confused by his question, but he looked genuinely serious.

"Um, no. We have science together." *Where your friends throw pieces of paper in my hair,* I thought, *where you sit back and laugh.*

A moment of understanding flashed before his eyes, but not long enough to matter.

"You're in Mrs. Green's homeroom, right?" Keenan asked.

"Yeah," I replied.

"Oh, that's a sweet deal. I wish I started with English. We're in Fuentes." He motioned toward Q, shaking his chin.

"Yeah," I nodded, "but, but I kind of like how formulaic algebra can be."

Why did I say that when I'm one test away from failing Mr. Fuentes' algebra class?

I wanted him to think I was cool, smart, and lean into the nerdy opinion he already had of me. I used words like *formulaic* and sighed at the sight of Keenan nodding his head as if he felt the same way. Q cleared his throat, placing his weight on one hip as he leaned closer to me. "The next time you see Mrs. Green, tell her I say hi. She loves me."

She did not.

"Bullshit!" Lila called out, waving a finger in the air, scolding him. "You never once showed up to class, and when you did, you were a dick about it! This all happened before you transferred, Maya." That she added for me, smiling intently, and I felt myself smiling back.

Q held a hand up to his chest. His movements were slower and more pronounced being stoned. "Barbara and I are best friends."

Bryce snorted at the claim and countered with, "Because you were a kiss ass!"

The rest of us laughed, shifting into easy postures and open hands. I envisioned myself walking down the hallway past each of them and calling out nicknames or inside jokes that tethered us back to this easy night. My shoulders dropped in utter relaxation during the roast of

Q. I wondered if this was what friendship felt like? Bryce fed off our reaction, angling his body away from Lila and toward the rest of us. "This fuck skipped class every day last semester to go to the 'bathroom'. Who goes to the bathroom for a full hour? But when the rest of us failed the final, he passed! Like what is that about?"

Bryce passed me the blunt, but again, I shook my head, so he passed it to Keenan who cranked up the music on the portable speaker he kept hidden in his pocket. I checked both ends of the alley, but still, no one came to interrupt them.

Us, I mentally corrected. *No one came to interrupt* us.

"I don't know, man, people just like me," Q shrugged, directing the full weight of his attention on me. I swallowed hard, and Lila shifted her attention back to Bryce. The lack of her presence made me feel oddly alone with this boy even though we were surrounded by his friends. His confidence unnerved me. He had oily blond hair and acne, yet he carried himself like the next cover story for GQ. Maybe that's why he always managed to have a girl on the hook.

"Or maybe you're just a memorable douchebag," I mumbled, and the circle went cold, waiting for his reaction. His tongue flicked the corner of his mouth, sizing me up. He nodded, his lips pulling at the side with a gleam in his cold, brown eyes.

Then Bryce cried out a great big, "Ohhhhh!" And the tension disappeared into applause.

He took the second puff of the joint and gave me a once-over that made my stomach lurch and toes curl. His eyes lingered on my chest a split second longer than I cared for. But I didn't exactly know what to say or do about it. And so, I ignored it.

"I like your hair," Q nodded, tugging lightly on the end of my ponytail. I swallowed so hard I could've sworn people turned to stare.

Keenan cleared his throat, checked his watch, and edged toward the emergency exit door. "Look, I'm not missing the opening credits. I'll just meet y'all inside." The group barely said goodbye as he vanished into the theater, leaving the four of us alone under the red glow of the neon exit sign.

The moment Keenan left, the energy shifted. With the click of the door frame locking into place, electricity prickled the air, and I had the distinct impression that this was how prey felt out in the wild.

Lila didn't seem bothered by the change. If anything, she relaxed into it. Expected it. Her neck pressed deep into Bryce's collarbone as his arms wrapped around her stomach. I had no idea there'd be so much tongue utilized while kissing.

Q nudged me with an elbow, swaying on his heels as he peered at me down the bridge of his nose. I looked up at him, trembling. He leaned into my ear, axe body spray radiating off his skin as he whispered, "You're cute when you're nervous."

A cold sweat crept across my body. Bile pushed up my throat, but I coughed it down, opening my mouth to ruin the moment. "Are Katie and them coming?" The name caught Q off guard, but only for a moment.

"What?" He asked, eyebrows pinched and a smirk playfully displayed across his thin lips.

Bryce fell silent for the first time all night.

"I just... remember her saying... you were her boyfriend. So... I just assumed she would meet us...?" Katie had never said anything to me, but their relationship was a point of common knowledge in the hallways. Pictures of him covered her Facebook, not to mention they spent science class sitting shoulder to shoulder.

What if he was my boyfriend? I thought. *How would he act then?*

Q shook his head as if he knew no one by the name of Katie. "Uhhh, cool, if that's what she's saying. Why would I invite you if I had a girlfriend?"

"Lila invited me."

Q wrapped his arm around the small of my back, taking a drag off the joint in his hands before blowing the smoke out of his nose. The act was mesmerizing. He held the joint out to me once again. Not pushy or forceful, just an open invitation.

"My mom would crucify me."

"She'll never find out," and for some reason, I believed him.

"What's the point?" I asked, taking the blunt from his fingers with fumbling hands.

Q shrugged, "experience."

I mirrored the way he smoked, taking too deep a breath and choking it all up in big gasping coughs. Bryce couldn't contain his laughter. Lila smacked him on the arm. This time, it wasn't playful.

"Fuck yourself," Lila hissed.

"Sounds good," Bryce moved to unbuckle his belt while Lila flipped him off. I decided that boyfriends shouldn't act like Bryce, either.

Q pushed a hair out of my face, and I immediately tensed up. My chest burned while my mind spun like a merry-go-round. I needed a change of subject.

"Do people ever call you Tarantino?" It was a genuine question, no matter how random it may have seemed to him.

"What?"

"Yeah, like...Q, like... *Pulp Fiction, Reservoir Dogs...* Tarantino?" I did a little nervous dance with my hands like a 1940s gangster with every word. Q smiled. I liked it when he smiled at me.

"Ahhh, the Nazi guy. Sweet."

"Yeah... whoa, my head hurts," I whimpered, clutching at my forehead, but no one seemed to care. Bryce was already prying open the exit door while Q hid the rest of the blunt in his pocket. Bryce motioned for us girls to follow. But I didn't. I waited for the boys to step inside, and then I latched on to Lila's hand.

"Let's go home," I begged.

But Lila simply gave me a reassuring look. "It's easier if you go with it," she whispered, squeezing my hand. I was no longer the kind of person who stood outside alone. The firm sound of a metal door slammed shut behind us, closing off the last patch of light.

VI

The theater was packed by the time we made it inside. Lila and Bryce fled to the vacant back row while I followed Q toward two empty seats nestled up against the wall at the end of a cramped lineup of boys I usually avoided at school. His friends greeted him as we passed, standing tall and uncaring if they blocked the screen. I hunched over and whispered apologies on his behalf. A disgruntled audience member yelled for us to keep quiet. Q faced the blinding projector light with a handheld over his heart.

"My bad," he hollered back.

Asshole, I thought, suddenly struck by déjà vu. I thought of another boy who floated through life with owl eyes, royal confidence, and a gap-toothed smile. I wondered how much of his self-assurance came naturally and how much was a poor imitation of the protagonists in the DVDs he left behind. I imagined what it might be like if he never moved away and if he'd be sitting in this theater with me, praising Q or rolling his eyes. I remembered the look on his face after he kissed my knee, my cheeks flaring red in the memory. It made me smile to think of him. Maybe one day, I'd find him again burning his way through the world.

Keenan offered me popcorn when I settled beside him. I took a few pieces and mouthed, "Thank you."

Q made his way to the empty seat on my right, flopped onto the fabric with a huff, and made sure the chair creaked as he settled in. "Thanks, dude," he said, grabbing the tub of popcorn from Keenan's hands before placing it directly into my lap. He took a handful of pieces and shoved them into his gaping mouth all at once, chewing loudly.

"Keep it," I whispered, gently passing it toward Q, but he just shook his head and continued taking pieces from my lap.

On screen a comedy played with no sign of Bella, Edward, or the Wolf Pack. But I did spot one of my all-time favorites: Stanley Tucci. He played a dad who spent his time cooking cozy meals alongside his wife and gifting comical yet timely advice to his children. I liked to call those scenes 'free therapy' for those of us who grew up without a father.

I was a bit more generous with my laughter than the boys beside me, but the laughter coming from behind us stole my attention. I didn't want to look, but a warm spot in my stomach made me.

The Beautiful People occupied the row behind us. More importantly, Katie Demarco sat directly behind my head. Her summer blond hair casually tousled to the side while her manicured fingertips dug into the small popcorn corn bag she and her cohorts shared. They giggled amongst themselves, throwing glances my way, but Katie did not. Katie focused on the screen, but it didn't seem like she was watching the movie.

I unzipped my jacket just a bit, slipping the fabric down so it sat just around my elbows. The cool air felt incredible on the nape of my neck. I'd been sweating for so long that I was positive there'd be stains to prove it.

Q's arm folded around the hood of my jacket, fiddling with the hem. He took my state of undress as an invitation that I was getting comfortable. And I was. It felt nice to catch him appraising my face, the slight curve of his mouth as he smirked at me, and ice-cold shivers ran down my spine as he took my hand.

"Aww," he mumbled, lips forming an endearing smirk. "You're shaking."

His fingertips grazed the side of my cheek, brushing back a bit of hair that was matted due to the humidity. I didn't like him touching my hair. It felt too intimate.

He inched closer, eyes closing, and it was then that I realized I was not ready. I needed a distraction. I took a handful of popcorn, shoved it in my mouth, and hollered, "LOOK, STANLEY TUCCI!"

It was loud, and people stared, but I did not care. I focused on the popcorn in my lap and the man himself dazzling us from the screen. "I just love him, don't you?" I whispered, chewing away like a madman.

"Stanley Cucci?" Q giggled.

"Stanley *Tucci*," that time the name hit the air in double. Keenan and I exchanged a glance of recognition before he turned back to the movie. It was too hot now, and I decided to abandon the jacket altogether, taking it off and placing it flat on my lap.

I heard a throat clear, and then I heard a word I didn't think would ever apply to me. Over my shoulder, one of the Beautiful People coughed the word *"whore,"* followed by a row of delicate laughter. I wasn't sure if they meant me, but when I turned around to investigate, I found Katie, arms wrapped tight and protective around her chest, while her ice blue eyes glistened in the glow of the movie screen. She was crying.

I felt a tap on my shoulder and turned to find Q leaning in close, smiling and clearly flattered by my erratic behavior. "Why are you so nervous?"

I couldn't stop thinking about the fact that I still slept with my childhood plushies while he dissected my body. I guess no one is ever ready; sometimes we all just go with it. Should I tell him to clean the crust from the corners of his lips? They're a bit thin, aren't they? If I moved even the slightest bit, our noses would touch, and my skin would melt off my body. I didn't fight it when he kissed me.

Our teeth clattered together in awkward motions. I didn't know whether to open my mouth or staple my lips shut. My heart beat like a jack hammer while his remained steady. He felt my body closing off and pulled back. He smiled at me, then he guided me to lean into his shoulder, wrapping his hand tight around my shoulder. My sweaty palm gripped the edge of the arm rest dividing our chairs.

Just as quickly as it started, it ended, and it felt like… nothing. Just two people whose faces touched one night and nothing more. It was not like my books, but I didn't think it was supposed to be. It wasn't earth-shattering. It was just… kind.

The Beautiful People were not.

Q was the first to notice the popcorn kernel in my hair. He handed it to me, and the moment the attack became known, the girls burst into laughter. They threw handfuls of popcorn paired with a coughed *"whore,"* in case I forgot the cause of my punishment.

Q turned over his shoulder and flicked a kernel at Katie's face. But she wasn't the one who threw the popcorn; she just sat there crying and staring at the screen. He even added a little air kiss and a douchebag wink to match. He leaned back into me, only this time his hands found perch on either side of my face, and it was not kind when he kissed me again. I didn't open my mouth, but his tongue found its way past the barrier of my teeth.

It felt like choking, and I wanted it to stop. But it didn't because I was finally fulfilling my true purpose of the night. I was a prop in his show, and I had enough.

I bit down hard on Q's tongue, and he howled in pain. The chorus of 'whore' bellowed louder. I could hear the people hissing from the crowd to shut up, but I did not move. Katie reached into the popcorn bucket and tossed a handful directly at my head as I stood to face.

I reached over across the aisle, snatched the bucket from her hands, and threw it hard against Q's head. The chanting stopped in place of shock. But it wasn't because of me or the fact that Q screamed, "bitch!"

The crowd stopped chanting the minute Lila poured soda on the Beautiful People, standing triumphantly behind their row with an empty cup in hand and five soaking wet teenagers angry as all hell beneath her.

"He's the whore," Lila called out. "Not her."

Katie rolled her eyes, wiping Coca-Cola from her brows. "I've seen your nudes."

It may have been the weed, but time snapped into hyperdrive the moment Katie spoke. The house lights came on as The Beautiful People chanted 'whore' once more, only this time it was directed toward Lila and I. If not for me holding Lila back, she would have mauled Katie in the middle of the theater. The movie paused on screen. An usher practically dragged us out of the audience, kicking and screaming.

I would do it all again in a heartbeat.

VII

WE STUMBLED INTO THE night air, shivering from the anger and the high of coating your childhood bullies in salt and sugar. Life moved in slow motion. I could see every dust particle floating under the fluorescent streetlights, and I wanted to count each one. If this was what smoking weed felt like, then I could see myself wanting more.

"I think we just got banned," I laughed, relishing how colorful and bright the world felt in her presence. I tugged on her shoulder, but it was rigid, immovable. She was looking past the parking lot, arms pressed tight to her side and chin wobbling. Her dark eyes appeared heavy, tired, like she'd lived this night a thousand times over expecting a different result but was cursed to end up here every time.

"Lila?"

She turned back to me, shoulders sagging under the weight of all the thoughts she refused to share. Her concealer was smudged with blue eyeliner and cheap mascara. She took a deep breath, and I mirrored it, moving toward her the way you'd approach an abandoned kitten on the street. We gripped each other's shoulders, balancing our body weight between us like wrestlers at the start of a match. It felt so peaceful to share in her silence. She pressed her forehead against mine until we formed a canopy of cascading hair and lashes.

"Fuck them," she said.

"Fuck them," I nodded back. But my voice was meek and hidden beneath the sounds of tires rolling into the parking lot behind us. She shook her head at me. Not good enough.

"Fuck them," she repeated, using her full chest to enunciate each syllable.

"Fuck them," I said, this time with a little bit more force in my throat.

"Fuck them!" She hollered, her chin pointing toward the sky.

"FUCK THEM!" My fists curled at my sides as my vocal cords strained to match Lila's fury. She smiled. She loved that. I smiled back.

"Lila?"

"Yeah?"

"He was just using me because I was new, wasn't he? Not because I was pretty or interesting."

Lila rolled her eyes. "Well, ugly people don't make pretty people jealous. But who cares? He's an asshole. She's a bitch. Everyone sucks. Why does it even matter?" Her voice trembled, and I looked at the floor, embarrassed that I cared about something she found so trivial.

"It doesn't," I coughed, kicking a loose bit of gravel off the sidewalk. "It's just a shitty thing to do, isn't it? Trying to make someone jealous."

"Yeah," Lila nodded, wiping her nose with the back of her sleeve. "It is."

I twirled in a circle, hands fiddling in my pockets as I found the courage to speak the subtext aloud. "So, you agree?"

Lila's eyes widened, lips parting in shock as she realized what I was so excited about. "Maya!"

"He was using me to make the prettiest girl in school jealous?"

"Yes, Maya, he was using you!"

"It's just," I gasped, placing a hand over my heart. "I've never been used before!"

"That's not a good thing!"

"I'm not suggesting it is! It's heinous, disgusting—"

"Why are you smiling then?" Lila cackled.

"He thought I was pretty enough to make Katie DeMarco jealous!" Her name became a battle cry, one I used to jump on top of Lila. We giggled into the air, jumping around in circles with our hands tied together through fingers and sheer strength.

"That is not the proper lesson to be learned," she grumbled, but we laughed too much to care.

"FUCK THEM!" We screamed in unison, clinging to each other as we laughed at the absurdity of it all. I stared at her then, sobering up as I wiped the moisture from her cheeks. She was crying, and I was too self-obsessed to care.

"Lila?"

Her lips quivered, and her eyes begged me not to ask.

"Did you two…did anything happen?" I asked. Lila wiped at the tears pooling in her eyes, but before she could elaborate, something over my shoulder caught her full attention.

Mami stood behind us with to-go ice cream cups. One was chocolate, while the other was strawberry. Mami's arrival meant the movie was coming to an end, and all those inside the theater would soon exit. We needed to get out of there.

"*¿Qué pasó?*" she asked, eyes focused on how disheveled we appeared and the obvious tears Lila wiped off her cheeks.

"Mami!" I cried out, grabbing her wrist and hauling her toward the parking lot. "We'll tell you everything in the car. Oh, my word! What a night!"

"Tell me now. What's going on?" Mami pulled us into the safety of her arms as we walked through the rows of parked cars. She ran soft hands across my cheeks with her long, big-apple-red painted acrylics and tilted my chin for further inspection. Then the scent got to her.

Pieces of fabric hinted at the truth before I could voice the slew of lies creeping up my throat. We wreaked of weed. Mami sniffed at my shirt and my hair, and then those once soft hands became vice grips, holding my cheeks in place to better scope out the red plumes of my eyes.

"Nothing happened—" I tried to lie.

Mami smacked me over the head, cradling me against her chest as she unleashed a tirade of Spanish threats. It was the one moment I was glad Lila could not understand us, but I knew she caught the gist.

I cried against the glass window as Mami berated us on the drive back home. Lila sat quietly in the back seat.

"One rule! Samaya, I trusted you, and you ruined that trust," Mami's voice trembled. We had never fought like this before, and it seemed to hurt Mami to say my name. I broke more than my mother's trust. I broke her heart. "You're grounded," Mami declared. There was no need to fight back. "You are grounded, and I want you to question why you would lower yourself for anyone. Ever. And especially a boy. And don't you dare think I'm not telling your father about this, Lila!"

But something in the night caught my eye, a flash of movement, a flare in the open ocean on a stormy night. I perked up at the sight of Keenan frantically running out of the theater, holding my jacket. For some reason, I could not explain, I stopped crying.

THE THIRD KISS

I

"Please, stop kicking the wood," Father Michael grumbled through the lattice paneling of the confessional.

"Sorry," I muttered between bitten nails and soiled fingertips. "I didn't realize I was doing that. Bless me, Father, for I have sinned. It has been thirty days since my last confession, and in that time…"

I heard my classmates chattering amongst themselves in the breezeway melting beneath the Florida sun, the air conditioner purred through the chapel vents, and if I focused hard enough, I could decide if I wanted to use this time to unload my soul or lie through my teeth.

I'd already confessed to smoking weed last month, and the penance didn't make me want to stop. I confessed to having impure thoughts about my boyfriend, and Father Michael's rather rude response made me realize I never wanted to bring it up again. But there were new developments this week that led to thoughts that made me question whether I was a good person or not. The type of events that left me lying awake at night, wiping tears off my cheeks, and praying Mami didn't notice the swollen skin when I left for school the next day.

"Be mindful of the students waiting outside, child," he muttered, his irritation palpable through his heavy breathing.

I cleared my throat, "I've harbored anger, kept secrets, and disrespected my mother."

"Elaborate." He replied, clipped and monotonous.

"I've raised my voice at her, Father."

"Not uncommon at your age, but I encourage you to work through that. The more you let your emotions win out, the weaker you become."

I chewed on the inside of my cheek until a hole appeared beneath my tongue. Only when it started to sting did I respond. "I received a letter from my father a week after my birthday passed. We haven't spoken in several years." That last bit of information escaped my tongue like it was being scraped out of me.

Father Michael hummed in understanding; he rocked in his seat, wood creaking beneath the weight of the past fifty years he dedicated to the church. "Well… it must not have been easy for him to write to you. Not all fathers write the letter. Not all children get a second chance. There is no undoing the past, and there is nothing that can fill its place in your heart. Forgiveness might be the only thing that's left. An olive branch is the kindest gift a father can grant their child. Mine never did. In a way, you're now faced with a choice: you can either accept and move forward, or you can choose to live in the past."

"Agreed," I lied.

"Why the anger?"

"I know that there are worse fathers, but there are also better ones. This is mine. We haven't spoken since I was seven, and now he's writing to me, but… he didn't really say anything. It felt like he was blaming me for the silence. I'm his only daughter, and he forgot my birthday. I'm just so… angry. I hate him so much my blood boils with it. It's coming out my eyes." I laughed, but it felt hollow slipping from my throat.

There was a rough, hot shakiness creeping up my chest. The walls of the confessional felt thinner than before. I could see Father Michael's patchy white beard between the cuts in the wood, and I imagined him judging me. It felt nasty to speak, and I wanted to get out of there as quickly as possible, but I knew I had to wait to be dismissed. Saint Anthony's required monthly confessional, which sucked, but it was cheaper than asking Mami for therapy.

I closed my eyes and let myself settle into the silence Father Michael provided. I pictured Mami screaming in the hallway of our old house, banging on Papi's office door as he blasted *Led Zepplin* on the other side of the wood. I could still hear her crying, young and thin, confused as to whether she should go back to bed or wait for him to come out. What is a woman meant to do when her husband would rather drink himself into oblivion than talk to her?

Sometimes I saw myself a bit older, years after we left him, during one of our visits to Peru. My mother's brothers would avoid me at first, catching glimpses of my cheeks, my hands, and seeing only memories better left forgotten in my laughter. They'd sip scotch and wax poetic about their childhood as they gained the courage to mention Papi any chance they could get.

Your dad was in a band when he was a kid, they said.

He had a record collection worth a fortune, they boasted.

You have his eyes, they mused. *His chin, and his nose, and everything down to your toes.*

With every passing drink, they came looking for me to tell me more about Papi.

What they didn't understand was how hard I tried to forget him. I tried to rewrite our history, pretending Papi lived an epic lifestyle that kept him far away from me. Papi wasn't an alcoholic. He was an explorer. He was busy hiking the Himalayas, running with bulls in Spain, or researching the cure for cancer. But then the email came, and I was crushed under the truth that Papi knew exactly where I was and how to contact me, but he didn't remember the day I was born. The rough guess of the month, for sure, but not the day.

He did want you, they clarified, *but it was your mother that took you away.*

"Ms. Ximena?" Father Michael cleared his throat.

I chose to pretend Papi was dead because I couldn't imagine any other reason that could keep a father away from his daughter. But I did not say that. Because to even think it felt evil.

Instead, I sighed and said, "I ask forgiveness of my sins and only those."

"Is that all you'd like to share?" He asked again with a tone that made my eyebrows crease.

"Yes?" I replied, but there was a teenage hiss in my voice I forgot to reign in.

He shuffled in his seat so I could hear every creek. "Ms. Ximena, to lie in the house of the Lord—"

"I'm not!" I spat, and this time I was loud.

"Do you recall last week's mass? You, Ms. Ximena, walked up the aisle on your own accord and accepted Communion from Father Barry." His voice skewered me through the slits in the wood dividing us. My mouth dropped open in disbelief. "You had the opportunity to accept a blessing from Father Barry but accepted Communion instead."

I sat up straight, eyebrows pinching together while my lips ran dry. "Yes."

"You admit to taking Communion when you had not yet completed your Confirmation requirements."

"You went on and on in class about the importance of Communion. Yes, I took it. I forgot. Father? Is this because I asked to postpone my Confirmation?"

"Lower your voice, Ms. Ximena." He warned, and so I did. "Consuming Communion when you have not yet completed your Catholic rites is a sin. A sin you are well past the age of understanding. Perform five Our Father—"

"Yep, got it," I sighed, pushing out of the box, not caring about the punishment waiting for me in class come Monday for the rudeness of my exit.

Sweat bubbled up along my cupid's bow as I stormed out of the church. I had to blink back at the force of the sun, contrasting the darkness I left buried behind me. I accidentally bumped into one of the baseball players on my way out, their face was a blur as I rushed down the hall, but their letterman jacket caught my eye as I muttered an apology. They didn't seem to notice the disturbance.

I pulled out my phone as I turned the corner, frantically checking to see if Lila had responded to my texts. I didn't notice a person standing beside me until I felt them press up against my spine, their feather-light touch cupped around my eyes, blurring my vision as their laughter wreaked havoc in my daydreams.

"Boo!" The word jumped out at me in fits of laughter. His lips skimmed the side of my neck, spilling honey in my ears as goosebumps spread across my skin. Freckled arms wrapped around my waist, pressing my spine flush against the soft paunch of a stomach I'd spent the last year curled up beside. I knew who it was, but I jumped at his touch all the same. I used to picture his hands caressing my cheeks, weathered, and calloused from hours tuning his electric guitar, and think, *wow, how lucky am I to date Keenan O'hare.*

"Jesus, Keenan, you know I hate when you sneak up on me." I tried not to hurt his feelings as I so easily tended to do.

I wiggled out of his arms, turning to wrap my hands lightly around his neck. He'd grown taller, and I had to tilt my neck too far back to look into his baby-blue eyes. I hoped the heavy eyeliner currently smeared across my waterline looked mysterious like Effey Stonem from *SKINS* and not messy like I cried for hours on end. He didn't seem to notice, which was one of my favorite things about him. Keenan smiled at me like it was prom night and I'd just been crowned queen. He scanned the hallway with a crooked grin, cutting dimples in his cheeks that I loved to trace with the backs of my fingertips. He leaned in close, kissed my forehead with the brush of his lips, and I swooned.

He liked me, and I couldn't remember what I did to deserve it.

"Who were you texting?" he asked, glancing down at my phone as if it were an open book waiting to be explored. I moved the screen closer to my chest, and he pulled me closer into his arms.

"Distance!" Sister Margaret shouted at us as she passed, hurrying down the hall with a stack of exams and an expression that could melt ice in a blizzard. Keenan and I jumped apart.

"Sorry, Sister," we shouted back. The scolding sent us into a fit of laughter that had me crumbling into his arms the moment she was out of sight.

"Why aren't you at rehearsal?" I asked, happy by his appearance but confused all the same. "I thought they were running your solo today."

His tongue poked the corner of his mouth as he smiled, leaning in close like a detective on the case. "Why won't you let me see your phone?"

"It's Lila," I caved, and he scoffed, but I chose to ignore it. "I haven't seen her all morning. I don't know. It's just weird. She would have told me if she was skipping."

"Have you checked the boys' locker room?"

"That's not funny," I snapped. My voice cut sharply through the open air as my shoulder blades stiffened.

"Kidding! It was a joke. She probably would've laughed. Relax." He sighed, already over whatever fight I was going to start before it began. "Are we still on for tonight?"

His hands folded through my hair, and I resisted the urge to purr at the tingles he sent rippling through my spine. I felt the presence of the students behind us trying hard to look away, but I didn't care.

I stepped on my tip toes to kiss the stubble budding from his chin. "I'm thinking we go a little bit classic, maybe a rom-com? I found a new one starring Renee Zellweger, and… fine. What do you want to watch?"

He laughed, holding my cheeks between his clammy palms. I loved it when he did that. "No, no! It's your turn to pick. I promise."

I rolled my eyes. "But?"

"But what kind of boyfriend would I be if I didn't bring options?"

There was a spark of confidence in the way he carried himself that I got to see bloom firsthand. I liked to think I helped water the seeds. His eyes wandered across my sweater, and my cheeks blushed. It was like I could step inside his mind as he imagined his fingertips loosening the messy top knot sloping off the edges of my head. He wanted to undo me. I never let him, but my smile deepened knowing how much he wanted to try.

"Seriously, what are you doing out of rehearsal?"

"Stepped out to see you, obviously," his nose pressed up against my forehead, pulling me close as I laughed against his chest.

"Liar," I joked, but there was something about the word that hit a little too close to home.

"Shh, no one's going to notice."

"Uh, you're one of three guys in the department. Trust me, they'll notice." I pushed out of his grasp, resting my hands on his shoulders. He clearly wanted to make out, and I really wasn't in the mood.

He once told me he developed a crush on me the first day I started at Saint Anthony, though I didn't know how much I believed him. Q invited me out that night at the movie theater only because Keenan mentioned how 'underrated' I was at lunch one day. I couldn't figure out if that was a compliment, but it made me blush all the same to hear him say it.

"Hey," He tilted his head to the side, searching my eyes for the answer to a question he was nervous to ask. "Is everything okay?"

I sighed, taking his hand in mine. *Tell him,* I thought. *Let him in.*

But something quiet in my stomach told me it wasn't the right time for those types of conversations. Especially when surrounded by high schoolers on either side sweating under ninety-degree heat. "I'm just excited to spend time with you."

"Keenan!"

We both turned in time to catch Sophia Gomez waving at us from the parking lot. She was a drama club junior, just like Keenan, who had a rather public infatuation with him. Everyone knew it. But Keenan refused to acknowledge it. I couldn't tell if he was stupid or if paranoia was slowly chipping away at my mental health. He waved back with a toothy grin and bright eyes.

His feet were already shuffling away as he said to me, "Listen, I've gotta run back to rehearsal. I'll see you after school."

Seeing him with Sophia left a pit in my stomach, but it wasn't a subject I wanted to get into again. Besides, I was already in a bad mood. I didn't need to pick a fight with my boyfriend to make it worse. A vibration in my pocket brought me out of my intrusive thoughts and toward my original quest. A single message sprawled out across my phone screen, and tension I didn't realize I had instantly eased off my shoulders.

Lila Park: Hey!! Sorry, I went MIA. I'm sick. Staying home today. <33

Maya Ximena: Are you "sick" or sick?

Lila Park: I'm sick.

Maya Ximena: K. Coming.

Lila Park: Maya. I'm sick.

Maya Ximena: I heard you.

Tiny gray dots formed at the bottom of the screen, but I wasn't in the mood for the fake back and forth.

Maya Ximena: Lila. Do you or do you not want me to come over?

No dots formed on the screen for a solid minute.

Maya Ximena: Dope. See you after class.

II

The second the final bell rang out for the day, I ran to the bike rack and pedaled as fast as I could to Lila. Her house was just down the street from mine, though I could count the number of times I'd visited on one hand. I was always welcome to come over, but Lila never saw the point in hosting when she was born to be a guest.

Mr. Park was a kind man, slowly losing the battle with male pattern baldness. He was older and needed the use of both arms to press up off the couch whenever a visitor came through the front door. I slipped my shoes into the rack by the door, nodding my head low and immediately feeling foolish as if I'd done the wrong thing. He sat in a leather armchair in the living room with Mrs. Park resting in her hospital cot nearby, eyes glazed over watching old reruns of *Jeopardy!* He tried to push himself up out of the chair with wobbly knees the moment he saw me.

"Come, come, listen to this," he said to me with a sleepy-eyed smile.

I reached out a hand to steady him, and his hand shook as it latched onto my wrist, equal parts excitement and necessity to keep steady as we strode across the tile floor. It cooled my blood to see Mrs. Park in the makeshift home care unit. To say she 'lived' at the Park residence felt incorrect. Mrs. Park was the nexus of the household, the control center from which every life altering decision extended. Groceries were not purchased unless articles and clinical trials backed the positive effects of the meal. It made sense why Lila's brother, Lucas, left for college at the start of summer. It was hard to breathe in her stratosphere.

There was a hospital bed pressed into the corner of the living room with multiple screens and wires connected to Mrs. Park's body. I did not fully understand their purpose, but I kept a safe distance. If I heard a beep or a hiss, I was convinced I'd done something wrong that had life-altering consequences. I hovered by the couch, nodding to the hairdresser, Carmen, whom Mr. Park invited over once a week to refresh his wife's roots. We smiled at each other the way strangers did on a hike, like we knew each other's faces but had no desire to exchange pleasantries past that.

"Good afternoon, Mrs. Park," I nodded at her as Appa rummaged in his desk. I knew she couldn't hear me just as I knew she wasn't really watching *Jeopardy!* Her eyes were open, lips relaxed, chest rising and setting like the sun. But we all knew the reality of the situation. This house was less a home and more of a live studio production created to support Mr. Park's glimmer of hope that his wife could recover from a medical anomaly that wouldn't stop disintegrating.

"Samaya," he waved over to me, enunciating every letter in my name with an accent that felt as safe and comforting as the one I heard back home. He was an accountant who shrank his practice to only a few lifelong clients and phone calls. I imagined that at one point he was a titan in his field. "The other night, Ji-Yeon's vitals dropped a little…" he added that bit of information with shadows in his eyes, almost as if he blamed himself for the drop as if he weren't watching closely enough to prevent it. "But when I ran to call the hospital, I heard her calling out to me!"

"That's amazing, Mr. Park," I smiled, but it didn't reach my eyes because I didn't believe him. "It's been like… a few months… right? Since the last time—"

"Yes, yes, but listen. I recorded it this time! Listen, listen." He gestured for me to lean in close as he cranked up the volume on the tape recorder. I held my breath and tuned out the volume from the television set just down the hall to hear the faint, staggered breathing of a middle-aged woman attempting to finish a word but only creating mangled sounds of consonants long forgotten. It wasn't beautiful or comforting. It disturbed me to hear Mrs. Park fighting just to speak. Tears prickled at the back of my eyes as my lips trembled. I guess if I tried to put myself in his shoes, I could hear her trying to say the first few letters of his name. But I'd have to use a bit of my imagination in the process.

"That's amazing, Mr. Park," I smiled, meeting his eyes head-on even when my body wanted to run away.

"If I kept Mrs. Park in hospice, they wouldn't treat her like I do," he whispered, shaking his head

"She knows," I whispered back to him, waiting for the opportunity to politely exit the interaction.

He lowered his voice, leaning in close, and I could see the telltale signs of wetness pooling in his tear ducts. "They gave her four months." The words came out gurgled, but he waved the emotion away like nasty ju-ju he wanted nothing to do with. "But with me, it's been one year. Almost. Almost one year."

"That's amazing!" I smiled, and he gripped my shoulder blade tight, his lips moving as if he wanted to add something but didn't know the right translation.

"Appa!" Lila shouted, and the loud noise felt too aggressive for the eggshell paint and Ikea furniture. "Stop scaring my friends."

Lila's bedroom was a blast of incense, succulents, and perfume. It felt like the greenhouse on a spaceship, a vessel for creation in a place that wasn't meant to sustain life. She cackled on her bed, still cuddled up wearing her pajamas from the night before, as she measured out weed on a dinner tray. I ignored the empty plates of food littering the floor beside her nightstand. I wasn't staying long enough to worry about the potential for mold.

"That perverted old fart doesn't care about your daddy issues. Why are you telling Father Michael your personal business?"

"I don't know, 'cause I'm stupid."

"He was just tired and wanted to go to lunch. Just tell him you cheated on a math test next time and repent like the rest of us."

"Easy for you to say, Father Michael thinks you walk on water," I plopped onto the foot of her bed, tucking my toes beneath my thighs as she measured out weed from the personal stash she kept hidden in a shoe box beneath her bed.

"Yeah, well, when your mom's dying, people tend to let you do or say whatever you want. So." She shrugged, nestling deeper into the pile of plushies crowding every inch of her lavender duvet. "Lucky me."

"Lila, your mom is going to be okay."

"I know," she lied right back.

"People let you do whatever you want because you landed on the honor roll without even studying." I rolled my eyes, accepting the baggy of weed she handed over, tucking it deep into my backpack for safekeeping. "How much do I owe you?"

"Maya, it's shake. Free of charge." She bowed to me with a wave of her hand, but I left fifteen dollars on her nightstand regardless. "How are you feeling?"

She scooched over for me to climb under the covers beside her. My uniform khakis felt foreign in the world of cotton and comfort Lila cocooned herself in. She leaned her head in my lap, grabbing hold of her favorite pink and purple stuffed rabbit while I combed the knots out of her hair with my fingertips.

"I'm sick," she coughed, and it was the worst performance I'd ever seen.

I nodded, tapping my chin like a doctor searching for a cure. "Hmm, symptoms?"

She covered her face with the rabbit and sighed. "I went through his phone."

"Huh, I thought I saw some gray strands here," I joked, tugging on her hair as she swatted my hands away. My head collapsed against the wall, already prepared for what she was about to say next. "And what did you see?"

"Um," she laughed, wiping her face while a hollow smirk pulled at her left cheek. "Exactly what I knew I'd find. With pictures."

"Did you say anything?"

She shook her head, lifting herself onto her elbows. "Are you going to respond to your dad?"

"You're changing the subject," I rolled my eyes.

"No, I'm just mentioning two conversations that sound worse than stabbing needles in my eyes." She nudged my shoulder, a soft smile illuminating her apple cheeks. "Your daddy issues are much more interesting than a baseball player cheating on me."

"I'm probably going to delete the email and forget it ever happened." I cleared my throat, staring off at the succulents slowly dying on Lila's windowsill instead of furthering the conversation. I spotted something hanging in her closet that made my jaw drop, shoving her head aside as I jumped off the bed. "Is that my skirt?" My voice jumped up an octave as I rushed toward the fabric I knew rightfully did not belong in the vortex of a bedroom.

"This is brand new with tags!"

"And it's been collecting dust in your closet for months."

"Because I was waiting for the right occasion." I huffed, gripping the fabric in my hands, grinding my teeth as I tried to lower the redness building in my cheeks by counting backward from ten. "We've talked about this. Just ask me, and I will say yes."

"Maya, I know you want to ka-boom on me—" I gasped, but she pressed forward like a shrink concerned for my mental well-being. "But I think we both know your anger is better directed at—"

"Do not make me sound like I'm some anger management nut case!" I yelled, and she leveled me with a smirk, eyebrows raised as if to say, *point made.* "You are not my therapist; you are a thief who has no concept of boundaries."

I slammed my hands onto her desk, accidentally knocking over the plastic pharmacy bag I skipped over when I first entered the room. Poking out of the white plastic was a pack of gum, lip gloss, and a pink box that made my stomach drop.

My throat constricted as I croaked out, "Lila?"

She leaped up off the bed, picked up the bag, and stashed it away at the bottom of her desk drawer. But the image of a white stick with a blue base was permanently seared into my brain.

"You should talk to your mom. If you don't, you'll just bottle it up and blow up on the next person who gets on your nerves." She leaned against the drawer as if she could protect that part of her life from my judgmental stare. I opened my mouth to say something, but she cut me off. "We're not going to talk about it."

"What made you buy it?"

She rolled her eyes, arms crossed protectively across her chest but answered anyway. "I haven't had my period in over a month."

"A month?!"

Lila smacked my shoulder. "Keep your voice down!"

"Does Jack know?"

"No? What? Why would I tell him?"

"Well—"

"Samaya. I'm 16. Whether or not that stick has lines or dots or changes colors, I'm not having a baby and let alone with Jack fucking Rodriguez." She cringed at the sound of his name rolling off her tongue. She laughed, shaking her head and trying to casually wipe moisture from her eyes as hysterical laughter shook her torso. "Oh my,

God, could you picture me showing up at his stupid baseball games with a baby? Over my dead body!"

"I thought you loved him," I whispered.

Jack Rodriguez was a baseball player who was decent in school and relatively nice when convenient. He was handsome in the way only a teenage boy with money and an overly affectionate mother could be. He smiled like his jawline could part the Red Sea. They'd been dating on again off again for the past year.

"Well, pregnancy scares have a real wild way of putting shit in perspective, don't they," she huffed.

"Do you want to take it?" I asked.

"I haven't decided yet."

My phone buzzed deep within my pocket, but I ignored it as a thought occurred to me that sent a wave of shock through my chest. "I can't drive."

"Um… okay?" Her eyebrows creased, head tilting to the side. "How did you manage to make this about you?"

"No, Lila, you can't drive either! We cannot drive. How will we… drive to… wherever we need to go… do not make me say it."

"Shut up! We'll cross that bridge when we get to it. In the meantime," she took a deep breath, her shoulders relaxing as she closed her eyes. "Can I borrow your skirt?"

"I'm sorry, I think I just hallucinated that question." My phone kept buzzing, but I was too focused on Lila to care. "Wait… are you going to Sophia Gomez's party? Without me?"

"Do you want to come?"

"Well… yes, but no. I can't."

"Yes, you can, you just don't want to. You never want to, which is why I never ask you to come. But, hey, enjoy movie night." Lila laughed and picked up my phone to see three missed calls from Keenan. She kissed the air, mockingly making out with herself by running her hands wildly through her hair.

"You're more than welcome to join us. Wait, no, that didn't sound right."

"Ew," she cringed. "I would rather poke my own eyeballs out and eat them with a fork than sit through your passive-aggressive love fest. Besides, I don't want to go to this party, I need to go. It is my God-given right to go to this party. I'm breaking up with Jack," she said it as if it were the most obvious conclusion in the world.

My phone rang again, and this time, a very irritated Lila answered on my behalf. "Hello—Hi Mami!" She smiled. I snatched the phone out of her hands.

"*¡Hola Mami!* Yes. I'm coming right over. I'm sorry, we can talk about it when I get there. *¡Te amo, adiós!*" I hung up and stamped my foot on the floor. "Fuck, she's pissed."

Lila smirked, falling back on her bed. "Well, have fun. Call me if you want to hang out. Don't get pregnant." She joked, and I scoffed at the idea.

"If I were pregnant, I'd be on a one-way flight to the Vatican to get canonized."

"Do they still canonize people?"

I grabbed my book bag off the floor, slowly walking backward toward the door, feeling like the worst person in the world. "Maybe I can come after—"

"Please, Maya, I'm not a charity case. I'll be fine. Promise." She said it, but I didn't believe her. The lump in my throat threatened to push its way out of my body as I hovered by the doorway. The soft, suede fabric of the skirt felt like liquid silver slipping between my fingertips and burning me with every inch.

"Okay, fine, I'll let you borrow it just this once, but do not spill anything on it. Promise?" I leaned forward, holding my pinky up and she gripped it tight with her own. I couldn't help but pull her close, wrapping my arms around her shoulders as if I could turn back time to when we used to stay up late giggling over *twilight* and boys whose names I'd already forgotten. She hugged me back just as fiercely. The future crashed up against us like tides on the shore, slowly overtaking the seawall. But I never feared drowning with Lila beside me.

I swallowed hard, my throat closing shut from the gravity of the situation. "… should we… pray?" I whispered, and she practically spat at me, shaking her head no.

"Ew, Maya." She threw a shoe at the door as I ran out, laughing so loudly I could hear her down the street.

III

He opened the door before I had time to pull out my house keys. I curled one ankle around the other, trying to hold myself in place, pushing back the desire to reach forward and touch him. I wanted to forget the whole wicked day and get lost in kissing him. But I understood the rules of the game. I knew to let *him* approach *me*. I tilted my head toward the wooden doorframe, eyes purring up at my boyfriend.

"Hi," I breathed, chewing at the inside of my lip.

Keenan looked over his shoulder to see if the coast was clear. I instinctively did the same, shrugging off my hoodie and backpack as I stepped inside. Keenan slipped the latter off my shoulders, hanging it up on the hook with one hand as he pulled me close with the other. "Your mom hates me," he whispered into my hair as if Mami had supersonic hearing.

Turns out, she did.

"*Tesoro?*" Mami called out from deep within the house, out of sight but very much in the forefront of my mind.

"Pfft, no," I shook my head, averting his gaze, and wiped the sweat off my brow from the bike ride home. His hands nestled low on my back as my eyes searched for Mami's shadow over his shoulder. When I found none, I planted a quick kiss on his cheek. "It's your whole gender that's the issue."

"What's that?" A stack of DVDs waited for us on the coffee table. Keenan raised an innocent hand, cutting me off to defend the greatest television series on earth.

"They're only suggestions. But until you've learned to appreciate the artistry that is the smash hit television series *LOST*, I don't think you can fully appreciate cinema." I didn't even try to suppress my eye role as he made himself comfortable on the couch.

"Fine," I whined, sticking my tongue out at him. The sound of Mami vigorously chopping in the kitchen lured me through the house like the sword of Damocles hanging over my head.

He bounced in his seat like a golden retriever, popping a disc into the player as I rounded the corner. "You're perfect!" It was a sweet thing to hear as I walked in on Mami chain-smoking cigarettes with the glass door to the backyard wide open.

"I thought you quit," I said, leaning against the archway with way more attitude than needed.

"*¡No empieces!*" Mami held up a single finger, blowing smoke outside as she rubbed the remainder of the butt against the bottom of her heel. She pointed toward the living room as if I had brought home a stray cat and forgot to mention it was covered in fleas. "You told me Keenan was coming over tomorrow night."

"Did I?"

"*Aye,* Samaya, you know I don't like being this mom." She shook her head, trying to decide if it was too late to call in sick and chaperone. It was.

"What are you talking about? You're a great mom. The best mom! You're also going to be late." I hurried toward the door, but Mami spun me around by the wrist, holding me back.

"*Samaya, sabes que tus amigas siempre son bienvenidas en esta casa.*"

I took a deep breath, controlling the urge to roll my eyes. "*Yo sé, Mami.*"

"*Pero no me siento cómoda dejando a ustedes solos.*"

"Mami, nothing is going to happen." I scoffed.

She frowned. "*Obvio, no va a pasar nada. Eres mi hija,* and I trust you one hundred percent. But I don't like being known as this type of mother."

"So, let me go to Keenan's house. Or do you still not trust American families and their loose moral values?"

"*Oye,* what's going on with you?" Mami leaned on the kitchen island, searching for her daughter buried beneath the eyeliner. She cut me off with a wave of her hand before I could say something flippant and juvenile. "You've been distant, rude, and I haven't seen Lila over here in weeks. You've been spending—"

"She's busy."

"—All your time *con ese cojudo.*"

"He can hear you!"

"Oh, now he can speak Spanish? How convenient. Wait, *tesoro,* were you crying?" Mami rushed toward me, her hazel eyes oozing with warmth while her candy apple red fingernails cupped my face in the safety of her hands. "Did you and Lila get into a fight?"

"What? No, never." I almost laughed, but the sound came out choked and odd.

"Is it him?" She hissed, her bottom lip bitten between her teeth.

"It's nothing, I'm just nervous." I sniffed, rubbing at my temples.

"Is he pressuring you? *Que cochino de chico. Nunca me gusto. ¡Jamás!*"

"What? No." I whined, shaking my head. "It's not him. It's you. I'm nervous to talk to you."

She stiffened, head cocked to the side. "Since when do I make you nervous?"

"Did you know Papi was getting married?"

Mami's neck snapped back at the shock of my statement. "Who told you that?"

I pulled out my cell phone, scrolling through my emails to show her.

"Hold on…" I pushed through the tremble in my throat. "Here it is. 'I know it's been a while since we last spoke, but I want you to know, you're in my thoughts always. I met someone, Samaya. We're welcoming our baby boy into the world next month,'… and it goes on from there, but yeah. You get the gist." I tried to keep reading, but the rest of the text appeared to me as if there were nothing more than a mush of black lettering on a screen.

"*Dámelo,*" she ordered, her palm facing up, waiting for me to hand over the phone. I passed it over to her the way you would an egg, fragile and prone to mess. Mami slapped it onto the counter, face down, eyes focused solely on me. "*Imbecil,*"

"Aren't you going to read it?" I asked, but she shook her head.

Her lips rolled between her teeth as she paced along the kitchen tile. "I told him that I'd tell you when it felt right."

I nodded, still chewing my nails. "And?"

"It never did," she whispered to the floor, sniffling as she choked down whatever heartache awakened in her chest. *"Ay, puta. Me voy a hinchar."*

"You're not going to look swollen, relax. He's an asshole."

"Samaya, your father was… a very interesting man—"

I held up my hand, eyes focused on the sky as I swallowed my tears. "Mami, I understand why you thought you were being nice. But, please, just let me call him an asshole."

"Déjame terminar," She ordered, searching the fluorescents hanging overhead for the right words to say.

We shared beautiful memories in our kitchen over the years, but this conversation felt like lightning struck too close to the canals. It was a hurricane, and we didn't heed the warnings to pull closed our shutters. I stood there, staring at Mami as the joy in her eyes deflated, and I was buried too deep in the water to do anything about it.

"Tu papá was top of his class at Stanford University. He was handsome, charming, and I loved him from the moment I saw him. And he loved me. When it came time to propose, my mother practically gifted me to him. Because he was the perfect husband she could have imagined for me. He was the type of father I thought my children deserved. Good family, great job, and maybe if I was older, we'd still be together. He was the perfect son but could have been a better husband. What do you need from him that I don't give you?"

Nothing, I wanted to say. But the word, *everything,* seemed to scream louder in my head. I knew my mother would love me to her dying breath. But to know my father was starting over with another baby, without even trying to start over with me, hurt deeper than I could ever explain.

Maybe someday I'd outgrow the hurt that he left in me, but until then, I swallowed it shut and pretended it didn't exist. My father wasn't around because he couldn't be. He was wrestling black bears and studying the meaning of life at a monastery.

But that wasn't true, was it?

Papi was a software engineer in New Jersey. He had a phone, he had a car, and he clearly had an email address. He just didn't have the will to know me. He replaced us. Maybe someday I'd understand his version of love, and maybe someday I would heal the heart he broke. Maybe someday, he'd remember my goddamn birthday.

But for now, I blew out my candles each year, wishing he would stay away.

We were quiet for so long that I could feel the room sway. Mami stared at me like I was an anchor at sea, and she was mine. I couldn't move, and if anything ever happened to her, I would lose my sense of being.

"Nothing, Mami," I said, swallowing hard. "I don't need anything else."

The only sound came from the *LOST* theme song playing out in the living room. The awkward placement of it all made my lips twitch, and I couldn't help but choke out a laugh. Mami smiled back at me, her hands covering her mouth as she rolled her eyes at the boy outside. Tears welled in our eyes, but they weren't from sadness. We were each other's family. I'd never leave her, and she'd never leave me.

"Come here, baby," she waved me close, holding me in the kindness of her arms. "*Disculpa*, Samaya."

"Why are you sorry?" I asked. "You're the one who stayed."

She let out a deep breath, and I did the same.

"What's Lila doing? You should invite her over. Have a mini party." She did a little dance just to emphasize how free and open this house could be.

"She's busy," I said.

Mami paused, waiting for me to elaborate. When I didn't, she prompted, "...with?"

"Homework," I lied.

"Oh?" Mami nodded, not expecting that answer for a Friday night. "Where's your homework?"

"We're in different classes."

"Hm, maybe I'll call the school and move you to the classes with work," Mami laughed, but I wasn't in the mood.

"Does it look like I've been crying?"

"*Pues, obvio, ¡Samaya! ¿Como qué no?*"

"Mami!" I whined, flailing my arms at my disheveled state, begging her to solve my problems.

"Just use my makeup. You know where everything is. Oh, *carajo,* I have to go."

Mami was on her way to work a double shift at the hotel, which sounded exhausting, but she seemed quite excited about it. "Remember that Norwegian couple I was telling you about? The one with the tiny Yorkie I pretend to talk for sometimes, like, '*Oye,* I want a pina colada!'" She performed with an over-exaggerated Hispanic accent she knew guests loved her to use.

"Ah, yes, the slightly offensive inner-puppy-monologue," I nodded, stepping through the archway connecting the kitchen and living room. Mami was too busy assembling her work lunch to argue with me, so she stuck her tongue out instead. "Mami, you don't talk like that. No one is forcing you to do that."

She waved me off, "It makes me happy to make people laugh. Anyway. *Ellos llamaron* the regional manager just to brag about me!"

"Oh my God, that's amazing!" I howled, grabbing her by the hands as we bounced up and down in the kitchen.

She loved it at her new job, and they loved her if the recent promotion was any indication. I wanted to celebrate. I wanted to pop open the bottle of wine I wasn't supposed to know she kept hidden beneath the kitchen sink and celebrate the life she built for us. But there was a boy outside whose patience for fresh popcorn was wearing thin.

I took a moment to fix myself up in Mami's bathroom and changed into a pair of black leggings and an oversized knit sweater that hung down to my thighs. Keenan made himself comfortable on the couch, setting up pillows and a single blanket for us to share. I grabbed a second blanket from the cabinet, an item he 'forgot' each time he came over.

I settled onto my side of the couch, scrunching my legs beneath the quilt. "You know, it would be nice if you at least pretended to care about what I want to watch."

Keenan made a goofy confused face, totally focused on the screen. "I always ask what you want."

"When?"

"This morning, when I texted you if you wanted to chill at my place or yours," he smirked, leaning in close to kiss me, but I swerved out of the way, conscious of Mami searching for her keys in the other room. His face planted into the cushions like a cartoon character.

"It doesn't count if you already know the answer."

He rolled his eyes, shaking his head as he turned back to the TV, his arm dangling along the back of the couch. "It's not like I'm going to assault you or something."

"That's not funny," I snapped.

"I'm kidding," he sing-songed, but he was clearly upset at my angry tone. But I didn't find it funny. "Okay. What would you want to watch?"

"There's a National Geographic documentary screening at the IMAX. It's about birds in the Amazon, and I don't know, I'd love to learn more about Iquitos," I breathed, melting into the couch at the idea of watching panoramic images of a Peruvian landscape I'd only ever heard about in stories. "I want to visit someday."

"Maya," he smirked at me like I was a child arguing the existence of Santa Claus. "Don't make me point out how boring that sounds."

"Fine," I grumbled, arms crossed and chin lowered in defeat. "*LOST* it is."

He bounced up off the floor to give me a big smacking kiss on the forehead. "You won't be sorry!" He scanned for the perfect episode, catching me up on everything I may have forgotten from our last binge. I placed a giant pillow in the middle, separating us, and pulled a blanket on top of myself.

"Can we share?" He asked, a little confused that he even had to voice the words. I nodded and handed him a different blanket to use.

He was clearly frustrated that I was not getting the hint but used the blanket anyway. He acted like that every time he came over and did not get his way. Like the rules were brand new. I stopped wasting my breath trying to remind him. He pulled me close, burying himself into my hair like Q did all those years ago, only Keenan was far too clumsy and easily redirected.

I grabbed the popcorn bowl off the table and tucked it into my lap. "If I have to pay attention to this, so do you," I said, taking an elaborate bite from a handful of popcorn. Keenan clicked his tongue but did not argue. Instead, he made a big show about staying on 'his side' of the couch.

Mami tried her best not to stare at us as she made her way out of the house. We talked about it a few times, and she was getting better. With a big breath, she smiled, a little too aggressive to be casual. She wanted me to be comfortable here. She'd rather I rebelled within her walls than repeat the same mistakes she made at my age. I popped up to give her a kiss goodbye, but Keenan didn't take my lead, no matter how many times I walked him through it.

Get up and kiss her cheek, I thought.

Instead, he put his feet up on the coffee table and reached out only to grab the warm popcorn nestled in the curve of my lap. With a mouthful of gobble gook, he waved a limp hand in her direction.

"Have a good day at work, Mrs. Ximena."

Mami caught a sexually charged scene on screen that made my cheeks burn. I slapped a hand over my face in embarrassment. She snapped back toward me with a disgusted expression just as I lunged for the remote to fast forward.

"Sorry, sorry," I chanted, completely ignoring how irritated Keenan appeared beside me.

"*Ay, dios mio,*" Mami sighed, mumbling under her breath as she made her way to the front door. "Make sure you can hear the door. Mrs. Baker might stop by later to borrow milk —"

"You never said that." I shouted, officially done with the helicopter parenting.

"Well, you never know—"

"Got it!" Keenan and I shouted in unison.

"*Te amo,*" she hollered as she rushed out the door.

I gestured toward the door for Keenan to say goodbye. He swallowed another mouthful of popcorn and called out, "Bye, Mrs. Ximena—" just as Mami slammed the door behind her. Slouching back into the cushions, he turned toward me with raised eyebrows. "See?"

Patience, I thought. *He just doesn't understand.*

Mami's car engine roared in the front yard, traveling out of distance until it disappeared completely. I twisted toward Keenan with a mischievous look on my face, elbow propped up on the back of the couch.

"Hey," I smiled, pulling a perfectly pre-rolled joint from my pocket. I leaned over and planted a heavy kiss on his lips before sprinting toward the other side of the house. He followed quickly after. Such was our routine.

IV

Smoke rolled out the open bathroom window in waves. I flapped my hands around, hoping it didn't stink up the house. I stood on the toilet, coughing from the two puffs I just ripped off the joint and blew the excess into his latest invention, a toilet paper roll wrapped in dryer sheets. It was so dumb; it was practically brilliant, and it made me smile remembering the night he first came up with it. We smoked under the pier with his friends beneath a full moon, the waves crashing against us as Lila and I chased the shoreline.

I remembered whispering to Lila that it was *'an engineer's wet dream,'* and the way she loved the joke so much she repeated it, only louder. The way everyone laughed afterwards made me wish I had said it first.

"We could smoke in the yard—" he suggested, sitting on the tile floor beneath me, legs flared out like the letter Y.

"Neighbors," I coughed, spraying the room with air freshener. It was toxic, yes, but I didn't care. I was too anxious at the thought of Mami coming home unexpectedly, but the paranoia was a regular occurrence I couldn't outgrow with practice. "What if she left something behind on the counter? Or-or what if the local police broke down the door from the smell because they thought I was some sort of drug kingpin?"

Keenan laughed beneath me, and it ripped me from my intrusive thoughts. "Right," he nodded, laughter bubbling in his throat. "Because your house wreaking of lemon pledge is a lot less conspicuous."

I sank onto the floor beside him, spreading my legs onto the cold tile. I liked pressing my hands against the solid texture of it all and the way my legs grew numb to the point of falling asleep. He pulled me closer, and I tucked my head into his neck, searching for shelter in the woods.

"You think she knows?" He whispered into my hair, and I shook my head, curling up against his side.

"She doesn't know what weed smells like, and even if she did, I feel like she wouldn't want to know. Does that make sense? Why? Do you think it smells? Don't you smoke at your house?"

"Nah, I quit after they caught my sister. Plus, I don't really want to spend money." He pushed a strand of hair behind my ear, but I was too worried about the smell to be wooed by it.

"I need water," I said, sitting up against the bathtub as I tried to steady my breathing. Keenan reached up toward the sink and filled a glass with tap water, handing it back to me. I smiled, letting the liquid calm me down. I took a deep breath, and all was fine.

"Fuck, I'm sorry," I placed a hand over my lips, embarrassed at how emotionally high maintenance I felt.

"It's chill," he shook his head, brushing off my panic attack like it never even happened. He sank down beside me, wrapping me in his arms so my face collided with his. He leaned in close and nibbled at my bottom lip. I froze... he had never done that before. He pulled back a bit, searching my eyes. But I had nothing to say.

"Did you like that?" He whispered, trying to be sexy. I saw this side of him before, but only in small doses. Tiny little micro-movements of trembling hands and fumbling choices. But that choice felt deliberate. His eyes lit up with delight at the blush creeping over my olive cheeks.

Yes, I thought, *I did like that.*

But I wasn't going to tell him that. I cleared my throat and changed the subject.

"What are Becky's plans for next year?"

He leaned back with a sigh. "Go to state school." He didn't care about the answer. He said it like he pointed out his left sock from the right.

I nodded, "That's cool. What about you?"

Keenan laughed at the thought, rubbing a hand aggressively over his eyes. "Kill myself before I have to go." He smiled, but I didn't.

"That's not funny," I swallowed.

"Yeah, well, maybe lighten up a bit." He huffed a laugh, but I didn't think he was kidding.

I knew the answer, but I asked the question anyway. "You don't want to go to college?"

"You don't need college to make movies." He said this a million times before.

"Yeah…," I swallowed, "but the connections get you into the industry, right? I don't know, I feel like if you're going to do something, why not set yourself up to be the best person for the job?" I leaned my head on Keenan's shoulder, and he pinched my chin between two fingers, his lips hovering centimeters apart as he stared lovingly into my eyes. It was romantic. It was quiet. And just for a moment, I felt brave enough to say the quiet part out loud. I traced his lips with my nails. "And you'd be with me."

But that seemed to be the wrong thing to say. Keenan pulled away from me slightly, and suddenly, the floor felt colder than it was before.

"I don't want to talk about this. It stresses me out," he scratched his head, "Hey, look at me a second."

He positioned himself sitting in front of me, knees touching, eyes locked on mine. He took a hit off the joint, burning without purpose in his fingers, sucking in hard, then leaned forward, gesturing for me to do the same. Centimeters apart, he blew the smoke toward my open lips, and I sucked it up without fail. I secretly loved it when he did this because of how intimate it felt. The idea of physical touch was sexier than the physical touch itself.

"You've been practicing," the smoke slipped between my lips as my thoughts raced to catch up. It was much smoother than he'd done in the past. He'd been practicing, but… how?

"Hey, are you okay?" he asked, taking his time as he came to a standing position behind me. I gasped so much I couldn't even lie to confirm it.

He moved closer toward my body, hands searching for purchase on my hips. He did that a lot lately, interacting with my hips, lips, legs, and chest, but not me. I did not know if he could tell the difference.

"Can I ask you a personal question?" he asked, hands holding mine and eyes staring at the floor.

"Of course."

Leaning against the windowpane with a smirk across his full, pink lips, he looked up at me and whispered, "What's your fetish?"

I must have smoked so much that I wandered out onto the street because the only sounds going through my brain were cars screeching to a halt, followed by a loud crash.

"Where'd that come from?" I asked.

"I don't know, just curious. Aren't you?" Before I could respond and kill the mood, as he knew I would, he cornered me against the wall. Both hands pressed along the window, barely caressing my shoulder blades as he forced me to meet his gaze. "Come on, what turns you on? Don't you think it's important we know each other like that?"

"That's just, like, really random," I choked on my own discomfort. "I don't think I have one."

"Everybody has one," Keenan scoffed.

"... You're freaking me out." I tried to climb out of his embrace, but he wouldn't budge.

"I think it's sweet. It shows we're comfortable with each other. Come on—"

"What's yours?" My chin jutted out, shoulders back. It was not a question; it was a dare. He took the joint, smoked it, and stared deep into my eyes before blowing the smoke out of his nose. He was trying to be sexy, but it came off as creepy.

His shoulders loosened. He was comfortable.

But my shoulders grew tighter, my body pulled itself into a pretzel.

"It's like, look," he stammered, laughing off his insecurity, "it makes sense if you watch porn, but...," he searched the room for the right words to use before settling on the crude truth, "big clits. Like, it sounds— yeah, it sounds weird, but..." He shrugged like he did not need to explain what was perfectly common amongst members of the pornographic community. I was not one. He took a hit off the joint and leaned in again, but I pulled away. He rolled his eyes at me.

"Come on, I told you mine. You tell me one."

"Guys who go to college," I smirked, pouring water on a grease fire.

He pitched forward, hands clutched behind his back as he chanted, "Ha. Ha." An impish grin crossed his face, waiting for a response. After a moment of thought, I gave in, offering my best guess.

"... Are British accents a fetish?"

"Oh, that's so your fetish!" He clapped. "I bet there's porn for that. If you want, we can look some up together. Only if you're down for it."

Instead of meeting his gaze, I turned toward the sink, examining my skin in the mirror. I hadn't had acne in years, but the scars were still there, no matter how much Mami said they weren't. I still saw them. My hair was still frizzy on account of the humidity, and flat ironing only made it worse. I got attention from the other girls every time I tried to look good and uninvited advice on how to look better every time I didn't. I swore I got uglier with every passing moment I stayed in school. I could see it in the yearbook pictures. Bit by bit, they were breaking me down until I had nothing left. But college was my chance at an escape, and I couldn't wait to go in two years.

I cringed at the memories creeping up from the vault I locked them away in. Shaking off a life I no longer lived, I focused on fixing my hair, twisting it back into a solid bun at the nape of my neck. I smoothed out any bits of frizz that escaped my attention. The skin on my shoulder felt hot and blotchy and I pulled up the neck of my sweater to cover it up.

"Porn's pretty pathetic," I said to my reflection. "Same with nudes. Like, if you really wanted to have sex, just find the real thing." This I added by facing him, but my eyes skipped a beat when they landed on his. "I didn't mean to say that. Well, I did mean it, but—" I cut myself off, finishing the thought in my head. I immediately regretted what it implied.

"By all means, lead the way," he gestured to the hallway toward my bedroom with Vanna White hands.

"Don't be a dick," I warned.

"I'm not. I'm being direct. But, out of curiosity, what would you do if I sent you a dick pic?"

"Delete it," I snapped. "Where is all this coming from?"

"Would you send me one?" He took a step toward me. I scrunched up my face in confusion as if he were an idiot.

"Send you a picture of my dick?"

"Why, no, thank you," he said with the worst British accent I'd ever heard. The sound of it escaping his ill-thought lips made my jaw drop. "But I'd love to see your breasts if your majesty allows it." He lightly poked my chest to emphasize his desire, and I smacked his hand hard.

"Ow?" He waved his hand in the air, shaking off the sting.

I wanted to vomit, but he wouldn't leave the bathroom. The calloused hands I used to dream about felt nightmarish touching my skin. I was angry, and it was all bubbling up to the surface, and I thought he could see it coming from the way his body seemed to sag. I mirrored him, taking deep breaths and keeping my eyes closed tight so as not to cry from how powerless I felt in my own home.

"Hey, look at me," he instructed, pulling me close to his chest and slowly I obliged. I stared at him with hatred burning in my heart, but I couldn't tell if he noticed the change. Instead, he held my hand. "I'm sorry."

Those two words melted me. I shuddered, wiping my nose, trying to shake off the anger. "What the hell has gotten into you?" I muttered as he pulled me close to his chest, rocking lightly left to right like an infant caused a scene. He moved one hand to the nape of my neck and extended the other taking hold of my palm.

"I'm sorry," he whispered, humming softly into my hair to a song I could not place.

"You are the one for me, for me, formi, formidable...," his voice trembled with a vintage French accent. I hummed along, melting into him as we swayed.

I picked up the next verse, *"You are my love, very, very, vertiablé—"* He dipped me, and the surprise sent us slipping onto the tile, laughing into each other's arms, pawing at our shoulders, and not giving an inch of room.

His phone buzzed, but instead of checking it, he ignored it. It buzzed again.

"Are you going to check that?" I asked.

He shook his head. "Nah, it's probably something stupid." I nodded, but I wanted to know more.

Between middle school and high school, Keenan grew up to be the kind of boy girls whispered about. He knew it made me uncomfortable, but he didn't stop them. If anything, he fed the frenzy. I did not have the stomach to say anything because it was all good fun at the end of the day, right? He could be a bit self-centered at times, but he was my boyfriend, and I should trust him. But really, I felt like I was trapped in a fish tank, staring out past the glass as the world poked and poked and poked at me until I exploded. And once I did, I was the crazy one.

His eyes focused on me, searching the freckles on my face with a monologue playing in his mind, but I didn't know the lines. He got like that sometimes, and I was too afraid to ask. Then he said it. Still in his incessant British accent, he peered down at me, bottom lip quivering ever so slightly. "You'd look so beautiful in a white dress."

Ah, there it was, I thought, slipping the joint from the countertop where it was discarded and reigniting it to take a long puff, avoiding his eyes.

Boys twirl the promise of forever like a cat toy, expecting you to chomp at the bit. I saw it for the Trojan horse that it was. It was not the first time he did, and most certainly not the last time he'd use commitment as a segue toward sex.

I was not stupid. I learned fast that pretty promises had hidden meanings.

I love you, was followed by a request for a blow job.

I'd never cheat on you, was said just after a group of girls giggled about how he could model with his bone structure.

I want to marry you, was followed by an angry rant about how unfair it was that we hadn't had sex yet.

I grew allergic to promises.

I ran into my bedroom, slamming the door shut. My chest rose and fell with each breath as I listened for his footsteps down the hall. I felt him creeping near, and something inside of me launched toward the door frame, pushing it shut as he tried to twist the knob.

"Samayaaaaa," The British voice sing-songed through the wood, "May I come in?"

It was all so ridiculous I could not stop laughing. So, I did my best southern belle impression to play along. "Sorry, puddin', but no boys allowed."

Keenan dropped the accent, irritation coating his throat. "Samaya, come on—"

"Too late, kid, I'm invested in the bit." Now, I was a seasoned Sheriff with spurs on my boots and a piece of straw between my teeth. "I don't make the rules, fella. I just enforce them."

Keenan pushed on the door, knocking me out of the way. My hair was a mess, and my legs were unsteady. I did not have time to react before he pulled me close, and our lips met.

We'd been 'going steady' for over a year now, and at this point, we knew each other's lips to a degree that felt practically rhythmic. But this was different. This was rough.

This felt like a full-course meal of whatever locker room advice taught him to bite my lip like that. To tug at my top the way he did then. That taught him to pick me up by the hips and practically smack me against the desk. It wasn't sexy. It was clumsy. The small of my back smacked the side of the wooden desk, and I cried out in pain, but he didn't stop. He covered my open mouth with his while his hands traveled down my torso until they flirted with the elastic waistband of my leggings.

I pushed him, breathing heavily as I shouted, "Stop!" He had the nerve to look offended.

He scooped back his yellow hair, adjusting his pants away from my view as he recalculated the scene. "Did I do something wrong?"

"No," I rushed to say the word even though I didn't mean it. "Just... cool it."

"Why do you keep pushing me away?" His eyes glistened as he asked the question. He even had the courage to sniffle. "Do you not like me anymore?"

"Don't be dramatic."

"So, it's okay for you to run away and slam the door in my face, but I can't be offended by it?"

I scoffed, "It was a joke—"

"Your girlfriend rejecting you isn't funny."

I wasn't expecting his voice to be that loud, and it made me whisper. "... I'm sorry."

Biting his lip, Keenan shook his head, hands flared in the air as if wiping the scene from his memory. "It's fine."

He leaned up against my desk, agitated, and made a show of his bruised ego. I looked down at his pants and saw a visible bulge growing. He noticed me looking and remarked, "You could at least help me out."

He said it like it was a class assignment. Like it was a chore around the house.

I walked right out the door without another word.

"What?" He called after me.

A moment later, we were sitting on the couch watching *LOST*, an arm's distance away from each other. I was seething, but when I looked over at him, he appeared almost nonchalant. Like it never happened.

His phone buzzed again, but instead of ignoring it, he picked this moment to answer. He smirked, standing in front of me, talking to someone else while I fought the urge to scream. I wanted to snatch the device out of his hands. I wanted to kick him out of my house. I wanted to pretend that none of this had happened and watch his stupid show like we were supposed to. My blood ran hot, my neck sweating, and I could feel tears burning at the back of my eyes.

It wasn't because we fought. It was because he didn't care. And somewhere between anger and sadness, a nasty voice crept into the back of my mind.

Maybe Samaya Ximena did not know the first thing about love.

I was never present when we kissed, and he knew it. Instead, I thought about what *he* might be thinking about and if kissing was supposed to make me feel something special.

Was I good at it? Was he? Was it rude to wipe my lips if I felt his spit all over them?

How was he supposed to know my limits if I didn't set one? What if I set too many, and they all started to blend into nothingness? Maybe the fighting was my fault. And when I looked at it through that lens, it was hard to see what I was even fighting for. Maybe sex wasn't as precious as I wanted it to be, and maybe the moments I saw in movies weren't supposed to feel special in real life. I felt numb all the time, and maybe that was normal.

In the beginning, Keenan would tremble when he was around me. Keenan and I were friends before we were boyfriend and girlfriend, and that's what made our connection so special. He'd send me movie recommendations and wait for my opinion every time. We walked along the boardwalk, just talking, and then one day, he took my hand, and I trembled, accepting it. Maybe I made him mean. Maybe pulling away and building brick walls hurt us. And the thought of ruining my own relationship made my temples sweat and chest close.

And just as tears welled at the corners of my eyes— he moved.

Laying out on the cushion toward my right was a hand, palm facing up and outstretched toward me. It was a white flag. An invitation. And when he met my gaze, there were tears in his eyes, too. I stared at him, and without another moment of thought, I leaped across the couch to sit beside him. His body reacted in turn, and I tried my best to go with it, not against it.

"I thought you were paying attention," he muttered against my lips while his hands snaked their way down the curve of my spine.

"I am," I mumbled back. But he didn't understand my meaning.

I nibbled at his lips ever so slightly, just to see how it felt. He loved it. Keenan's lips trailed down my chin, my ear, and then down the nape of my neck. But he did not stop. The feeling of his tongue pressed against the soft curve of my collarbone sent a shiver down my spine, sinking further into his lap in a position that felt too close for comfort. I felt him move beneath me, his body igniting at the touch of me, and it woke me up from pleasure to fear. After too long of a moment, a gasp escaped my lips. I pushed against his shoulders to stop, but he kept going, closing the grip around my torso.

"Wait, Ke-Keenan, stop it!" I pushed at him, concern washing over my face, until he finally let go, his head slammed back against the pillows, irritated.

"What!?" He snapped, but I was already halfway across the house, running to check my skin in the bathroom mirror.

"Fuck!" I shouted, rubbing vigorously at the bright purple bruise on my neck that wouldn't go away. "One fucking rule, dude. ONE!" I tore through the room, snatching a decorative pillow off a nearby laz-y-boy just to chuck it at him.

He blocked the pillow, curling away like a cartoon to avoid it. "It's not a big deal." He laughed, exasperated by my reaction.

"It is to me!"

Keenan just shook his head, "Of course it is." And raised the volume on the TV. Exaggerated suspense music floods the room. He gasped, hands clutched to his face in a comedic copy of *Home Alone* as he wailed, "Oh no, not the boat!"

I turned off the TV and rushed toward the kitchen.

"Dude, chill," Keenan called out behind me, but I did not stop until I reached the freezer.

I grabbed an ice cube, shoving my thumbs against the tray and making a mess of the countertop. I did not care how red my neck got as I rubbed my skin; I just needed the hickey to go away.

"My mom is going to crucify me. Why is this so funny to you?!"

He gestured to the room like a mime in a house fire. "What? Babe, I'm nervous!"

"This isn't funny!"

"No, but it's so fucking typical," he clapped, and my jaw scraped the floor in shock. Off my glare, he continued scolding. "You only want it when you want it. No more and no less."

"The fuck?"

"Samaya, we've been together for, like, a year —"

"And three weeks," I finished the factoid for him, biting off his tirade with gritted teeth.

He plopped down on a stool beside the counter, hands gesturing to me as if to say, *exactly my point*, "— and you won't let me go further than your bra."

I shook my head, "What's wrong with that?"

"Samaya," he sighed, "I love you. But you can't even come to my house without my parents calling your mom first. Is that normal to you?"

That time, the tears won the fight, spilling freely over my cheeks. "So, what? You want me to fight with my mom because it's inconvenient for you?"

"No," he slapped the counter, standing straight and bounding toward me. "I want you to stop being such a little tease!"

I recoiled at the way he looked down at me. My eyes shivered into slits, veins throbbing in my neck as my voice dropped an octave. Slowly and with a clipped tongue, I said what had been on my mind all day. "Stop being a desperate fuck!"

He shook his head, jaw falling off its hinges as he backed away from me. His blue eyes chipped away at my image until I was nothing but a naked figure. The sweater felt like it was too thin of fabric. I wanted to run and grab the blanket to wrap around my shoulders like a cape and save myself from what came next. This was a new chapter. This was a new kind of conversation. I wished I could turn back time, but I knew it would always end here, in this kitchen, with his lips moving and cruel words coming out.

He mocked me with an impression of my likeness. "'Wait until Valentine's Day, Keenan! Oh, no, I meant our anniversary. No, wait, your birthday!' But fuck, man, I bought condoms for my birthday, and you got me socks!"

I swallowed the bile building at the back of my throat, tossing spare strands of hair from my forehead, and met his gaze dead on. When I finally did speak, it was like I had to deadlift the words out of my throat. "You needed socks."

Keenan just stared at me, exhausted and done. "That's not the point."

"Don't tell me you love me just because you're angry I won't fuck you!"

Keenan shook his head but did not say a word. I stood there in the aftermath of my words. I felt so much lighter. Better. Stronger. I wished I could say it three times over.

As he turned around, his body language poised to strike with an insult, I saved him the trouble by throwing his DVD collection at him and locked the door once it slammed shut.

"Those were fucking Blu-rays!" He cursed through the door frame, but I did not care. I wished I could have kept them just to smash them. I stood there for a beat, my back pressed tight against the wooden frame and my chest bouncing with adrenaline. I felt high in a way I never felt before. My skin vibrated, and I could not stand still. I paced around the house, but the walls felt too small to contain this newly formed part of myself.

Running back to my room, I grabbed a jacket and dialed the one phone number I kept on speed dial. My shoulders physically sagged at the sound of her voice on the other line. "Don't leave! I'm on my way over."

There was a newly defined swagger in my hips as I ran toward my bike. I wasn't going to spend my Friday night crying on the couch over a boy. That wasn't the girl Mami raised.

V

THE WIND RIPPED THROUGH the strands of hair that poked out from beneath my helmet as I flew through the neighborhood, pedaling hard toward the Park Residence. The faint gray glow of the full moon hid behind a wall of rotten cotton candy threatening rain. There was always the threat of rain in Florida. Maybe the impending storm would help my cause with Lila, and if I pedaled hard enough, I could save her from the omens begging us to stay home.

I pedaled until my lungs threatened to give out, discarding my bicycle onto the gravel the second I saw her front door. Hunched over and heaving, I stumbled through the yard, searching for lavender curtains and the flickering life that meant Lila had not left her house yet.

"Lila," I tried to call out her name, but I was too busy hacking a lung into Appa's rose bushes to form the word. I banged on the glass until I felt it shudder beneath my knuckles. The pane slid open, and as usual, Lila looked straight out of a movie.

"Keep your voice down. My parents are watching *Password*," she hissed, tossing me her satchel and helmet. I caught the helmet but scrambled for the purse before too many grass stains set into the fabric. "Is that what you're wearing?"

"Yes," I coughed into my hands while a vein fluttered in my throat. "Wait, what? No," I coughed again, hands pressed to my hips as I tried to find my balance. I could feel an arrhythmia threatening to send me to the hospital. "I… gotta stop… smoking."

The suede mini skirt I loaned Lila rode up her thighs as she climbed out the window, combat boots coated in fresh dirt from the rose bushes as she settled onto the flat earth. Appa thought she was fast asleep in her bedroom while Mami would not be home in time to notice I left.

Not that Mami would be upset at me for attending a party. Knowing I kicked Keenan out of the house to have a good time with Lila would probably send her over the moon. But tonight was not about me or some stupid party. Tonight was about Lila finally getting the redemption arc she deserved, just not how she might have planned.

"Don't go tonight," I wheezed, standing up straight as she took her belongings from my arms, not stopping to process my words as we skulked through the yard.

"Maya," she sighed, crouching down so her parents didn't spot us through the living room windows. "If you're going to be a buzz kill, just go home."

Lila pre-staged her teal blue bicycle at the edge of the driveway, standing up tall on its spokes, ready to carry her through the dark toward whatever movie moment she'd rehearsed in the privacy of her bathroom mirror.

"Just run me through how you want this to go," I jumped in front of her path, legs spread out in a hero stance, unshakable. "How will this benefit you?"

"Samaya Ximena, let go of the handlebars," she warned, settling onto the leather-coated foam of her bike saddle. I gripped the bars with all my might.

"Ew, don't be rude."

"Well, you're acting like a child. So, I'll address you as such."

"So, you agree? We're both children who have no business racing off to a party to do—what, exactly? Hurt our feelings? When we could go get ice cream instead?"

Lila hopped off the bike, shoving me further away from her house. She walked the bike down the road, not meeting my gaze but keeping pace with my steps in a passive-aggressive display of independence. "Will you leave me alone if I promise to go tomorrow?"

"If we take a left up ahead, we'll be two blocks away from the best soft serve in town. Strawberry and chocolate. All my treat."

"Let's go tomorrow—"

"We can go back to my place, rage dance to whatever playlist you want, take that test—"

"I don't want to take the test, Maya," Lila's voice hitched up an octave, her words spewing out fast and defensive.

"Fine, we will completely ignore the test on our fun night in," I had to pick up the pace to keep up with her. Lila was practically running down the street. "I think it's going to rain soon."

"I think my patience is wearing thin, and you should run along home to your boyfriend."

"Keenan went home. Well, I don't know where he went, but I kicked him out."

Lila stopped walking, and I stumbled at the abrupt change in her attention.

"Why?"

I sighed, staring up at the sky as the storm clouds bloomed overhead. Thunder tumbled through the air, sending shock waves down my spine , warning me to run home. But I wouldn't leave without Lila.

"He pressured me," I said. Her mouth dropped open, but I cut her off with the raise of my hands. "But nothing happened."

Lila nodded with her classic far-off stare, the one that made me feel she was talking to herself, not me. "Guys are always going to pressure you."

"Yeah, well, this time it was mean."

"Did he hurt you?" She stepped forward, hands curling into fists.

"No! Not on purpose. It was... it was just mean. Like all the quiet parts came out, ya know?"

"Are you okay?"

"I'm not trying to make this about me—"

"Are you okay?"

"Yes," I said, stepping back to consider my words. "Right now, I kind of hate him. But maybe I'll feel sad tomorrow? Is that weird? I love him, but he's been mean."

"I think that's normal. But then again, maybe that's a red flag."

"I'm sorry I didn't cancel my date to stay in with you."

Lila shrugged, tugging the bicycle out of my grip. "It's fine," she said, stepping forward down the sidewalk. "I didn't ask you to."

"Lila, we should head back. It's going to start pouring any minute."

"You're pissing me off, and I don't want to get into this with you—"

"It's a 20-minute ride down to the party. You'll get soaked before you even make it to the front door."

"I would've been there by now if you weren't holding me back," she sang, trying to keep her tone light, but her eyes kept avoiding mine.

"You deserve better than Jack Rodriguez." My voice practically echoed off the houses, stopping Lila in her tracks. She turned to me as I told her the sky was blue.

"No, shit, Maya."

"If the point of going tonight is to prove you're better than him, don't worry; everybody already knows." A giggle slipped through my lips as I considered the post-high school downfall of this subpar boy. "He's a high school senior who got sidelined by every recruiter in the area. I'm not making fun of him because that's awful, but it's also fucking karma. He's awful. Handsome? Sure. But you, Lila Park, are not some girl people forget about post-graduation. You're the character in the movie people show their grandchildren, flipping through the yearbook to show off. You will forever be the girl he let slip through his fingers because he wasn't smart enough to hold on. You are the star, and if you go tonight, you'll gift him his fifteen minutes of fame that he does not deserve."

Lila stared at the asphalt, her lip quivering.

"Don't give him the satisfaction of seeing you cry."

"Is that why you still let Keenan hang out with Sophia? To avoid a fight?"

"Ow," I winced, taking a step back.

"I'm sorry," Lila whispered. "That was mean."

"Yeah, it was," I sighed. "But if the roles were reversed, you wouldn't let me go either."

"That's not true—"

"Yes, it is."

"Well, it's not about you. It's about me." Lila spat, biting her bottom lip until it disappeared between her teeth. "I've spent the past month freaking out, and he's barely called me. He doesn't text me; he responds. I don't want to spend Friday night hiding out at your house, crying over a piece of plastic for the worst five minutes to eighteen years of my life. Where is he? Why am I here fucking screaming into my pillow while he's doing... what? Telling some girl all the same shit he used to say to me? How does that make me better?" She wiped her eyes, smudging her makeup until black streaks formed at the corners of her cheekbones.

"You look like Effy Stonem," I smiled, but she did not.

"I don't want to be Effy Stonem," she said. Hands pressed to her eyes as we sat down on the curb. "I don't want to be a yearbook picture he feels bad about. I want to be happy. Girls like Effy Stonem don't get happy endings."

"You're going to be fine, Lila."

"Shut up, Maya," Lila huffed into her arms, her face hidden in the crook of her elbow while her fingers dug deep into mine.

"Okay. But you will be. We can stay like this all night if you want. We can go back to your house or my house or move your bed onto the driveway and camp out in the front yard if that makes you feel better."

"I want him to say sorry," she whispered.

"I'm sorry, honey," I whispered back. "One day, the universe will send you someone who never lets you cry on the sidewalk. I know that with every bit of my heart." I smoothed the hair from her face as she nodded into my palm.

"How can you be so sure?" she sniffed, turning to me with a soft smile marred with fresh spilled tears.

"Because if it doesn't happen for you, how will it ever happen for me?"

"That's an awful thing to say," she laughed, but it was not the kind of sound made when hearing a funny joke. It was the type of laugh a beautiful person made after being complimented by someone less attractive.

When I looked back up at the sky, I saw a sliver of a crescent moon trying to fight its way from out behind the clouds. I heaved a sigh and prayed to the thunder crackling overhead as if I had a one-way line to God.

"Give me your hands," I ordered.

"Ew, Maya, don't make the moment weird."

"Just humor me," I knocked my shoulder into hers, and with a shake of her head, she placed her palms in my mine. "Dear God, please hide us so only our husbands can find us. Let it be easy and let them know who we are without us having to beg."

"There are so many problems in this world, and this is what you choose to pray for?"

"Your father would move the earth just to hear your mother laugh again. My mom freezes whenever I mention my dad, and I have zero memory of him ever being worthy of that response. But she does. If falling in love wasn't important, I wouldn't want it this bad. I don't want to be someone's second choice ever again."

"You're never my second choice, Maya," Lila said, gripping my hands. And it was my turn to laugh.

"Yes, I am," I sat up, dusting the debris from the sidewalk off my leggings. I turned back to Lila, smiling down at her with my hand outstretched. "I'm asking that tonight you make an exception."

Lila smiled, her dimples poking through as she nodded up at me, melancholy and understanding. I leaned forward to pull her up. She nodded at me, searching through the street with that far-off stare she used whenever she shut me out of her inner monologue.

Rain splattered against her nose, abrupt and cold. As we scrambled for our bicycles, I noticed a small dark stain on the back of my suede skirt glaring at me beneath the streetlamp. I closed my eyes, shaking the irritation burning at the back of my neck.

"What?" Lila asked, scanning the area to understand the change in my mood.

"Nothing, let's not get into it."

"We just had this deeply profound moment, and then you huffed like I drank the last coke-a-cola in the fridge. Just say it!"

"You stained my skirt," I spat, grabbing Lila's bike while she scanned the fabric for the blemish.

"Wait, what?" She said, spinning the skirt until the back facing the front. "Oh, my God."

"It's fine. I'll just ask Mami to take it to the cleaners—"

"Maya, shut up. I got my period." Lila's voice was a breathy bit of sound hidden beneath the onslaught of rain crying from above.

"Oh, fuck, Lila," we started running, dragging the bicycle alongside us to flee the storm. "Blood is never going to… wait… you got your period!"

"I think I was just so stressed out that…" she smiled, practically skipping through the street. "I got my fucking period!"

"Fuck yes! Don't you ever scare me like that again."

"The same goes for you," she smacked my shoulder as we hid in the safety of her garage. "I'm too young to be an aunt."

We sat there in the darkness of her garage until the storm died down, holding hands and hugging each other as our teeth shattered. But mine never did. I couldn't shake the fear that something was off.

It had been an emotional evening, but that wasn't it all. I kept waiting for the rain to wipe away the nasty fear that one day there would be stains that laughter, ice cream, and friendship couldn't erase. Perhaps that fear never went away. I learned to smile through the fear, hoping one day I'd be brave enough to never need the rain again.

THE FOURTH KISS

I

PROFESSOR IRMA WAS A forty-something year-old Portuguese woman who sported a buzz cut and harem pants as her daily uniform. She was a bit of a celebrity on campus for her work in trauma response and childhood development, and I became obsessed with her from the instant I stepped into Introduction to Psychology. There was something about the way she carried herself that made me want to become her. She did not care if you found her entertaining or approachable. The only thing Professor Irma cared about was that her students understood that psychology was a vocation, not a job.

We were studying children, how they operated, and how our choices affected their potential growth. In learning about others, I quietly dissected myself, where I came from, and why I desperately wanted to appear approachable and entertaining. Twenty years from now, I wanted to look into a mirror and see Professor Irma's influence staring back at me. The only issue was that Professor Irma was not known for being a ball of sunshine, and even though I was doing well in the course, I still could not tell if she liked me.

"Class is canceled next week to give you more time to study for the final, but I will be here bright and early if anyone wants to come by with any questions." My knee bounced in time with the knocking of Professor Irma's expo marker against the whiteboard. Her brush strokes matched the slightly listless inflection of her accented vowels. "As George comes around with last week's pop quiz results, please take a moment to self-assess your standing in this course. Your first semester is ending, and it would be a shame for your GPA to start off on the wrong note. At this point you are all aware of my infamous red pen and how happy it makes me to use it. Do not be proud. See me if you need help."

I could have sworn she avoided meeting my eyes as she turned back toward us. I took a deep breath, my satchel already slung across my shoulders as the clock ticked closer to noon and students on all sides of the auditorium packed up their belongings to race out the frigid classroom. I needed to get to her desk before the line of students begging for extra credit took form.

A voice cleared beside me as the crisp sound of paper sliding across a wooden desk forced me to break eye contact with Professor Irma's briefcase. "She'll respect you more if you try less," George didn't break concentration as he scanned his stack of quizzes, offering me the same bit of advice he had repeated since I started the course. I ignored him in favor of glaring at the B mocking me in big, bold loops on the top right-hand corner of the page. It was not a minus or a plus, but an average B.

I stood up, bag heavy on my shoulder with binders filled to the brim with notes. He was right. On the back of the quiz, written in red ink, was a single phrase: "Keep going."

"Thanks, George," I beamed. I barely caught the thumbs-up he sent my way as I shimmied down the aisle, trying not to knock into any students on my way to the pit at the center of the classroom. I was third in line to speak with Professor Irma.

Crap.

"Samaya?"

I turned to find James Williams standing beside me with my laptop charger in his hands.

"Oh, shit. Thank you, I totally forgot," I slipped the charger into my backpack before he noticed the way his amber eyes crinkled at the corners when he smiled affected my disposition.

James Williams was the typical sun-kissed fraternity type, with broad shoulders and chapped skin from too many hours spent chilling by the local beach. He always managed to smell like suntan lotion and summertime no matter the time of day and never managed to remember his own charger before coming to class.

"No, please. Thank you for lending it to me again. I'm bad with details, ya know?"

"Right, right," I nodded, side-stepping the girl in front of me to catch a glimpse of Professor Irma chatting with another student in our class. She patted his shoulder, and I became second in line. She already looked tired, but I did not have another shot before exam season ended and holiday break began. But as I stepped forward, so did James. I scratched a nonexistent itch at the nape of my neck as I turned toward him. "Sorry, I'm a little distracted. Is there something else? Not to be rude! I just—" I gestured toward Professor Irma, and he nodded in turn.

"Understood. I'm not doing too hot in this class, either," he sighed.

My eyebrows creased. "What? No. I'm fine."

"Yeah, I figured. I saw your test—"

"You what?"

"When George handed it to you. I wasn't like looking, looking. I just saw a little. And you are always asking mad questions and taking hella notes, so I figured you'd be fine to go out this weekend. You know what? Hold on. Back up." He sighed, scratching his jawline as his lips curved to the side, and a soft chuckle slipped from his chest. "I'm trying to invite you to a party at the house tonight."

"Oh, really? Wow. You're doing an excellent job," I laughed, and he laughed along with me. I clutched the satchel at my shoulder firmly between my palms. My shoulders curved inward, toes curling in my sneakers as my weight drifted to the left along with the flyer James handed me with poorly photoshopped fraternity letters sprayed across the center as if drawn on by a paint can.

"It's Anything-But-Clothes themed, but no one cares if you don't do it," he smiled up at me beneath long eyelashes, but the way he said it made it sound like his brothers would most definitely care.

"Oh, really?" I asked because I could not find the words to say anything else.

"Yeah," he nodded, taking a step closer to me on the exhalation of his breath. I stopped breathing in turn. "Most girls come in bikinis or…whatever feels comfortable. You could come in a trash bag," he chuckled, his eyes roaming over my body in a way that made my lips go slack. "But definitely come."

"Okay," I breathed, eyes darting to his parted lips and back. I could tell he noticed from the way his shoulders pulled back. "I'm a bit busy," *I wasn't,* "but I'll try to make it happen."

"Dope," he murmured back.

Out of the corner of my eyes, I saw the girl ahead of me in line, edging away from the desk, and my position became clear. "Listen, I gotta focus—"

"For sure," he said, his hand brushed my shoulder as he backed out of the line, not taking his eyes off me. "Bring your friends!" He stopped to fist bump George on his way out of the lecture hall, shooting me one last wink over his shoulder like a John Hughes movie.

What the hell just happened? I thought, but I shook off the confusion as I braced myself for an already tired Professor Irma.

I stepped forward with an eager smile. "Hi—"

"No," she shut me down, packing her briefcase with random files splayed out across her desk.

"You don't even know what I was going to say," I tried to hide the teenage sass from my voice, but it was unfortunately prevalent in the way I held every bone in my body.

With her hands pressed firmly across the handle of her bag, Professor Irma stood up and gave me a once-over as if she already finished our conversation before it began. "Is this any different than the last three times you have approached my desk? Exactly. The internship at the women's shelter is for graduate students only, not college first-year students."

"That is totally fair! But what if we did not look at it as an 'internship,' per say, but more of a 'volunteer experience'?"

A bemused smile formed at the center of the professor's lips. "You need more experience."

"But how can I gain more experience if you don't let me work for that experience?" I walked alongside her as she made her way through the exit.

Students milled through the courtyard of the humanities department chatting amongst each other in an open way that was only found on college campuses. Everyone greeted each other like potential friends they could borrow homework from, or hold over a keg stand, or take shots with at a tailgate. Strangers I'd only ever met in the laundry room of my dormitory waved at me, and I waved back. I knew their names without having to think too hard about it because I paid attention. I was a social butterfly, and it was like everyone around me laid out pretty flowers for me to rest upon.

It was beautiful. It was glorious. It was the reinvention of Samaya Ximena.

Professor Irma smiled at me, and I knew she was about to reject me, but she had never seemed so happy to do it before. "Listen, I appreciate your enthusiasm for the course, but do me a favor? Enjoy this time because it does not come back. Take a bunch of different classes and approach them with the same amount of curiosity. Have fun. If you are still interested next year, you can stop by my office, and we can work something out."

"Thank you!" I practically screamed. "I can live with that. And if anything changes—"

"It won't," Professor Irma shook her head, her voice finite, but her lips still curved in a smile.

"But if it does?"

"Enjoy the winter holiday, Samaya. I'll see you at the review session?" She asked, already making her way back toward the faculty parking lot.

"Yes, ma'am!" I hollered back, practically skipping across campus with this 'almost' win.

II

I FOUND LILA IN the library with her biology textbook open and discarded on the table in favor of the *Twilight* Tumblr account she'd maintained since middle school. I tugged on one end of her signature chunky headphones until they slipped off her head and assumed occupancy in my unofficial-official reserved seat beside her.

"I think I just got asked out," I leaned close to her so that only she could hear me, and the words struck their mark as I knew they would.

Lila twisted until she faced me directly, her books completely forgotten. "You think someone asked you out or you know?"

I shrugged, searching for the folded flier I kept secure beneath the cover of my psychology textbook. "Well, it's never happened before. I don't want to read too much into it." I handed the sheet of colorful printer paper to her how an archivist would manage an ancient relic. She accepted it with equal respect, a small smile creeping at the corners of her lips like a proud mom.

"Miss Maya, since when do you hang out at frats?" She teased, her voice bubbling with excitement.

I shrugged and snatched the flier back. "Since I was invited to."

Lila leaned forward onto the table, her chin perched in the crook of her palm and her pointer finger pressed to her cupid's bow. Mischief danced in her eyes as she searched for her words in a wistful hum. "Hm, was this before or after he asked to borrow your charger?"

I swatted at her arm, scanning the surrounding tables filled with college students cramming for finals to make sure no one heard her. "Don't be rude!" I hid my face between my hands as she slouched back onto the wooden chair, laughing in that low rumble only cats and loved ones seemed to do right.

"It is cutesy. You like him," she held onto the vowels like a *Kidz Bop* ballad. I tried to cover her mouth, but she twisted out of my reach, grinning like the Cheshire cat. "He clearly likes you, or he smoked so much weed his short-term memory is just nonexistent."

My fingers split open, eyes peering out at her from behind the safety of my hands. "You think he likes me?"

"Maya, don't fish for compliments."

"I compliment you a million times a day! Can I have some?" I gestured to the open can of *Red Bull* sitting beside her backpack, highlighters scattered about to give the illusion of studying where there was none.

"No."

"Too late," I sipped the last remnants of the can while she rolled her eyes at me.

"Obviously, he likes you. Inviting a girl to a frat party is like bringing sand to the beach."

"Would you come with me?"

Lila shook her head, turning back to her books and notebook as if I were the distraction and not her own attention deficit disorder. "Can't. I have a biology exam next Friday."

I nodded, my pointer finger tapping my lips, mimicking the same face she gave me. "Hm, of course. So, tell me, how was Tumblr helping with your studies?"

Her face went slack as she closed her laptop with a soft click. "I was taking a break."

"You have a solid A in that class—"

"B+," she corrected.

"Plus, there is over a week's worth of time to study. You can't say no because you know I'll never go unless you come with me. Please? What is one night off?"

Lila removed her headphones from her neck, wrapping the cord around the center as she stared at me as if I were a stranger. "What the hell has gotten into you?"

I shrugged. "Don't know what you mean."

"I am the bad influence, okay? Not you. Don't steal my thunder."

"Huh?" I leaned back in my chair, leg folded beneath my thigh as I took a closer look at the pink tint coloring her eyes. "Did you smoke?"

Lila flipped through the pages in her textbook, intently scanning each line as she tried to cement the structure of the human cell to memory. I took her silence as a cue to drop the conversation, but I never enjoyed loaded silences with Lila. It made me nauseous not knowing what she was thinking when we were together. Every sentence that entered my mind spewed from my lips without a second thought. There were no secrets between us, at least not from me. But I learned to keep my opinions to myself in the months after her mother's funeral.

"I'm not judging you," I muttered.

"I know," she said, but her voice felt flat and dutiful.

"I just… there's smoking, and then there's smoking too much—"

She turned to me with sharp eyes and an energy that made me back up in my seat. "And who are you to say what's too much for me?"

"I'm sorry," I whispered. The words fell off my tongue like seeds from a grape, painful and unwanted. I cleared my throat. "I'm going to go scan a few things," I slipped my student ID from my back pocket with the tips of my fingers, uncurling my body slowly from the chair as if waiting for her to invite me to stay.

"You do that," was all Lila said, flipping through her book without giving me a second glance.

The library's main lobby spread across four quadrants, each comprised of large, rectangular wooden desks for students to scatter their belongings across and bookcases at least six rows high, filled to the brim with books abandoned since the 2000s. All rows led to the printers, and standing with his back turned to me was none other than my favorite TA.

"George!" I called. He turned over a shoulder, spooked by the disturbance a firm *shh* cried out to me through the stacks reminding me where I was. "Oh, sorry," I mouthed, claiming a spot beside him at the copy machine.

"Hey, good job on the quiz," he said, reaching a handout to high-five me as quietly as humanly possible.

"Eh, could have done better. But I am trying," I shrugged, rifling through my book bag for my textbook, flipping through the pages until I landed on the diagrams that felt too tedious to copy by hand. "Are those the exams for next week?"

He quickly pressed the pages beneath his underarms, away from my prying eyes. "Absolutely not. I have my own finals to worry about." His tortoiseshell glasses slipped down the bridge of his nose in emphasis.

"Noted, just making conversation," I mumbled, focusing back on the scanner. "What are your plans post-graduation?"

"Med school, hopefully. If I can survive statistics."

"Ahh, you'll be fine. You're like a genius."

"No, I'm just grossly type A. Blame my parents. Hey, can I give you some unsolicited advice?" He shoved his documents into a crisp, clean white binder as he turned to me in what can only be described as sage kindness. "Stop asking for Irma's approval. You are never going to get it. Instead, be direct. Go to her office every day until she says yes. She responds well to determination. And coffee. With extra sugar and no milk."

"Noted, thank you."

He nodded at the flier sticking out of my books, leaning back against the printer. "You going to that?"

"Only if I can get my friend to come with me." I gestured toward Lila, and for a moment I understood the high of being cupid as I witnessed George flip from a wise upperclassman to a bumbling fool, blushing at my friend as she flipped pages in her book. My cheeks hurt from smiling. "Hey, George, can I give you some unsolicited advice?"

"Sure," he sighed, chewing on his lips with an eager curiosity.

I pointed over at Lila, "Lila also responds to directness."

He giggled, folding over at the waist in a way I would not imagine someone with his broad shoulders and muscle mass even know how to do. "Thank you."

I was so excited I practically ran back to the table.

"Lila," I hissed, catching my breath as I barreled back into my seat.

She did not look up at me but rather groaned, "yes?"

"That boy standing by the printer – do not look! He has been staring at you for like an hour."

"We haven't even been here an hour," she corrected.

"Same difference."

Lila nodded ever so slightly, but her face didn't change. "Mm, ready to go?"

"What are you going to do?" I asked, head dropping down low and re-opening my laptop to pretend I had work to do. "He is kind of cute. And he blushes, Lila." I grabbed hold of my chest, pouting from the cuteness overload.

Finally, she said, "Nothing."

"Nothing?"

She looked up at me with a thin smile and knowing eyes. "He can come to me."

"Oof," I nodded. "Bold, amazing."

She laughed, slamming her textbook shut and randomly shoving her belongings into the various pockets of her backpack. "He has been staring at me for a week. First, it was over by the table at the exit. Then two days later, he was one table closer, until today. His friend looks sick of it. I am sick of it. I am thinking we leave and smoke out the arboretum."

George sat at a table at the other end of the study area with a stranger whose only identifying features were a black hoodie, dark wash skinny jeans, and a tactical backpack covered in patches haphazardly sewn onto the material that told of trips to various national parks, rock concerts, and history channel memes I hadn't encountered since middle school. He was the total opposite of George's clean-cut, navy-blue polo shirt and boot-cut jeans. George made a comment to his friend, who barely looked up from his textbooks but seemed to say something back that had George snapping at him to "keep your voice down!"

The boys laughed together, and the blush from earlier seemed to coat George's olive-toned skin. I liked that he was the type of guy who giggled, blushed, and smiled when my friend flipped pages in her textbook.

"I'm kind of proud of him. You have an intimidating stare."

"Thank you," she smiled, flipping another page.

"But what if he never comes over? What if he's a really sweet guy who's just too shy to make the first move?"

"Then I didn't waste my time."

"And what if he does come over?"

Lila shrugged.

"Oof," I nodded again, snapping my fingers. "The wisdom at this table, ladies and gentlemen. How do you do it? Teach me to be cool like you."

"Cool people are cool because they say they are," she stuck her tongue out at me like we were still children at snack time.

"Amazing. Just give me a moment while I find my pen," I panto-mimed, pulling a pen out of my purse, clicking the top, and jotting down notes on my hand. "Okay, perfect, note to self... do less." I clicked the 'pen' closed while Lila burst into laughter.

"Let's get out of here," she stood up abruptly, pushing her chair into the desk so that it scraped the floor beneath it. Something about the sound of her impending exit from the building sent her admirer into action. We passed through the front exit, walking out into the court-yard under the cover of night, with my only sense of direction coming from the elbow Lila linked with mine. But I could feel someone running after us. The sound of footsteps clattering against the pavement betrayed whatever cool approach George might have had planned. Lila stopped walking before he even spoke. Though she played it off well, she had secretly observed her admirer just as closely.

"Hey," George ran up to us, his figure was only a shadow in breeze-way at this hour of night, but there were multiple sheets of paper flapping between his fingers announcing his pursuit. "You forgot these at the scanner."

I pressed a hand to my forehead, shaking my head as I took my notes from his hands. "Oh, geez, did I? Ugh, my bad."

He stopped beside me, hands pressed to his hips, looking at Lila with open lips and not a thought behind his eyes. He was working out of instinct, certain that he would know exactly the right opening line when he reached us, but his brain betrayed him. I felt like an anthro-pologist hiding in the trees as I documented a rare animal mating ritual. It was painful to watch.

"Oh, um, Lila, this is George, my TA," I gestured toward George, hoping he would pick up from there.

He reached a hand out to her the way you would when meeting the father of your soon-to-be bride, full of fear and ready for battle. Lila tracked its movements with her eyes, smiling in a way that made George shake. He looked a bit awkward just standing there, but he didn't walk away. He took a deep breath, cleared his throat, and recov-ered. "Hey, uh, are you taking bio this semester?"

"Yes," Lila replied, cool and clipped.

He nodded, "Cool, um, do you like it?"

"Yeah," she smirked, crossing her arms as she let her eyes roam from his shoes to his eyes. "I mean I want to go to med school, so I better like it."

"I didn't know that." I waited for Lila to elaborate, but all she did was shrug.

"You never asked," she said, her eyes never leaving George.

"If you're up for it," George said, drawing my attention back to him. "Our house is throwing an ABC party tonight. There is going to be a keg and a bunch of people dressed like assholes. *I'll* be dressed like an asshole. It will be fun. Y'all should come."

"You're a part of a frat?" She asked.

He rocked back on his shoes, brushing an invisible bit of lint off of his polo. "I'm the president."

Lila rolled her eyes so far back I feared they pop right out of her head. "Of course you are."

He laughed, running a hand through his combed-back chestnut brown hair. "Did that just ruin it?"

"No," she said softly.

"Dope!" I said, smiling ear to ear as I jostled Lila on the shoulder. "We'll be there!"

He smiled back at me, shoulders loose, happy that the rejection he braced for never came.

I had seen Lila around guys before, but this was different. This was simple.

Lila's lips curved softly across her cheeks. She hooked an arm through mine, pulling us away from George and back toward our dorm on the other side of campus. Just like that, our plans for the night were set in motion.

I nudged Lila's shoulder with my own, wiggling my eyebrows at her.

"Stop, I'm done with boys," she shook her head.

"I'm just impressed. I mean, look at us?" My shoulders rolled back as I stepped out of Lila's arms and strutted down the sidewalk like it was my own personal runway. "We have dates tonight."

"We're probably one of the many girls he invited to this party."

"Who cares? He invited you." I tapped the tip of her nose, spinning around Lila as if there wasn't a cluster of students passing us on either side. "I feel like I am floating on a cloud. He's a cutie, Lila."

Lila's tongue pressed against the inside of her jaw as she scanned the cement, her hands adjusting the straps of her book bag unnecessarily. "He is, isn't he?"

"Who, George? I'm talking about mine!" I practically sang my words to the rooftops. "I think he's going to kiss me."

Lila let out a breath of air, looping her elbow through mine to keep me in place. "Oh, I'm sure he'll try."

"And I will be super cool about it. Just you watch."

"No, you won't," Lila shook her head at me.

"Yes, I will!"

"Maya, you haven't kissed anyone in the past two years. You will catch feelings."

"But what if I don't!" I cheered, teeth stretching from cheek to cheek. I clutched her arms, shaking her shoulders until she smiled with the same amount of excitement as I felt.

"Fuck yeah," she said.

"Fuck yeah," I said back.

"Fuck yeah!" she hollered.

"FUCK YEAH!" We cried out in unison.

People turned toward us, but we did not care. We were too busy jumping around the college lawn, twirling with excitement, to notice anyone but ourselves.

III

DANIELLE STAUD WAS MY college roommate, a pairing Lila believed to be an error made on behalf of the housing department but was an active choice on my part. I loved Lila but needed someone to push me out of my comfort zone. The comfort zone in question was isolating myself in my bedroom while I waited for Lila to produce our social calendar.

"What's in this?" Danielle asked, twirling a section of her strawberry blonde hair around a hot curling rod.

"Honestly, a little bit of anything I could sneak off the trolley before the housekeepers took notice," I explained, swiping deodorant under my arms, admiring my favorite pastel pink bralette and matching pajama shorts in the mirror. I needed a confidence boost, and I would take it wherever I could get it.

Lila emerged from the bathroom wearing nothing but a sports bra and joggers. Her washboard abdominal muscles were on full display, and I tried my best not to body-check my figure in the mirror. It was hard not to run a hand across my belly, comparing the soft curves of my flesh to Lila's taught gym-toned edges. "Well, beggars can't be choosers. Bottoms up."

"Wait! Who's driving?" I asked, clearly not volunteering.

Lila pulled out three pencils of varying sizes from my desk drawer and lined them up equally in her hand. She presented them to us like a game of straws. Each of us pulled a pencil, leaving Lila with the short stick.

Lila laughed. "Fuck me. Fine. I will drive. Bottoms up."

I poured a bunch of mini-liquor bottles into an unlabeled bottle of water the student union handed out for free during orientation week. As someone who didn't really play sports or go to the gym, I put the bottle to good use as the designated home for what Lila and I affectionately called 'So-Duh'. The drink tasted more like battery acid than sugary syrup. I took a swig from the bottle, shaking my head as the liquid burned its way down my throat.

"I should have snatched a chaser." The words practically clawed their way up my throat through hacking coughs.

Danielle matched my gulp and did not fare any better with the aftertaste. The moment the drink touched her lips, her eyes shifted. I did not have the chance to move out of the way before she spewed the drink back up. Bits of backwash sprayed across Lila and me, and all I could do was stand there in shock.

"Ah, Christ, Dani! Aim down!" Lila ran into the bathroom, grabbing a towel off the hook to wipe the spittle off her exposed skin.

"I'm so sorry!" Danielle whined; her southern drawl sounded more like a bad Judy Garland impression than a college freshman. "I didn't expect it to taste like that."

I rushed over to the sink, eager to wash the droplets of vomit off my hands while Danielle gasped at the horrid taste of whatever poison we gifted her.

"It's all good, love, just breathe through your nose," I walked back over with a damp wash cloth for her forehead. Danielle looked up at me through ragged breaths and eyes full of gratitude.

"Thanks. Maybe I'm allergic to Schnapps?" Danielle looked between Lila and me for approval.

"Texas Barbie, why don't you hop in the shower? It will make you feel better." Lila suggested, her smile sharp and posture ready to be rid of Danielle like a carton of putrid milk.

"But I just started my hair—"

"Then I suggest you clip it back," Lila smiled, plopping onto my bed as if she owned it.

"Honestly, you'll feel refreshed. You can borrow my shower cap. It's on the hook inside." I needed distance between Lila and Danielle before any more comments arose that couldn't be erased. Lila placed a *Pink Floyd* record on the vinyl player she bought me for my birthday last year, cranking up the volume loud enough to end any conversations that didn't entertain her.

"There's no shame in Texas Barbie staying back if she's not feeling up to it," Lila called out over the music. I bit my lips between my teeth, hoping Danielle did not feel the disdain in the air as she waited for the nausea to pass.

"I'm usually not like this, I promise," Danielle clipped back her hair with an oversized plastic flower. I handed Danielle my shower cap, nodding along as I backed out of the bathroom. "I have had drinks before. I am not a prude. But Utah's weird with their alcohol percentages. So, it's not really drinking, yeah know? Just a glass of wine at dinner now and then." She took a deep breath, exhaling like she had just gone on a wild ride.

"Of course, love, it's all good."

Lila popped up behind me, resting one arm around my shoulders while the other elbow pressed into the doorframe. "Everyone gets shit-faced, okay? The first time Maya—"

"I SAID I WAS SORRY!" I yelled, but it only made Lila want to tell the story more. Without permission, Lila gripped the back of my kneecap and hauled my leg up in the air, knocking me off balance. I clipped my shoulder on the green tile to steady myself as she pointed out a slightly faded jagged scar hiding in plain sight.

"She blacked out off of three shots of vodka from my dad's liquor cabinet and fell off the bottom step of my front porch," Lila laughed.

Danielle took a closer look at my skin. "I never noticed how many scars you have."

"I'm clumsy. And it was more than three shots." I yanked my leg free, tired of being gawked at like a circus attraction. "Show and tell is over!"

Danielle cringed at the sight of the wound; her nose scrunched in apprehension. "I don't want to get like that."

"You won't," I promised, but there was more bite to my words than I intended. The sound of Danielle's judgmental tone made me want to crank the music louder.

"You might," Lila corrected, sauntering out of the bathroom with an impish smile. "But it's human."

"But what if—"

"Hey, Dani? You have vomit on your cheek." I scratched my nose for added effect. I was sick of being a cautionary tale.

"Oh, my God!" Danielle gasped; I had never seen her run so quickly to wash her face.

I left the bathroom with a soft click of the door on my way out. Lila pulled my weed stash from the shoe box I kept hidden beneath the box spring. A habit I adopted from Lila back in high school.

"We should move that to my car. If the RA does an end-of-semester room check, I'm screwed." I sat in front of the megawatt lights lining my vanity mirror, covering up the blue hue encasing my under eyes with drugstore makeup.

"Please, if you only knew what she kept under her bed, you wouldn't worry," Lila rolled joints like grannies knitted sweaters. It soothed her.

"How the hell do you know—"

She shushed me, not taking her eyes off the wrapper in her hands as she sealed the edge with the tip of her tongue. "Don't ask questions you don't want to know the answers to."

I grabbed a sweatshirt off the dresser and hurled it at her head.

"Hey!" She gasped.

"We are not ditching Dani. Quit asking. Be nice. And stop calling her Texas Barbie! She is from Utah." I plopped down onto the bed beside Lila, the backs of my hands pressed against my forehead. "It's only 8 o'clock, and I'm already exhausted."

"So, let's stay in."

"Don't be ridiculous."

Lila wiggled her eyebrows at me, placing the joints inside a plastic sandwich bag within her canvas tote bag. "You're nervous."

"No," I lied. I hated to admit it, but I was nervous, and when I got nervous, my mind shut off, and when my mind shut off, I looked to Lila to guide me through the dark. "What are we wearing?"

Lila rifled through her tote bag, searching for a yellow roll of caution tape. She presented it to me, and all I could think about was the time we used several of these to decorate our door frame on Halloween. It took me a second to realize what she was suggesting.

"No," I gasped, feeling like Eve after she ate the fruit and discovered the concept of shame.

"Oh, yes," she nodded, laughter tickling her cheeks. "It's an Anything *But* Clothes party. You could go, right now, as is and be perfectly dressed. Well, you'd fit the theme perfectly for Sigma's *Risky Business* party, but—"

"You're insane," I hissed, but she had a point. "I can't wear that."

"Why not?"

I opened my mouth, but I did not want to fill it with words. Instead, I stared at Lila, the curve of her hips, her flat stomach, and the carefree way she strolled through the room, knowing she was undeniably perfect.

"You have gotten sloppy drunk plenty of times. I just don't mention it." I pressed up off the bed determined to find something respectable hidden within the sea of hoodies in my closet.

Lila raced after me, thrusting her arm out in front of me as if my clothes were radioactive. "Please, Samaya, I beg of you. You're young. You're hot. Do not wear a garbage bag to this party." She grumbled, and I know she said it as an unfathomable joke, but it gave me a brilliant idea.

"Absolutely not!"

"But it would be so cute!" I pleaded, bouncing on my toes with my hands folded in front of my face. She rolled her eyes at me, fighting back a smile with the edge of her teeth. "What's that noise? Do you see my phone? Wait, Lila, don't!" I jumped across the room, trying to snatch my cell phone out of Lila's hands before she could answer it. Mami's picture filled the screen as Lila pressed the phone to her ear.

"Hola, hola!" Lila's impression of Mami's accent was exceptionally good. "Please tell your daughter that wearing trash is unacceptable—"

"Give me that," I slipped the phone from Lila's hands, pointing at the vanity like a mother sending her child to time out. Lila obeyed, smiling to herself as she resumed makeup touch ups while I hid in the corners of my closet as if she couldn't hear me. "Sorry, Mami, ignore her."

"Ay mi bebe! Ugh, you have no idea how much I needed to hear your voice." Mami gushed.

"Are you drunk?" I whispered into the phone, laughing at the thought of what Mami might act like without someone to guard over all the time.

Mami gasped over the phone and the dramatics of the gesture made me snort. "How dare you say that about your *Santa Madre?*"

"No, but seriously, what's up? You called like four times. Mami?"

"Nada, I just miss you. I ran into one of the moms from your old high school at the bar, and I don't know… *ay, mi, hija,* when are you coming home?"

"Mami, we talked about this." It was kind to be missed, but Mami

and I had this same conversation several times throughout the semester.

"I know, I know. But you're only an hour away."

"I'll be home for winter break in a few weeks."

"Okay, but you said you'd visit—"

"If I visit, does that mean I get to meet your new boyfriend?" I knew it was a saucy question. Discussing her love life was never a part of our relationship, but I wanted Mami to be happy. As I grew older, it became more apparent that she had spent her twenties playing house with me, and I always worried if she felt lonely, even if she did not say it. "Am I getting introduced to the new boyfriend anytime soon? Robert, right?"

"No, no, stop it!" Mami scolded, but I could hear the voices in the background, and I tried to picture their faces no matter how wildly inaccurate I might be. "How's school? How are your classes? When does sorority rush start?"

"Good, good, and never," I laughed, but she did not join me.

"*Bebe*, I know what I'm telling you! Do it! Do not be your own worst enemy. Those are the friends you will keep for the rest of your life!"

"Mami," I hissed into the phone. "*Ninguna de esas chicas* would have looked at me in high school. Why should I pay to be their friend?"

"Honestly, Samaya, I can't keep up with you. You want to reinvent yourself? This is how you do it!" She cheered, her drunken bliss creeping back into the conversation along with loud jazz music wafting through the background noise.

I took a deep breath, exhaling through my nose. "I'll think about it."

"Fine, Samaya," Mami grumbled. "Do what you want."

"Why are you mad?"

"The point of you living on campus was for you to grow. Transform into who you always wanted to be!"

"I like who I am," I spat.

"Don't twist my words, Samaya. That is not what I meant *y lo sabes.*"

I scanned my clothing rack in search of the one item I had not had the courage to wear out yet. It was a skintight tank dress with the tags still attached. Lila and I bought matching dresses to wear to parties we never attended. It was short, and the fabric left little to the imagination.

I remember feeling so powerful when I first tried it on. I loved the way it cascaded over my body. I loved the fact that I owned something like it. And yet, for some reason, I gripped the jersey cotton in my hands, utterly paralyzed by the idea of wearing it outside. I could feel the panic attack creeping in, but I could not find the words to express it. If Mami knew I had panic attacks she would make me come home. I was not ready to go home.

"No offense." I bit out the words with a hand pressed to my neck, monitoring the rising speed in my pulse. "But you're drunk."

"Samaya!"

"Did you call just to fight with me? *¿Que, Mami?*"

Mami whispered through the phone like a prayer I was not meant to hear. *"Sólo quiero que seas feliz."*

Lila tapped me on the shoulder, and for a moment, I completely forgot she was even in the room. She gestured for me to hand over the phone and mouthed, "Go try it on." I nodded, tension dripping off my shoulders the instant I handed over the phone.

"When are you coming to visit?" Lila asked, and I could hear the joy returning to Mami's voice through the speaker.

I stepped inside the bathroom, sighing out all the negativity building inside my chest.

"It's just me, Dani."

"Okay, I'll be out in a minute," she responded.

I slipped on the dress and let every negative intrusive thought I ever had about myself win out. I braced myself against the sink and examined my reflection in the mirror. The dress caressed my stomach fat in a way that made my skin crawl. I wanted to rip the fabric in half and throw it in the trash. But I could not move.

The cool texture of the porcelain sink was the only thing keeping me upright. I turned on the faucet just to stare at the hot water pounding through the pipes, wishing it would wipe my mind clean of every negative opinion I had of myself. I slipped my fingers beneath the water, letting the heat numb my skin as I focused on the rushing water and the steam hiding my reflection in the mirror.

The door cracked open, and Lila held the phone out to me as Mami shouted over the speaker. "Have fun, girls!"

"We will," Lila and I hollered back.

Lila looked at me up and down, hand on her hip and words missing from her tongue. "Come on," she motioned for me to follow her out of the bathroom, and so I did.

"What's going on?" She asked, facing me with open arms and understanding.

"Nothing," I sniffed.

"Is it Texas Barbie? Cause there's still time to ditch her."

"No," I giggled, "it's nothing."

"Am I being a cunt? That happens sometimes. It's on autopilot at this point."

"You're not a cunt," I sniffed, wiping at my nose. "Stop saying that. Don't ever say that."

"Is this about James?" She asked like she already knew the answer and hated me for it. "Jesus, Maya. Is he a Rockefeller, and I am just unaware of it?"

"Would you ever join a sorority?" I laid back on the bed, staring up at the ceiling as I focused on my breathing and the sound of the shower roaring through the walls.

Lila was startled by the question but delivered a quick response. "No."

"I don't know... it was just an idea," I said more to myself than anyone else.

"Okay. But just because I don't want to do something doesn't mean you can't."

"I know that it's just hard to actually commit to that." I tried to find the right words to describe how I was feeling but did not feel safe enough to say.

Lila looked around the room, flipping over pillows and moving my bed sheets until she finally found what she was looking for. Without prompting, Lila snatched my phone off the bed and quickly undid the passcode. I did not stop her. She scrolled through my phone until she stumbled on a certain app and a certain picture she was not supposed to see.

My blood ran cold. "Give it back," I jumped off the bed, but Lila was too glued to the screen to listen.

"Oh my," Lila gasped.

"Stop it!"

"Is this who you've been *lusting* after? Maya! Girl!"

"Please, stop."

"He looks like such a dick!" Lila cackled, but I was getting redder by the minute. I snatched the phone out of Lila's hands, but not fast enough.

On the screen was James and his Instagram profile. He had arms like a Greek god, but the attitude of someone who said they were six feet when they were really five foot seven. I whirled around and snatched the phone from Lila's hands, pushing her in the process. But Lila won out, giggling into my phone screen, brushing me off without a care in the world.

"Knock it off!" I snapped, eyes blazing, and the carefree attitude I had all morning evaporated.

Lila typed on my phone, commenting on a certain shirtless ab picture from his profile. "Hi, James!" She mocked, doing a generic impression of a swooning teenage girl, "I want to suck your—"

"Lila!"

I tackled Lila to the floor and accidentally pressed the send button in the middle of the brawl.

We froze, and I could feel my veins pounding beneath my skin, but there was nowhere to run. Lila scrambled to delete the comment. She was not laughing anymore.

"No," I whispered, running into my closet, and slammed the door shut.

"Maya," Lila whispered, pulling open the closet door and climbing in after me.

"It's okay," I mumbled, my voice cold and wobbly. I kept my eyes glued shut, wishing for her to leave, but she wouldn't. Lila crouched down closer to me, arms wrapped around my shoulders, and all I could do was tense up.

"I'm sorry," she promised, and I knew she meant it.

I shook my head. "It's fine. It's my fault." Lila held me close, and though I was angry, I hugged her back.

Lila rubbed soothing circles into my back, "I deleted it. Okay? He didn't see it. I doubt he will ever see it. I mean, guys are shit with their phones. And on a Friday? He is kind of… I bet he won't see it. I just wanted to make you laugh."

I gasped, pulling away from Lila's shoulder. "But I don't want to be a joke anymore."

"Hey! No one is laughing."

You are, I wanted to say, but I didn't.

Lila grabbed me by the cheek, forcing me to meet her eyes. "But you're so funny! And pretty! And smart!"

"You're not listening—"

"I promise you, I am. I just feel horrible, and I want to change the subject."

I pushed off Lila. And like a good friend, she did not stop me. "I just need a minute," I sighed. I pulled myself up off the floor and into the twinkling string lights of my dorm room. "We don't have to go anymore. Let's just stay in."

"Absolutely not."

"What?"

"You're going. You're wearing that dress. And we're going to have a good time." Lila slipped her joggers off, discarding them onto the floor as she started wrapping her hips in caution tape. "By the way, your makeup looks really good." She smiled at me, and I took deep, grounding breaths as I chugged the So-Duh.

"Wait, or what if I wore—" I peeled my white bed sheet up off the bed and held it up over my figure in the mirror. "Maybe like a toga? I could wrap it around like this?"

Lila skipped over to me, searching through my jewelry. She held up two dangly gold hoops in the mirror for me to get the full effect. We smiled at each other in the reflection. "Thank you."

Danielle stepped out of the bathroom wrapped in a towel. Taking in the palpable silence of the room. "What did I miss? Ah, I always miss everything!"

"Well, that's kind of the side effect of puking all over yourself." Lila shot at her, and she was too nervous to do anything but giggle uncomfortably.

"Hey," I snapped, glaring at Lila. It was such a foreign experience that it instantly made my skin crawl. I held up the So-Duh as a peace offering. "How are we sneaking this in?"

"By offering it to people as we walk by," Lila demonstrated, passing around the bottle as if it were the most obvious solution.

"Or wait!" Danielle gasped, excited to show off a new contraption buried deep within her bag. It was a wrapped tampon. "I have this flask that's shaped like a tampon if you want to use it." We just looked at her. "It's not a real tampon!"

I drank the last bit of So-Duh until the bottle ran dry. "Better make another for safety."

IV

FRATERNITY ROW WAS THE closest thing we had to nightlife on campus. The sidewalks bustled with girls navigating their way to whichever house coordinated with their outfits. Bikini-clad babes headed over to Pi Kappa Alpha's annual Beach Bash while the others dressed in calf-length socks and over-sized button-up shirts ran toward the brothers of Sigma.

"Maya, I'm freezing," Lila shivered in her two-piece caution tape tube top and mini skirt.

"So-rry," I sang, closing the car window before climbing over the center console to steal the French fries Danielle kept hoarded in the back seat. I held one up to her as if we were treasure hunting in the deepest parts of Egypt. "This is the best decision you ever made."

"Thank you," she smiled, happily chewing away at the box of chicken nuggets sitting in her lap. "I feel like a completely different person now! Honestly, I think I was just hungry."

My cell phone buzzed beneath my thigh. I practically stopped breathing at the sight of the name etched across my phone screen.

"James followed me back," I gasped. And then I saw the DM he sent me. I was way too out of my depth to handle that alone. "Oh, my God," I muttered, already handing the phone over for Lila to see the name on the screen.

She went quiet at the sight of his name while her lips parted into a soft *oh*. "Well, open it."

"Open what?" Danielle popped forward between the seats, trying to be a part of the action.

JAMES: Hey! You coming tonight?

"What do I say to that?" I asked, eyes frantic but smile wide.

"What? Oo! Gimme!" Danielle practically ripped the phone out of my hand, and I had to breathe to keep myself from snatching it back.

"First, let me ask you something?" Lila asked.

"Always," I answered.

"What do you want to happen tonight? What's the end goal?"

Danielle scrolled quietly through James's online profile, examining his well-shaped abs. "Jeez, Samaya, this guy's a little much. Don't you think? Like… he's hot and all, but he's a little show-y about it." Danielle grimaced, handing the phone back to me. "I don't know how people are so comfortable exposing themselves on the internet like that. Last summer, my riding coach's daughter, Libby, sent nudes at Bible Camp. I don't know how, but they leaked, and it just left a sour taste in everyone's mouth—"

Lila turned to face me, eyes locked on mine as if we were the only two people in the car. "Answer the question."

"Honestly?" I spoke in a hushed voice, not whispering exactly, but not confident I wanted the world to hear me either. "I maybe… want to flirt and feel pretty." I blushed, and Lila smiled at me like a mom dropping her kid off at summer camp. *Maybe,* I blushed.

"Maybe," Lila nodded back. "Well, if that's the case. Don't respond," She put the car in park, unbuckling her seat belt. "If he really wants to see you, he'll find you. And if he doesn't, it's probably for the best. No one worthwhile met the love of their life in college."

"My parents met in college." Danielle leaned forward between the seats and placed a hand over the neckrest. "I'm getting a weird vibe tonight that maybe we're not all on the same page. I don't want to go home with anybody."

"Ditto," I added. But Lila said nothing.

She reapplied lip gloss in the rearview mirror, ignoring Danielle and me. She focused her attention on the frat house's front lawn, trap music bumping through the glass windshield, fingers floating off the steering wheel in limp defense. "I like exploring what wants to explore me."

I turned around in my chair until I faced Danielle directly. "No one's going to ditch you," I promised.

The phone buzzed again.

I smiled at the three gray dots vibrating at the bottom left-hand corner of his message. Lila had a point. Sometimes, the only right thing to do was less.

"Okay, you win," I smiled, dramatically tucking my phone into my bra strap. Out of sight, out of mind. "Let's have a good night."

I adjusted the hemline of the bed sheet Lila helped Danielle and I convert into dresses as we stepped out onto the curb. Tonight, I was finally the girl with the right clothes, with the right friends, at the right place, at the right time. And just as I was about to bask in the change, I stepped out of the car and tripped over a loose bit of gravel, punching my knee directly into the pavement.

"Motherfucker!" I cursed through gritted teeth.

Danielle dropped down beside me. "Are you okay?"

"It's all good," Lila reassured me, coming over to my side of the car. She scooped an arm around my waist as casually as possible. "Just grab my other side and smile."

I wrapped my hand around Lila's shoulder, leaned into her body weight for support, and laughed as if she had said the most hysterical joke ever. But Lila wasn't looking at me anymore. As we made our way closer to the front entrance to the party, a familiar face caught her attention.

George stood on the front porch wearing a *Bud Light* box as shorts and Hot Topic brand suspenders to hold them up. He was with the same shaggy-haired boy from the library, wearing the same plain white T-shirt and dark wash jeans he had worn before.

The boys chatted with two girls wearing matching blue and pink bikinis that they interchanged between each other. One wore a blue top with pink bottoms, while the other dressed in pink top and blue bottoms. I wondered if they made the decision before leaving their dorms that evening or sometime throughout the party.

To the untrained eye, Lila appeared cool and collected, but I knew her tells. I could see her jaw clenching at the way the girls fawned over George, and even worse how he enjoyed it.

"Hey," Lila called out, and George instantly turned toward her, a thick blush crossing his cheeks. I had a hunch he knew she was on the property from the moment she parked the car. "You guys got a first aid kit?"

George sipped from his beer can, smiling in a way that made him bite his lips, trying not to look too eager.

Lila was calculated even when you thought she was not. The streetlight beamed a bit brighter on the exact spot Lila stood. She was glowing. So, while the other girls circulated around George, tipsy and a bit wobbly, Lila remained a relic. She didn't move closer to him. Lila made him come to us. He took the stairs two at a time, trying to reach her.

"Is it a gunshot wound? A broken rib? Blood loss?" He asked, making his best impression of an ER doctor. I matched his energy in turn.

"Oh, what a world! What a world!" I howled, leaning into Lila with a hand pressed over my forehead. "The agony. The pain! It's scorching through my—"

"She fell and hit a rock," Lila cut me off. Danielle and I fell into a giggling fit beside her.

"Oof, that's the worst of all," he grimaced, and that time, a small burst of air rippled through Lila's throat. He seemed so grateful to hear what her laugh sounded like.

"Hey," Danielle whispered in my ear, "his friend's kind of cute."

I nodded, observing the shaggy haired boy with more interest than I anticipated. His face felt familiar. He looked like an actor or a cartoon character I used to watch when I was a little girl. Or like someone I saw at the movies but never spoke to. The shaggy-haired boy was tall, with long limbs that seemed to sink inside of his skeleton and disappear entirely. It was a neat party trick that reminded me of a turtle.

"Agreed," I whispered back.

The beautiful girl in the blue bikini top wore a black denim jacket over the top that melted off her shoulders in a way that perfectly accentuated her sun-kissed skin. I assumed it belonged to the shaggy-haired boy.

The girl leaned in close, her face hidden by his ear, but he didn't say anything. The boy just nodded, tucking his phone back into his pocket with a heavy sigh. His hands absently settled onto the straps looped around his neck, holding a high-quality film camera close to his chest.

"I love shy guys," Danielle whispered, clutching at my wrist as she swooned. Shy didn't feel like the right word to describe him, but I hadn't settled on the right word yet.

"The Uber will be here in 10 minutes. Keep an eye out for a black

Mazda. The driver's name is Steve. So… yeah. Can I get my jacket back? It's freezing?" He tried to make it sound casual, but the girl still appeared a bit hurt by his tone. George called over to his friend with a farmer's whistle loud enough to wake the dead. I covered my ears for fear of bursting an ear drum. "Yo, Isaac! Can you get us some ice? We need 3-CT and a 10-blade, stat!"

Huh, what an interesting name.

Lila huffed a laugh, shaking her head at him. "None of that made any sense."

George shrugged, the blush deepening along with his smile. "I know, but I watch a lot of *Grey's Anatomy,* and it sounded cool."

Isaac looked more than happy to have a task. He slid his jacket on, and I smiled at how his shoulders loosened the second his armor was securely in place. He stepped up to the door frame in a fluid motion, hands buried in his pockets and wide, round eyes searching in the open air until he locked on mine. I couldn't stop looking at his lips and wondering what he might have looked like with a gap between his front teeth — if he ever had one. He had a perfect smile. I shook my head, laughing to myself at the stupid obsession I needed to move on from.

"Wait for us!" I called out before I could think better of it.

Lila turned to me with raised brows, "You sure?" She phrased it like a question, but her tone said, 'Thank you'. I gave Lila a tight squeeze on the wrist and tried to play it cool when she squeezed me back.

Isaac waited for us by the front door, arms folded on his camera strap as he gestured for us to wait a moment while drunken partygoers in various stages of undress pushed through. I watched him physically count out a proper number of people to let pass before he stepped up into the doorway, his back pushing against the crowd, as he secured a moment of reprieve for Danielle and me to pass by. He gave me the impression of someone who lived on high alert, always searching for the nearest exit.

"Well, that was very polite—" I tripped on my way inside and accidentally grabbed onto Isaac's t-shirt to catch myself. "I'm sorry!" I blurted out, but he didn't seem phased. He didn't move while I steadied myself against his shoulder blades. He just waited for me to let go, and so I did, shaking my hands behind my back as if I'd done something wrong.

Isaac glanced down at my knee and replied, "You're bleeding." He said it the way someone would tell you you've stepped on chewing gum, or a bird relieved itself on the hood of your car. Sure enough, I saw a thick strip of crimson dripping down my leg.

"Huh, would you look at that," I shook my head, wiping at the blood dripping down my leg with the edge of my bed sheet. I took one last glance over at Lila, giddy at the sight of what was unfolding.

Lila laughed at George's costume. "How did you make that?"

He blew out a puff of air, shaking his hair while flexing his sculpted chest muscles. "Many, many, bottles of hot glue and too many casualties to talk about." He smiled, giving her a once over. "I like your, um—" he cleared his throat.

She took a step toward him, "Thanks." He matched her expression with a goofy grin of his own.

"George," he said, reaching out a hand to shake hers.

"I know," she laughed, accepting the handshake.

Lila's mother passed away in the spring of junior year, and in the years following the funeral, I watched Lila barrel through life like the Kool-Aid man, until one day she hit a wall too hard and never got back up. She never liked to talk about what happened, and I didn't know the right questions to ask. I wanted my friend back.

I wanted to see her smile so badly that I found myself performing in her favor, and sometimes, when I drank a bit too much or smoked a little too often, I realized that hanging out with Lila felt like one long audition. But then there were little moments when hands were squeezed, tears were shed, and all felt right again.

I wanted Lila to be happy.

George looked like he could make her happy.

V

A FOOTBALL FLEW PAST my head, causing Danielle and I to huddle together like squealing crows shooed off the lawn. Isaac cleared a path through the dancing bodies, guiding us toward the kitchen. He looked over his shoulder every other second to make sure we were still following him. When we reached the kitchen, he held open the door for us again in a polite yet begrudging way.

Mami would've swooned over him, scolding me as she said, you see Samaya? *That is how a boy should behave. It is the bare minimum.* It is funny how the bare minimum doesn't seem so bare when you rarely come across it.

"I don't think we have to worry about anyone calling an ambulance on me," I spoke like a late-night comic, begging for a laugh. No one supplied one. The music faded into white noise behind the wooden door, leaving us in the silence of strangers. I hopped up onto the countertop, sitting back against the kitchen cabinets while Isaac walked about the room with the comfort of knowing where everything is.

"I think you'll be okay," Isaac affirmed, closing the cabinet beneath the sink, sliding a plastic container with a red plus sign painted across the top onto the counter beside me. He crossed his arms, long legs tucked into each other like the sliver of a shadow beneath the bright neon lights.

"Well, that's kind," I nodded, and he bowed his head in response. I took a band-aid out of the kit.

He scratched his head, searching for something in the kitchen, and produced nothing. He glanced over at my bed sheet dress, his hands pressed around the hollow of his neck. "Um, there aren't any more paper towels. Would you mind if I?" He pointed at the edge of the sheet already covered in my blood. I lifted my leg for him, waving him closer with my hand.

"Be my guest."

"Okay, um, grab the counter."

"Excuse me?"

He didn't elaborate as he gripped the edge of the bed sheet between his hands and ripped off the marred bit. My jaw dropped open, mirroring Danielle's look of astonishment. He handed me the torn piece of cloth, head hanging low and eyes avoiding mine.

"Thank you," I laughed, dabbing at the blood dripping down my knee with the cloth. "Is this the chivalry that won over your fans?"

It took him a second to realize I referred to the girls from earlier. "No, I think they were just tired and looking for a place to crash."

"And you were a place to crash? Nice. And they say *gallantry* is dead," the bad French accent rolled off my tongue before I could keep it in check. He laughed and it was a pretty, quiet kind of sound that rumbled in his chest like an accident. His shoulders loosened from the vice grip he'd held them in.

Do it again.

Danielle hopped up on the counter beside me, shoulders back and hair falling delicately into place. "So, are you, like, going to get fined for not dressing in theme?"

"I don't think that's how fraternities work. I think that's just sororities," he sighed while his arms pressed further into themselves. "But then again, this is George's frat, not mine. They just pay me to take pictures for their social media. I doubt they care how I look as long as… everyone else is dressed, well… yeah." He shrugged, not wanting to state the obvious.

"As long as the girls show up half naked, you could wear a burlap sack, and everything would be fine?" I laughed at his silence. The reason for any themed party was for girls to show up looking hot. The guys were incidental.

Isaac smirked at me. "What's so funny?"

I waved him off, still dabbing at the wound. "Nothing. Don't worry about it." I was about to put the band-aid on the wound when Isaac came over. I didn't even feel him move.

"You have to put Neosporin on it, or it's going to get infected," he warned me.

"What? Are you pre-med too?"

"No. Do you need to be pre-med to know how to use Neosporin?"

I looked up at him with creased eyebrows. "It's not bad enough to get infected." His face shifted into a slight bit of shock, and it made me laugh even harder.

"Yes, it is." He was so indignant it made me push back harder.

"What about the cavemen? Hm? Did you ever think we're being fed big pharma just to buy things we don't really need?" I said, wiggling my eyebrows.

His stare was flat like he couldn't decide if I was being serious or making a joke. But he could see my lips quivering. "Are you messing with me?"

"Absolutely not. You clearly take infectious diseases very seriously."

Laughter bubbled in his chest. "No, I don't. But the average life expectancy for prehistoric humans was around 35. At most. You should shoot for higher."

I waved him off as I crossed my ankles and palms in my lap. "Puh-lease, 35 was the new 65 back then."

Isaac's jaw pulled to the side, his perfect white teeth poking through a smile he fought hard to keep at bay.

"No. It wasn't. 35 was 35." Isaac's voice rose just a bit, but not in anger, with enthusiasm. "Either they got infected, or a wildebeest killed them in the night. There is no honor in living like a caveman." He smiled at me. My jaw tightened.

"How do you know? You weren't there."

"I watch a lot of History channel," he said, eyes closing as if it were something to be embarrassed by.

"Ah, I understand the patches now."

His head cocked to the side. He leaned back against the kitchen island, looking at me through the slits of his warm brown eyes. "Do I know you?"

"No," I shook my head. "I saw you in the library with George before this. There was a big *Ancient Aliens* logo on your backpack."

He swallowed hard, his Adam's apple bobbing in his throat as he stared into my eyes. "Will you please put on the Neosporin?" It sounded almost like a question but also a warning. Like the type of tone you would use for a rebellious child. It made me laugh.

I turned my head to the side, searching the air for an answer as I chewed on the inside of my cheek. I turned back to him, chin held high and shoulders back.

"Make me," I shot back, and I did not anticipate the rose-coated blush rush across his brown copper cheeks. His neck moved back, and his shoulders scrunched and suddenly, I worried I read the room wrong.

My arms slipped, and I almost changed the subject when he said, "Well, no. I'm not going to make you. But may I?" He gestured to my knee with the Neosporin in hand. I nodded, and he knelt by my ankles with the first aid kit. Ever so gently he took the bit of cloth from my grasp and dabbed at my knee himself.

Seeing him kneel beneath me made me squirm, and I couldn't tell why. Suddenly, I wished I wore sweatpants or a full flannel onesie. I felt too exposed sitting above him. This felt oddly intimate. I didn't want to look at Danielle. I could feel her irritation through the gaps of breath between us. She was staring down at Isaac, wishing he moved over to her.

My phone vibrated between my breasts, and for a moment, I forgot I even owned a phone.

Isaac looked up at me, doing a great job of meeting my eyes than staring at the vibrating lights emanating from my bra.

"You going to answer that?" He asked, voice low and soft.

I nodded, wishing I could evaporate into thin air rather than dig within the halter top of my dress. My heart raced. I felt like an on-call doctor who did something horribly wrong, but I could not put my finger on what exactly. What if it was Lila? What if something horrible happened, and she needed an escape plan?

JAMES: ETA?

Fuck, I thought. For a second, I thought I accidentally said it aloud because Isaac stopped moving below me. I was shaking, and I didn't know why. I forced myself to look down at him, and I saw him sitting back on his ankles, staring at the scars on my knee. His fingers brushed along the curve connecting my knee with the small of my thigh, and I melted toward him, hoping for more of his touch.

What's wrong with me?

"My Lord on High," he mumbled, running a hand on his chin. "Where'd you get this scar?"

Danielle laughed, smoothing any invisible strands of hair off her cheeks as she jumped at the chance to tell my story. "Oh, she was drunk back in high school—"

"No, sorry. Sorry," he cut her off, still staring at my knee when he asked again. "This one, right here. The one with the little tail going around your knee."

"Oh," I shook my head, pressing my fingertips to my temples, trying to remember where I'd gotten that one. "Oh my God, that was so long ago I forgot about the scar altogether," I lied. Tonight was the first time in years I had thought about that day and how funny it was that he had made me relive it now. "Some douchebag pushed me off the monkey bars when I was a kid. I hurt myself, obviously, and this scar is my little memento."

I scoffed, giggling in the back of my throat, but Isaac didn't join me. Instead, all he did was look up at me with inquisitive eyes and a thousand-watt smile.

"What's your name?" He asked me. But I didn't want to respond. I could feel myself shrinking inward.

"Maya," I whispered, soft and quiet. I almost wanted him to miss it just so he could ask me again.

He shook his head, bottom lip curling between his teeth. "No, it isn't."

I smacked my hands onto my thighs and let go of the breath building in my chest. I hopped off the counter not realizing how hard my head would spin, but not really caring either way. Isaac reached out to catch me but held himself back from physically touching me.

Instead, he stood up and moved to the opposite end of the kitchen island until his back was fully facing me. He cupped his hands over his face, but I could tell he was smiling. "No, *fucking* way." He huffed, his shoulders curling with a sigh. He turned to me with arms crossed and mouth gaping wide. "Do you know who I am?"

I placed my palms face down on the kitchen island, head rolling but trying to stay as steady as I could while he inspected every inch of my face. I couldn't help but do the same. "You wouldn't by any chance have had a huge gap in your teeth, did you?" I giggled and could not stop once I started.

He gestured toward his now perfect smile. "Five years in braces."

"Am I missing something?" Danielle asked, clearly annoyed. Her smile faded, and seeing it made me realize that this interaction might fall into promise-breaking territory.

"Isaac was my childhood bully," I answered.

"I didn't bully you," he muttered, sucking on his tooth while he inspected his shoes.

"What would you call it then?" I spat back, but there was humor in my taunting.

"If anything, you bullied me," he countered.

I gasped, "What?"

"You were so rude to me!" He smirked, his tongue coasting along the inner corner of his smile. "Gosh, you walked around like the second coming. Never played with me, or anyone for that matter—"

"There's no way you could turn that around on me. You pushed me off the monkey bars!" I was screaming, flailing my hands around in emphasis.

His face turned serious, but his smile never faltered. He looked like a debate captain who spent hours rehearsing for this very moment. "That's not true. I reached out for you. Okay? But! But!" He held a handout to stop me from interrupting him, and with a deep breath, I complied. "My hands were sweaty, and you stepped off the beam too soon for me to readjust... and I am sorry. It was an accident." He smiled, but I turned away before that smile could make me rethink the past fourteen years of my life.

"If that's how you want to spin it," I muttered.

"... wow. Samaya Ximena..." he sighed, and a slight shiver ran down my arms at the way he said my name. He said it like the answer to a question he had spent years searching for. "You still live down here?"

I shrugged, slightly offended at the tone. "There are worse places to live."

He shook his head, hands sliding across his face. "No, I know. I just meant... ya know... most people leave or go away, and you—"

"You came back," I waved at him, palms pressed to my hips, searching for structure as I felt my walls collapsing.

He smiled at me. "Yeah, well, there are worse places to be."

"You look so different."

"You look exactly the same."

"Excuse me?"

"Yes," he nodded, pacing around the kitchen island with the energy of a golden retriever. "I should have said something. I just— I knew it was you. You always did this thing with your nose whenever you were not getting your way." He scrunched his nose at me in what I believed to be a terrible impression of a haughty girl.

"You have me confused with someone else. I have never made that ridiculous face a day in my life," I crossed my arms, pacing in time with him on the opposite side of the island. "You look like you just finished telling your dad, 'It's not a phase! *Slipknot* is for life.'"

Isaac leaned his elbows onto the counter and pressed his head into his elbows as he lost his composure into a fit of laughter. With his chin tucked into the safety of his arms, Isaac peered up at me behind long lashes and endless kindness. I froze, and my smile fell along with my center of gravity.

The silence that followed sent visible shivers down my arms. I closed my eyes, wanting him to disappear. I was drowning under the weight of his stare and everything I could not read. I did not want this.

I wanted to get out of that kitchen. I did not want to be that little girl sitting on the swing sets waiting for someone to play with her. I was different. I wasn't going back to that. The room spun, and I could hear him ask me, "Do you want to maybe go somewhere and talk—"

"You guys want to get a drink?" I spun back towards Danielle and grabbed her hands in mine. "Let's go do something fun that's not hiding in here?"

"Yes!" Danielle jumped off the counter. "No offense!" She gasped softly, a hand demurely hovering over her lips.

"None taken," Isaac bowed his head. "I think I'm going to pass for now. But you guys go ahead, and I'll catch up."

I could not tell if the pain in my stomach was disappointment or relief.

We rushed out of the kitchen too quickly to know where his next steps led.

VI

The memory of that night grew fuzzier every time I tried to piece the timeline together.

I remember hands twisting around my shoulders, pulling me deeper into the throng. I brushed them off at first, but when they kept pulling, I just gave up. It didn't feel scary. It felt like I was floating. I remember the music pounding through my ears. I remember swaying beneath a silly string-covered chandelier. I leaned my head back into the warmth of the crowd, staring up at the crystals until they burst into stars.

I remember a pretty redhead wearing thin wire rimmed glasses. It was loud, but she was welcoming all the same. Her name was Leslie or Cynthia, but it was her skirt made entirely out of red solo cups that made a lasting impression. She was a junior who'd somehow put off taking college algebra until the very last minute and was stuck in a class full of freshmen. She borrowed a pen from me at the start of the semester, promised to give it back, but never did.

I remembered beaming at the sight of her.

"Hey, you're in Gamma Phi, right?" I asked, pulling Danielle along with me. It was a polite kind of question, the type you ask after you have stalked someone on Instagram but didn't want to look like a psycho when you finally met. The girl nodded, fast and repetitive, with a big smile spread across her glossy lips, "I'm planning on rushing next semester."

Leslie squealed; hands folded across her chest like she had just seen the cutest little puppy. "Awww, oh my God! That's so sweet. Thanks for telling me!"

"What? I didn't know that!" Danielle gushed, clapping a hand across my shoulder in mock offense at my secret. It was not a secret because it was not a plan. I just saw Leslie-or-Cynthia, and I said it. It was a Freudian slip I did not realize would be a helpful lifeline until it was. "My mom was a Gamma Phi! But over at Texas A & M."

"Oh, so, dude, I'm not crazy. I didn't just make up Texas!" I rolled my eyes laughing while Leslie called out to a few girls at a nearby table. Several rectangular tables were set up across the den of the house with teams and observers equally distributed among them. Leslie took my hand and declared we'd join her sisters for the next round. I remembered feeling special. I remembered feeling like one of the Beautiful People.

Danielle and I transformed from strangers to potential new sisters.

After a couple of rounds, three things were made abundantly clear. First, that I was awful at beer pong. Second, the others were not. Third, when you're awful at beer pong you end up drinking a lot of beer.

I spent my losses dancing beside the table, not caring who was watching or the amount of beer spilled all over my costume. No one cared, so, neither did I. A hand gripped my wrist, pulling me off axis. We moved through the wall of bodies dancing on either side, and I remember having to grip the bed sheet with my hand to keep it from sliding off.

"I need air," I said to no one in particular.

Danielle guided us toward a dimly lit hallway. A few people were waiting in line for the bathroom, but other than that, it was private. I pressed my back up against a wall while Danielle berated me. I had never seen her quite this distraught. My forehead felt heavy, and it hurt to keep my head straight. It took me a minute to fully click into what she was saying.

"Dude, you spilled your drink all over me," Danielle scolded. Her shoes were ruined, but how much of that was me and not collateral party damage? It didn't matter. It hurt too much to lift my head to care about sneakers.

"I'm sorry, Dani," I whined, head bobbing in shame. "I'm so sorry."

"It's fine. I just… You drank too much."

"What?" I blew a raspberry, pressing my hands against the tops of my thighs. I landed on the floor hard. I drank too much to feel any pain. "That's… crazy."

"Whoa," Danielle reached out for me but did not catch me in time. I was too heavy. She scanned my face, not understanding why I stared off into nothingness. "Maya?"

"Mhm," I kept staring at the wall behind her.

"Are you—"

That's when I started gagging.

"Oh good, God," I swallowed whatever bile crept up my chest.

Danielle dipped down as if she could tackle whatever would come next. "Whoa, whoa, not in the hallway."

"Of course, yeah—," I held up a single finger, concentrating harder than a high school math class to conquer the moment. When I did, I pumped two fists in the air, triumphant. "We're good!"

"You sure? Look, I'm going to go get Lila? Can you wait right here?"

I nodded.

"Samaya?"

I nodded again, but this time, I shooed her away and curled my legs close to my chest. I remember her leaving and the discomfort of sitting in my silence. I did not like silence. It was too easy to think about everything I ever wanted to forget. I rubbed at my temples, pushing, and pushing until the headache disappeared. It didn't. Instead, I saw my phone lying flat on the ground beside me with a giant crack down in the middle. I still do not know how it happened exactly, but I blamed the fall.

The next morning, I read the texts I sent out and assumed that was where the night turned. They looked like this:

SAMAYA: &minees

JAMES: ...?

SAMAYA: S0ry 7

I spent an embarrassing amount of time staring at the screen, waiting for tiny gray dots to show up, but they never did.

"But I need air," I muttered to myself.

I had two options that, at the time, appeared inconsequential but ultimately changed the course of my life. If I stepped out onto the front porch, I would've stumbled into Lila and George falling in love.

"What's your major?" I would've overhead George ask.

"Bio," Lila would have replied, *"just like everybody else."*

"Why?"

Lila would shrug and say something cool and aloof like, *"I like money,"* she would turn toward him with warm eyes and a hooked eyebrow. *"Just like everybody else."*

I would've ruined the mood. But I would have gone home. Lila would have taken me home even if she had to drag me down the front steps, kicking and screaming.

But I did not step out onto the front porch.

Let Lila have her fun, I remember thinking. I peeled myself off the floor, and with unsteady feet, I reentered the party. I could barely register the bones in my body, let alone whoever wanted a piece of them.

The smell of weed canopied the backyard in a familiar way. A circle of stoners sat beneath the privacy of an overgrown oak tree, passing around multiple blunts. Then I saw James. He squatted beside the group, clasping hands with one of the guys while a girl in a trash bag dress passed him the blunt.

He was chiseled, as could be seen by his shirtless nature and swim trunks. He had a horrible farmer's tan only lacrosse and skimboarding could supply. Seeing him made me stand still.

Then he saw me. I knew he smiled. Or at least I thought he did. It doesn't matter now. I blinked, and he stood beside me. My bed sheet was less of a dress and more a cape wrapped tight around my body. I looked like a child who escaped from bed after having a bad dream.

I knew he was talking, *I knew that,* but I couldn't make out any of the words. Somehow, he guided me toward the circle.

I remember he called me *Savannah,* his *psych buddy.* I wanted to correct him, I knew that, but when I opened my mouth, I couldn't speak.

He laughed, nudging the girl on his other side a little too flirtatiously for my taste. The stars overhead were so pretty that I focused on that instead. They were faint, and when I closed one eye, I noticed they looked more like bundles of string lights than glowing orbs in the sky.

When a glass bowl entered my fingertips, I did not say thank you, but I thought it. I took a deep, long hit, and smiled when the smoke blew out my nose like the dragons I grew up reading about. James whispered something in my ear, but it was too loud to tell what it was. I turned toward him, and his palm cupped my chin. His fingertips turned my head in the opposite direction, where the girl, Abbey, whose name might have been, blew smoke into my gaping lips. We did not touch each other, but it felt sexual all the same. I did not like it, but I was too tired to speak.

Instead, I laid my head on Abbey's lap and curled my knees close to my chest. My eyes drifted closed while James rubbed soothing circles on my hip.

Perspective was everything.

From my perspective, I was taking a nice little nap beneath the oak tree.

From Danielle's perspective, I was letting a boy I barely knew touch me in places best kept hidden beneath my bed sheet.

I woke up with two sets of hands dragging me up off the ground. My bed sheet was discarded somewhere far away from me with my gym short and bralette on full display. Lila tried to cover them up as best as she could.

My arms were wrapped around both Danielle and Lila's shoulders, and I distinctly remembered my bare toes dragging across the grass. I didn't question where my shoes went. I just didn't like the chill of dew.

The bathroom was locked, but that didn't stop Lila from pounding on the door like her life depended on it. She nearly kicked it down before some guy whose face meant nothing to me opened the door.

"Do you mind?" He yelled, trying to block his girlfriend crying by the sink inside.

"There's only one GD bathroom in this place. Do *you* mind?" Danielle clapped back.

I pushed past them both, heading directly for the toilet. Not caring if the door was open or closed, I pulled down my shorts and relieved myself in the toilet.

"Out! Now!" Lila physically pushed the guy from the room. He didn't fight back.

"Hey. Hey! Stop it," I remember advising the crying girl. "It's not worth it. They're ne-never worth it." I was right.

Lila locked the door the second the crying girl ran out after him.

When I looked up again, I saw Lila staring down at me while Dani paced the cramped room.

"You're embarrassing yourself." Danielle scolded me.

"Hmm, nope," I gagged. "Not to me."

"You're letting him touch you-"

"Back off," Lila growled.

I plugged my ears, shaking my head back and forth. "Whoa, whoa, Whooooaaa. Don't say that. LALALALALLAALALA!"

"Do you realize everyone at this party just saw you—?" She addressed Lila as if I weren't in the room. She had a point. I felt like I was not in the room.

"Fuck off!" Lila spat; her nose dug into Danielle's personal bubble until she was forced to step back.

"Shhhh! Stop! Just stop, why, why, why are you doing this? I'm having fun!" I crawled off the toilet, not caring if it flushed. I gripped the lip of the tub and crawled inside. Lila helped me not to hit my head.

"Maya, this isn't fun for anyone," Lila whispered, talking to herself.

I turned on the shower head to tune out Danielle's voice and let the water wash over me. "Sorry, I'm not the Virgin *fucking* Mary," I grumbled, eyes closed and limbs splayed like a chalk outline.

"Give me your phone," Lila instructed, "I'm calling an Uber."

I patted myself down with closed eyes but found nothing. "I can't."

"Why not?" Danielle huffed.

"I lost my phone."

"Samaya!"

"Jesus Christ, just go!" Lila cursed at Danielle. "Go! Now!" She practically pushed the girl out the bathroom door. Sometimes, I wanted to say sorry about what happened. But then I remembered the morning after the frat party and immediately changed my mind.

"Fuck, Maya, you couldn't keep it together for one night?" Lila spat, slapping her hands to her thighs in exasperation.

"Just… calm down."

"No, fuck you, dude!"

"What?" Water sloshed at the insides of my mouth. I spit it out and rolled toward the tile wall.

"Fuck you, dude. I'm the one always cleaning up your mess! All I wanted was a night out. I asked you. Specifically, asked you if you wanted to stay in. Multiple times, I gave you an out, and you did not take it."

"…what?"

"Get up, Samaya. Now. We are leaving." Lila lunged at me, hands gripping the sides of my torso, but I pushed back. Instinct and anger curdling my blood. I could not open my eyes but maybe if I fell asleep, I would wake up to find it would all be a bad dream.

"You don't get to judge me—"

"I'm not judging you, I'm sick of you—"

"The girl who blew Alex Gilmore by the dumpster of the Phi Beta Kappa party." I laughed, gurgling water. To this day, every time I hear myself laugh, the moment is soured by the memory of Lila's silence. But the words just kept coming. "Everybody knows, Lila! Everybody fucking knows, but I'm the whore who hasn't even touched a dick yet. Call the Uber. Go home!"

"Shut up, Samaya," Lila whispered. It was hard to hear over the water, but I faintly heard her add, "... you have no idea what you're talking about."

"If I'm so embarrassing, leave! Fucking go! But I'm not going to be lectured by the bitch who sucked dirty dick—"

That's when Lila smacked me across the face. Stars splayed out in my eyes as my cheek smacked against the tub.

"Ow," I moaned, rubbing at my cheek. Water from my wet hair blurred my vision. I felt like I was going to be sick.

I don't remember Lila leaving, only that she wasn't there by the time someone else found me. When I closed my eyes, it was like I was reliving the party, floating over the crowd. I needed silence. I didn't need his hands running over my hair or the smell of smoke flooding my nose.

"Shhhh, you're okay," he whispered, his lips tugging at mine.

"You're cute," he moaned, leaving hickeys on my neck while I was too numb to feel it.

I remember my head falling upon something soft and the glow of streetlights passing overhead. A seat belt kept my head from falling against the glass. I remember the glass, the blue glow of the radio, and his knuckles gripping the steering wheel. He tried to make conversation with someone dripping wet and battling consciousness.

I remember pushing him away. I remember trying to say 'stop' but the words came out all wrong. "Sss, ow. Slow down-st-"

He kissed me. Hands pressed into mine, and the world spun behind my eyelids. The dark night blurred into a thousand little stars before cutting to black. I remember an alarm ringing in the distance, hard, repetitive, and the nauseating feeling of waking up.

I shut off the cell phone ringing on the nightstand beside me. It was not mine, but I didn't notice that until I noticed the color of the walls, the texture of the sheets, or the bathroom door where it shouldn't be. I was in a place I should not have been. My skin had goose bumps to prove how cold he kept his room.

His.

I never used that word to describe a space that was not mine before.

Lying on the pillow, I stared up at the ceiling fan that was not mine, too scared to turn to the side. Instead, I gripped the lip of the bed sheet and pulled it up higher to cover my naked body. I did not remember taking my shorts off or where I might have placed them. I do not think I even touched my undergarments; that was all him. My body felt raw and sore in places it should not be.

I turned over to the side, sitting up on my forearms to take a better look at him. James slept soundly beside me, a bit of drool pooling on his pillowcase. I peeled back the bed sheet and saw a small patch of dried blood beside my vagina.

No, it was not my room. However, it was my reality.

I stared down at him, wishing he would disappear. I did not understand why he was naked and where his clothes had gone. The alarm clock went off again. I accidentally snoozed it. I did not turn it off this time. Instead, I waited for him to wake up.

He stirred into consciousness beside me. "Mm, good morning," he moaned, stretching his toes and calves beneath the sheets. He rolled over, eyes filled with sleep and peace, wrapping an arm around my chest. I did not move. I just let him. "Headache?" He asked.

I nodded.

"Here, drink some water." He reached out to the carafe he kept on his bedside table, filling a glass, and passed it to me. "There's some aspirin in the top drawer, too, if you need it. Can you pass me some? My head is killing me."

I nodded again and passed over the pills he asked for along with the empty glass. I chugged the water he offered me. Sitting beside the carafe was a muffin, blueberry to be exact, waiting for me to eat it. I stared at it for an unknown beat of time.

"Can I use your shower?" I asked. My throat felt like sandpaper.

"Of course. Towels are in the cabinet." He gestured to the door, and I nodded.

"Cool," I said. The word felt foreign, like a pleasantry I memorized in a guidebook. It felt like the kind of thing you said, so I said it. I wrapped myself in the bed sheet, not caring if he lay there naked and cold, just as long as I didn't see it. I had never seen a naked man before. Not like that.

"Hey!" He hollered, pulling me back with a light hand gripping my wrist. I sat back on the bed, staring at his neck but not his eyes. "I really didn't care about the bleeding. It's fine, okay? Nothing to be embarrassed about. We always try to keep some tampons and makeup wipes in the bathroom. Help yourself."

He smiled at me. And I said, "Thank you."

I closed the door to the bathroom quietly, slowly, languishing in the sweet click of the lock. I was a ghost who'd risen from the dead, walking from room to room, doomed to watch other people live a life I had no control over. I felt like a character in one of the novellas Mami watched. The one where the main character switched brains with a stranger at a hospital without their knowing. *Mami,* I cursed, stress weaving through my muscles. I needed to find my phone and call her. I needed to make sure she did not send out the National Guard for disappearing off the face of the earth.

My face was smeared in makeup. Bags under my eyes mixed with mascara and acne spots already forming beneath the caked foundation I did not take off the night before. My hair knotted at odd angles. Bruises covered my neck, and I had a hunch that if I let the sheet fall and really looked at my body, I'd find that his lips left bruises in more places than one. But I could not think about that right now. I could not think about that ever.

I pushed aside the grid-patterned shower curtain and turned the faucet on until it churned out the hottest water I could find. I pushed up against the wall, slowly pulling the curtain to either edge of the shower until there were no slices of the bathroom left visible. I needed privacy.

Steam rose fast as I stood beneath the scolding hot water, scrubbing myself raw. Tears flowed down my cheeks just as effortlessly as the water poured from the spout. I did not sob. I did not think. I melted and prayed the memories would melt along with the makeup, dirt, and blood spilling down the drain. I lowered myself onto the base of the shower, legs splayed out in front me and hands limp on my thighs.

The porcelain boiled beneath my skin, yet I could not stop shivering. I felt nothing about this moment. Not anger nor shame, just nothing. I pinched myself hard on the inside of my hand until the skin was about to break just so I could feel a sense of pain. Mascara dripped off my face until it rushed down the drain, and I was captivated by the sight of it.

James offered to drive me home, and I accepted. Only, I could not stomach the idea of sitting in my bedroom, seeing Danielle and all that would entail. I showed up at Lila's dorm with no bag, and miraculously, she answered. She looked like she had not slept. I wore his clothes, but we did not talk about it. I walked through the door and noticed her roommate was not there.

"She's staying at her boyfriend's place," Lila explained, and I nodded. "You didn't answer any of my calls."

"I'm tired."

She let me lay beside her in bed, and I chose the side with the window. The curtains were pulled shut, but streaks of sunlight managed to find their way through the cracks. I curled into a ball, pulling the blanket close to my chin as Lila climbed into bed beside me. There was an energy to her that I did not want to address. She was angry with me, but there was another emotion hiding beneath the surface that I did not have in me to dissect.

"I'm sorry," I muttered, my lips pressed close to the pillow.

"Are we not going to talk about it?" She asked, but I didn't respond. She cleared her throat, and I could feel Lila cross her arms beside me just as easily as I could hear her choke up as she spoke. "I'd really like to talk about it, Samaya."

"I'm tired," I said again.

But I did not fall asleep.

The Fifth Kiss

I

Loneliness looked a lot like lying still on my unmade bed while my best friend caught me up to speed on a life I had no desire to take part in.

"He's oddly clean," I could barely hear her voice through the speaker on my phone. She and George had recently moved into an off-campus apartment, and though she sounded quite happy about the situation, she always called me from remote corners of their home, trying to debrief the lifestyle change.

"I can't believe your dad agreed to this," I rubbed a hand across my eyes, twisting my fingers into my temples until the headache subsided.

From what I gather, George slept with a rainforest simulator, which Lila loved. He quickly adopted her 'no big light' rule whenever the sun went down and ordered a shoe rack for the front entrance before Lila even agreed to move in with him. George often hopped onto our phone calls to brag about how Lila hid lavender soap bars in every nook and cranny of the space, making their lives feel calm and delicious.

"That's cool." Though I tried to seem interested in the conversation, I knew my voice gave away the fact that it was the fourth day in a row that I rotted in my bedroom wearing pajamas until five in the afternoon.

"It would be fun if you came over tonight. George got me into this new board game—" The laugh that slipped out from my callous tongue was like an echo that forgot where it started. Lila did not like board games, but I didn't have the energy to say that, and so she carried on as if I hadn't interrupted. "A bunch of his friends are coming over. You should meet them."

"Um, maybe," I cleared my throat. "How many people are going?"

"Ten or so. Not sure," she replied.

I nodded, a slight shake of my head along the pillowcase, even though she could not see me. "Anyone I know?"

"Isaac isn't coming if that's why you're asking. But he did ask about you, again." I could hear the smile through the phone line. My skin tingled at the use of the word 'again'.

"Oh?" I cleared my throat, sitting up on my pillows. "And what did you say?"

"That you hate me and never want to hang out."

"That's good." I wanted to ask more, but I also did not know how to open my mouth. "Did... did he get that internship he wanted?"

"Yeah, I think so."

Isaac Haas was the focal point of my solitary hours. I wanted to know more about the boy who grew up to be the man I did not recognize. We were like moons sharing the same gravitational field. I'd hear about Isaac when speaking with Lila or George, but I'd never see him. He kept himself busy with school, work, and photography. I knew from hours of listening and observing that he was very enthusiastic about photography. But, apart from side-long glances in university hallways or the occasional sight of him in the passenger seat of George's car, we didn't interact much.

I couldn't remember a year of my life when I didn't have someone on my mind as a point of affection. Isaac Haas was just the latest one.

"Samaya, it would be nice if you came." But what she meant to say was 'if you tried'.

It was difficult for me to explain to Lila why her request was not as simple to fulfill as she thought. It was difficult, because Lila knew what happened a year ago, but unlike Lila, I did not have the luxury of forgetting. I loved her for trying, but I wished she would stop.

I lost all desire to drink after that party, but George didn't know why. He thought I didn't feel comfortable around him or that I was insecure about him taking my friend away. It was neither, but it's not exactly like I wanted to chat about it.

Since the ABC party last year, nights out with Lila & George went one of two ways:

A: George tried to play drinking games with me, which I knew he did to make me feel more comfortable around him, but it just made me uncomfortable saying 'no' so frequently.

B: Lila watched over me all night, counting the number of drinks I had to the point where I just wanted to go home. But I did not want to fight with Lila, and so I mentioned none of those things.

"I have a club meeting tonight."

"Ahh, movie night," Lila held on to every syllable as if movie night meant I was visiting my imaginary friends and not an actual club on campus. "Well, that's nice."

"It is." I checked the clock on my phone, my legs unfurling from my bedspread just as a knock wrapped along my bedroom door.

Mami pushed the already-opened door until it was half ajar, only poking in far enough to announce her presence but not crowd my space. She carried a plated turkey sandwich and a mug of coffee. This was her way of saying I love you.

"I have to go. Send George my best." I hung up, tossing my phone to the side with the same reverence as a spoiled child who finished their dinner with green beans left untouched and forgotten.

"How's Lila?" Mami asked as she always did.

"She's good," I confirmed, as I always did.

I didn't tell her about the housewarming party as she'd probably force me to go. I didn't like her thinking something had happened between Lila and me, but it was easier to let her believe that than to keep asking questions.

She pushed the hair away from my forehead. "*Tesoro*, if you don't leave now, you're going to be late."

"Oh," I mumbled as I took the coffee from her outstretched arms. I knew exactly what time it was and how long it would take me to drive to campus from my house. I just didn't care. "I'll do it right now."

She lingered on my bed, waiting for me to say something.

I moved back in with Mami at the start of my sophomore year and did not regret it. I told her I missed her, and it was not a lie. I did miss her. But I couldn't stomach another minute on campus. My grades skyrocketed after one semester because I never left the house, if not for class. I read every book in my childhood bedroom twice, annotating the pages and color coordinating sticky tabs for sentences I barely remember caring about.

I wanted to tell Mami what happened, but I couldn't. Every time she caught me crying, I'd lock the door and hope she stayed on the other side. I wanted to believe she would hold me and tell me it was not my fault. I was in the wrong place at the wrong time with the wrong guy. But this little voice in the back of my head kept growing more obnoxious every time I tried to ignore it. And I was certain that Mami would feel the same way.

I should have known better.

She raised me better.

I spent so many years splitting couches in half, keeping my door cracked open, guarding my virginity like it was my birthright, and then, in one night, it was over. The thought of her eyes darkening when she heard what happened chilled me to my bone. I kept Mami out. I kept my friends out. I was conscious of every stranger near me to the point of paranoia. I monitored the way I spoke, the way I walked, and the way my lips parted when I smiled. It took months to learn how to make eye contact again. I wondered what my smile said about me now. I was ashamed, scared, and just felt so alone.

I moved to the dresser, ignoring Mami in favor of folded T-shirts.

"Aye, no!" She scolded me as she stood and ripped the clothing from my hands. "Shower! Now! *Estas tu loca?!* Samaya, you smell horrible. Wash your face, put on some makeup, and don't you dare leave this house unless you're wearing the cute new blouse I bought you. The one with the red ribbons on the arms."

I rolled my eyes. "That top is heinous."

"*Pues* wear something else, but it better have buttons, and it better not be black!" She stormed out of the room, doing a sassy finger snap and leaving me in the wake of her warning. "Now!" She called out to me.

To be fair, I did smell, and I was glad someone finally said something about it.

II

Mami gave me an ultimatum at the start of the semester: either I got more involved in school, or I got more involved in school.

The cinema society meets weekly at seven o'clock to project movies onto the white walls that fortified the building of arts and sciences. Despite my best efforts, I was the first person there, which meant I got to catch the sunset behind the downtown skyline all by myself. It was my third time attending one of their events, and my first time remembering to bring a beach chair so I didn't wind up sitting cross-legged on the dirty concrete. I planted myself at the center of the parking lot, marking my territory as I waited for the others to arrive. Cars pulled into parking spots scattered across the lot, and I shouted warm greetings to the names and faces I was proud of myself for memorizing.

A girl with large portrait tattoos running down both arms ran up behind me, chanting. "One of us, one of us!" She high-fived me for remembering to bring a chair before running off toward her friends, setting up blankets and a blow-up mattress closer to the main wall.

It was easy to slip into polite conversation as everyone had the same question on their mind. Throughout the week, members submitted anonymous suggestions for movies across all genres, but the movie selected wouldn't be announced until it was plastered on screen for all in attendance to see. Most people submitted a new title each week while others repeated the same title, hoping one day it would pay off. But, if you missed movie night and your film was selected, there were no replays. It was an addictive concept perfect for small talk.

Cassidy, the president, rolled into the parking lot lugging in an AV cart while the rest of the leadership committee played *Lion King* soundtrack, and we sang along like good little cult members. She had the kind of smile used for kindergarten classrooms and political campaigns, holding her laptop high overhead like Simba presented at Pride Rock while the rest of us cheered, excited to find out who this week's winner would be. While Cassidy did her weekly welcome speech, three boys from the leadership committee fumbled behind her, attempting to hook up the outdated projector. I searched through my tote bag for the silver pencil case that had become my comfort toy.

I purchased a brand-new moleskin after my first meeting when I saw everyone else taking notes for the group discussion after the film. I tore off the cellophane wrapper earlier that morning. My favorite part of the evening was the crisp sound of the spine breaking as I opened a new page, and the unmarred pages waiting inside.

I needed a life.

Hands smacked against thighs, pens against notebooks and chairs, and a drum roll erupted as we waited for the projector to light up. Credits rolled, and a title logo filled the screen: *Mermaids.* I smiled, *my pick.*

A blur of bodies moved in my peripheral as multiple guys in matching club merchandise clustered around a dark-haired boy, as if he were a legend to anyone apart from me. Isaac shooed away his fans as he tried to melt into the background. I turned my gaze back to the film, but my attention was already stolen by the owl-eyed boy hovering in the corners of the crowd, quietly observing from the comfort of his camera's viewfinder. In the aftermath of flashing lights and behind-the-scenes pictures for future recruitment reels, Isaac lowered his camera and met my gaze with the curves of his cheeks dimpling into a warm smile.

We clapped once the film ended as if the cast and crew were present to hear us praise them. As the lights came up, Cassidy turned to us with her butterfly journal clutched in her lap. "Who wants to kick off the discussion?"

Clustered on the floor, we shared our favorite scenes from the film, lines that stood out to us, and newly converted Cher fans made themselves known. Cassidy singled me out as this week's victor, and I received the rousing round of applause I was due.

I tried to look cool packing up my belongings, but I never really knew what to do with myself once the entertainment ended and everyone started mingling. It felt like everyone around me had been friends since the start of college, with stories and inside jokes that I did not know how to navigate. I was always so mystified by the effortless way people would just hover at the edges of a group, waiting for the perfect moment to introduce themselves. We were waiting for someone else to come up with a plan to continue the evening.

"Hey, do you guys want to go get a beer?"

Isaac called out the order, running a hand through his hair as if confused that the words had come from him. My lips quirked into a smile, watching as he gripped the back of his throat with one hand and slipped his phone back into his pocket with the other. The herd formed effortlessly, in that casual, breezy way that palm trees sway in the winter wind and college students knew exactly where to go to get a pitcher of beer for the cheapest price possible.

I hesitated between the comfort of my car or the excitement of joining a group of strangers turned friends. An arm slipped through mine as if I were speaking directly with the universe.

"Whoa! Sorry, I didn't mean to spook you," Cassidy giggled. "You joining?"

"Yeah… yeah, I'd love to." I smiled, dangling my car keys in my hands. "Just let me drop off my things really quick."

"No worries, we'll wait." She smiled, nodding over to the others. Cassidy took it upon herself to guide me into the fold. The walk over to the bar was filled with easy small talk that didn't ask more out of me than I was willing to give.

As a collective, we migrated through the parking lot toward the heart of the college bar scene, chatting about nonsensical factoids of our personal lives and laughing nervously in the hopes of prolonged friendship as we headed through what had to be the sorriest excuse for a downtown district in the state of Florida. Cassidy pulled a cigarette from her bag and offered me one. The buts sparked as she puffed and handed it back to me as I filled into a spot beside a guy wearing a flannel over a graphic t-shirt while Isaac lingered at the outskirts of the group. I didn't fully understand his dynamic within the club, but I was terribly curious to find out.

I turned over my shoulder, watching him sway quietly beneath a canopy of chattering old friends. Their body language seemed so comfortable around him, and yet his shoulders pinched, smile soft, and hands searched for purchase in the pockets of his blue-black slacks. He looked up, and when we locked our eyes, I waved over at him, cigarette in hand and poisonous smoke flowing from my lungs.

I puffed on my second cigarette of the night, hopping across puddles in the brick-lined sidewalks, wondering why on earth he hadn't spoken to me yet. *Probably because you're self-centered and obsessive,* I thought, which was fair but didn't offer the answer I was looking for. I hated to admit it, but I slowed down my pace just to see if I would casually line up beside him. But he beat me to the punch.

"I haven't seen you around the apartment," Isaac stepped up beside me with quiet strides and eyes trained on the floor. It took me a moment to figure out how to answer that.

"I've... been busy," I swallowed, and he accepted that as an adequate answer.

Our shoulders brushed, and it was awkward and quiet and charged. But it didn't make me want to step away from him. If anything, I wished I could sink closer into the fabric of his white linen button-down shirt. Isaac wasn't exactly my *friend,* but he was a friend adjacent and that was good enough for me. There was no reason to be nervous.

I noticed a subtle stubble growing around his chin, and I wondered when he last shaved. I wondered if he wore cologne or aftershave that tasted of evergreen or spearmint as it splashed upon his cheeks. He seemed like the kind of guy who preferred long hair and a fluffy beard. But, today, his hair was cropped tight to the scalp, and his chin looked brushed with a fresh blade.

"You cut your hair," I noted, eyes focused on the crosswalk flickering a giant red hand. My hand-held firm on the bag draping over my shoulder so that it didn't bump into him as we all clustered close together waiting for the timer to end and the drinking to begin.

The observation made him smile, and it wasn't small or shy. It was ear to ear, made more prominent by the scalped edge buzz cut that cut lines along his cheekbones. I could see his teeth and how he tried to bite his lips back together, but he still stared at the floor.

"You seem very proud of this decision," I joked.

"I am," he nodded. He licked his lips, breathed through his nose, and leaned closer to my ear. "I was invited on a trip at the start of summer, and I wanted something that I wouldn't have to maintain." His words were faster than typical, as if the sentence had played out in his mind, and instinct won over whatever voice told him not to speak. I understood that feeling.

"You're nervous," I poked his shoulder lightly, and he shook his head as the others ran across the road. Isaac hovered back with me, checking both ends for oncoming traffic or drunken idiots.

"I'm not." But the shiver on his shoulders made it clear that he was. His hands dug deep into his denim jacket, teeth gleaming beneath the streetlamps. There was energy coursing through his body, and I had to fight hard to take my eyes off him.

I stepped back, pinching my chin between my thumb and forefinger, and stared up at him like an art collector appraising a new museum collection. His laugh rumbled through his chest just the way I remembered it did, but his eyes skidded across my figure in a new way.

"You look good. And whatever it is… congratulations, that sounds exciting." The heel of my shoe caught in the edges of a pothole, my ankle twisting to the side as I yelped. Isaac jumped out in front of me, grabbing my arm and holding me steady. "Whoa… I swear I'm not this accident-prone."

"It's pretty sinful to swear on a lie like that, Samaya." He smiled wide, only letting go of me when we made it safely to the other side of the road. I could feel the others staring at us, sizing up our body language for more than it was worth.

"Thank you," I cleared my throat, fixing my hair as we passed beneath neon signs beckoning us inside for cigars, vapes, and overpriced incense sticks dipped in glitter.

"So, I um… I heard you moved back in with your mom," he asked.

"Yes," My smile slipped. The question felt like an attack. "I did."

"Are you happy?"

After a moment of deliberation, "Yes, I am."

"Why are you laughing?" He asked, but there was a hint of laughter in his voice as well.

"Because it was just such a specific question. I kind of expected, 'Wow, it's a nice night out, isn't it?' 'What's going on in your life, Samaya?' 'Wow, that test last week whooped my ass,' or something like that."

"Huh." His eyes shot up to the sky, pondering. "I'm doing pretty well in school."

"Well, if only we could all be more like you," I teased, bowing my head at him in reverence. He scoffed, pointing his chin toward the buildings opposite me.

My feet shuffled to a stop as the group mindlessly formed a line outside the local dive bar, with an open patio perfect for smoking until your throat ran dry and multiple pool tables scattered around inside. We waited for the bouncer to check everyone's ID. Isaac pivoted on his back heels and leaned closer toward me but didn't lift his shoulder off the steady wall behind us.

"So, what do you and your mom do for fun?"

I whipped toward him, confused and intrigued all at once. "Why are you so obsessed with my mom?"

"I'm not." He blushed, slack-jawed and eyes wide. I watched him shut down. He was finally standing tall, and just for a moment, I accidentally made him shrink. "I just— It's okay, I'm sorry. Never mind."

He scattered back, hand curling around his chin as if he could eat his own words. We fell into uncomfortable silence, shuffling toward the entrance, when he took a deep breath and tried again. "Nice weather we're having, isn't it?"

"Oh, simply the best." I lifted my hands to the sky like a Baptist church. "And the humidity? Barely there. You can breathe without choking on water."

"See? But that's my favorite part about flying into Florida. Even the air has character. You know that gap of space between the plane entrance and the jetway?" He paused, and I was suddenly very aware of how close his body stood beside mine. I nodded, and he pressed on. "Any time I get off a plane, there's a bit of time where I'm just disoriented and forget where I'm going. But I never feel that way in Florida. Every time I land, and that thick air hits my face, I instantly feel grounded."

My lips twitched, and I forgot that we were holding up the line for a moment. We took a few steps forward, Isaac walking with soft steps behind me fully unaware that I was picturing the shape of lips every step of the way. "Well," I cleared my throat, turning back to him as we waited patiently for the bouncer to check IDs. "If it makes you feel better, I'm pretty sure it's supposed to rain the rest of the week."

He put a hand over his heart. "You think so?"

"Oh, I know so. There might even be a heavy storm warning."

He shook his head, smiling at the floor, utterly moved by my announcement. "Thank you for that gift."

I laughed as he handed over his ID to the bouncer. The man guarding the door to what had to be one of most decrepit dive bars in the area was about 6'3, built like a bear, and only had a few teeth to his name. He examined each card like Nicholas Cage, searching for a hidden message in the Declaration of Independence. He let Isaac pass begrudgingly, and then it was time for me to hand over my ID. He handed it right back without a second look.

"Get lost before I call the cops," he coughed, cigarettes and beer nuts radiating off his breath.

I cocked my hip, full irritation welling in my chest. "For what?"

"I'll take it back. Don't push me," he warned, but I didn't understand why he was yelling.

I lowered my voice, hands waving toward the ground as if I could physically deescalate the situation. "Sir, I'm not pushing you. I am inquiring as to why you're denying me entry."

He laughed at me, "I know a fake when I see one."

"Oh, come on!" I flapped my ID around, irritated. "Just because it's pealing doesn't make it fake! It's an old license. If I was going to get a fake, why not get one that's horizontal and doesn't literally say that I'm 21?"

Isaac watched the scene play out from the entrance of the bar and was now stepping forward to intervene. "Hey, calm down. We're all in a big group in the middle of a college town. There's no need to give her a hard time."

"Get out of line before I call the cops on both of you." He moved on to the next person in line without a second glance in our direction.

"It's fine. It's fine. I'll see you around," I tossed over my shoulder, already rushing back down the sidewalk, trying to shake off the embarrassment of the scene and the fear of walking through the streets in the middle of the night. I pulled out my phone, ready to dial Lila, before I realized how messed up it would be to ruin her night by telling her I went out without her. I hid my phone back in my purse, gripping the straps tight to my chest, eternally grateful I wore something long-sleeved and warm for the chilly seaside air. I made it all the way back to the parking lot before I realized someone was following me.

The parking lot was desolate at that time of night. But Isaac didn't try to walk with me back to campus. It was dark, the streets were bare, and Isaac remained yards away from me without another word. He walked toward his parked car on the opposite end of the lot. I searched for my car keys at the bottom of my tote when I caught him glancing over at me. I smiled, and he nodded back, ducking into the driver's side door of his car, and I did the same.

I sat in the parking lot, hands resting on ten and two of the steering wheel, clucking my tongue in confusion.

What the hell just happened?

I blamed what happened next on a lack of impulse control and a strong gut.

III

"Hey!"

My voice echoed back to me off the abandoned cars prepared to spend the night under the watchful glow of fluorescent streetlamps until their owners returned in the morning, hungover from too many pitchers of cheap beer and potato chips. My car jerked to a stop, and I tried to look cool as my seat belt slammed me back against the leather cushion, but it was a lost cause. I tried to catch my breath, but my lungs were heaving far too much for a girl my age.

I need to stop smoking, I thought, but I knew it was an empty promise.

Isaac stopped short at the sound of my voice, turning over a shoulder to search behind his vehicle, afraid he had hit something. His face melted from concern to curiosity all in the span of seconds.

"What are you—"

"Why didn't you walk me to my car?"

I allowed the question to fill the air, his mind, and slowly, he stepped out of the car. My lungs collapsed the moment he closed the door behind him, hands firm and purposeful while the ghost of a smile soaked every corner of his deep brown skin. He practically loitered as he stared at me, leaning against his car, hands clasped in front of his thighs and camera dangling from his neck.

Finally, graciously, he cleared his throat and answered my question with one of his own. "Was I supposed to?"

Was he supposed to walk me to my car? No one else ever had, but for some reason, I wanted Isaac to offer the service. I wanted Isaac to stall by the doorway until I was safely in the building. I wanted him to hold the door open for me, pull out my chair, and offer me his seat on the bus just because he knew I was tired. I wanted to re-introduce him to Mami. I knew he'd stand up, kiss her on both cheeks and be exactly the type of gentleman she wanted for me.

After a moment of searching the asphalt for a reason, he released me from my mental torment. "It would have been inappropriate." His answer left me wanting more. I needed to stop wanting more from Isaac Haas.

"Oh," I nodded, and I wanted him to elaborate but I didn't want to ask. "Well, alright then." I shifted the car into drive like a cut scene from *Fast and the Furious*. The tires screeched as I tried to race out of the parking lot.

But he didn't let me.

Isaac came running up to the car, hands flailing, and shock painted across his face. "Hey! Wait! Was that wrong? Should I have?" His hands landed flat on the open driver's side window, gripping for purchase, but he didn't crouch to meet me at eye level. I enjoyed the way his Adam's apple bobbed at the touch of the metal between his fingertips. He kept me there, but he was also trying to keep himself still.

"No," I smiled, "that's sweet. I can accept that answer if that's really the reason."

"But?"

"I'm just a little confused. You set the plan for everyone to go to the bar. But you followed me back here to do… what? You ask about me when I'm not around," I stared at my fingernails, and I got the impression he stopped breathing. "You know, you could just ask me, right?"

"I don't know where to start with you," he cleared his throat, adjusting his footing.

I laughed, my head shaking as I looked up at him. "You could walk me to my car."

"Okay, okay. Noted, next time." He laughed, scratching at the back of his scalp. "Why'd you take off?"

I gestured in the direction of the bar blocks away from us with my eyebrows held high. "Seriously? For the obvious. That was embarrassing."

He laughed, leaning back on his heels. "Yeah, I know, I just thought—"

I leaned forward, eyebrows raised. "Thought what?"

He shook his head, biting his bottom lip, and left me in the silence of almost words.

"I didn't feel like making a scene," I continued. He nodded at me, but there was a slight smirk on his lips that made me think he wanted to make a comment but didn't have the confidence to voice it. "Plus, he was right. It was a fake. Well, no, it's very real. It's just not mine. It's a hand-me-down from a friend of a friend of Lila."

He bit his lip, nodding his head as if he expected as much.

"Okay… Why did you follow me? It was very Jack the Ripper for someone worried about being inappropriate." I pressed my chin to my fist, leaning on the armrest. I sounded like a child asking for a compliment. I wanted him to list out all the reasons he couldn't take his eyes off me.

A small laugh bubbled at the back of his throat, "Because we parked in the same lot."

"I *meant,* why did you leave the bar."

"Ahhhh," His body weight bounced between his heels and the balls of his shoes. His shoulders pinched his ears, and it was then that I saw the scars of piercings long ago forgotten. Two tiny holes punctured his freckled lobes, and I wondered what he looked like when they were filled. His eyes focused on the ground when he spoke again. "Yes," he coughed. "Well, it would be inappropriate to say."

"Isaac, we must get past this!" I practically growled, moaning into an exasperated heap as I crumbled into the driver's seat. "What are those from?" I pointed at the piercings, and he covered the faded marks with his fingertips as if he had forgotten they existed.

"I snuck out one night when I was… my mom had just gotten remarried, so I was 14? I think. And yeah. All my friends were lining up to get pierced by a sewing needle in someone's kitchen. I followed suit." He shook his head at the memory, laughing into the warmth of his hands. "I think I was trying to be rebellious."

"And how'd that work out?" I asked.

"Well, they got infected, and I was grounded for three months. So…" His smile slipped, his eyes went cold, and his eyes drifted to memories I wished I didn't trigger. "Not well."

"Three months? That's wild. Like under what terms?"

"No phone, no computer, except for school," he added that bit like a judge trying to be reasonable in a courtroom. "No Xbox and no friends." He held up his fingers, sounding off his punishments with the flat understanding that he could not change the facts of his past, only laugh at them. "Yeah, I think that's everything."

"Would you consider yourself a rebellious kid?"

He kicked the earth at his feet, spinning in a circle like a Golden Retriever. "Me? No way! No, never. I didn't have the freedom to be. But you were." He planted his feet in my direction, pointing at me with two hands pressed together in the shape of an arrow. My mouth fell open, and I pointed an exaggerated finger at my chest as if he must have me confused with someone else. "Yes, everything about you says it. You moved back in with your mom so what leash she kept you on clearly benefitted whatever fun you were having."

I covered my face with my hands, leaning my forehead on the steering wheel as my chest drummed with joyful laughter. I did not like how comfortable I felt beneath his eyes. I did not like the way Isaac stared at me when he finished his sentences or the way I never wanted him to stop. More than anything, I hated how curious he made me. I couldn't tell if I was curious because I was supposed to be or if I was just accustomed to being curious about boys like Isaac. The boys with sullen eyes and quiet minds. More than anything, I did not like how deeply I wanted to be his friend.

"Okay, if you must know. I barely show up to any of the meetings, so I try to take pictures when I can for club use later when they want to shmooze potential new members. Like yourself. And I didn't really think it was rude to leave. I just figured, if you weren't going to be there, I didn't see the point in sticking around." His breath came out in soft wafts of gray matter. He let his words fill the air and my mind. He crouched down, legs spread out and arms folded politely at the window. "I apologize for not walking you to your car. Would you like to take a walk now?"

I searched up and down the sidewalk but saw nothing but empty college buildings. "Around here?"

He shook his head. Slinging his backpack across his chest and unzipping the top. I tried to sneak a peek at the vials upon vials of products he rifled through. "No, I was thinking—, well, I was *hoping* you'd have a suggestion. As you're the Floridian and all."

"I might. What's in the bag?"

"Chemicals."

"As if that's such a casual thing to say?"

"It is to me." He twisted slightly to better display his camera. "For developing film."

Red flag. Red flag. Red flag.

Run, Samaya. We've been down this road before.

I leaned back against the leather seat as the light bulb went off in my head. "Ahh, you're pretentious."

From within the backpack, Isaac pulled out a plastic, metallic, pineapple container. It's the kind of item you'd find in the home decor department of a Marshalls or JC Penny. If you'd given me a million guesses, I would never land on that. He unscrewed the leafy green top and pulled out a perfectly rolled-up joint. I spotted a bowl, grinder, and bag of weed lying inside.

"I don't see it like that," he mumbled as the joint slid between his plump lips. He brandished a lighter from his back pocket. "I'm passionate. If I'm going to pursue something, I want to understand it fully. For me, it's photography, and for you… I don't know. But I'd really like to know if you'd like to share. But yeah. I'm pretentious, okay? I know." The lighter took three turns to finally catch a good flame. "But you know what, that's fine because so are you."

"You walk around campus carrying drugs?" I was so flustered I nearly jumped through the window. I didn't realize I touched him until I tracked his eyeline to my hand closed around his forearm, but I didn't take my hand away. He didn't seem upset by it.

"Not always," he smirked. "And correct me if I'm wrong, but isn't weed decriminalized? If it bothers you, I won't insist." He took the joint from his lips and twisted open the metal container he used to hold it. Both waited patiently in his hands, waiting for my decision.

I backtracked into the seat, trying to feign coolness. I didn't sell it well, considering I kept scanning the sidewalk for campus police or thugs or real police to pop out, arrest us, and ruin our lives all because Isaac was too cool for me.

"Hey," he looked down at me with understanding etched into his eyes. "I do this all the time, or else I wouldn't offer it to you. Nothing is going to happen. If you don't trust that I wouldn't get you arrested, which is fine and understandable, just know that I don't feel like getting arrested either. Do you not smoke?" Isaac asked, worried that he had made a faux pau.

"I do. But not tonight."

He nodded, and just like that, the joint went back into its case, and the pineapple was once more stashed in his backpack. "I'm sorry."

He stood in front of me like a shadow of someone I couldn't put my finger on. He did everything the way I wished he would, but it felt off to me in some way. He didn't fuss or push or… he just simply existed. He smiled down at me as if he had nowhere else to be.

"I want to get to know you," he said it like an order, not a request. "We don't need to smoke to do that."

I opened my mouth to speak, but all I could say was. "Thank you." Then I remembered what he said earlier, and my head stirred at the realization he'd commented on my character. "What do you mean I'm pretentious?"

He laughed, and the moment fizzled into comfort as I dropped my hand away. "I mean, you're pretentious the way normal people with culture and interests and heritage are pretentious. You like to read, but you don't shove it down everyone's throats. You like movies, but you openly call the 2000s *Charlie's Angels* trilogy cinematic classics. You—"

"—which they are. But how did you know that?" When I joined the cinematic society, there were fun mixers that had us go around the room to introduce ourselves, our majors, and any controversial film opinions we may have had. Some were off base, like '*Titanic* is overrated' while others elicited little gasps of encouragement. But Isaac wasn't there for any of that, I would've remembered.

His head cocked to the side; lips pressed tight as his eyes scanned mine. He sighed through his nose, pausing to make a choice I couldn't read through his expression. "We have more mutual friends than George and Lila. I know things. Like how you pronounce your last name with a heavy H when it starts with a X. Even when you've lived in this country your entire life."

"Well, that's not pretentious. That's just being culturally accurate. Also, it's how every member of my family says it. I'm the only *gringa* who says it like an American."

Isaac shook his head, eyes never leaving mine. "You say your name beautifully." I didn't say a word. I let his compliment wash over me, not filling the air just because I was uncomfortable with the silence. The idea of Isaac asking around about me made my stomachache. Suddenly, the seat belt was too tight around my torso, and I felt stupid still sitting in this ridiculous car.

"My dream is to backpack South America," he said.

"Oo, that sounds like quite the adventure."

"Mm, maybe a little more intense than the walk I'm thinking about tonight." He shook his head from side to side, mischief in his smile.

"I want to see the Peruvian Amazon. And Egypt. And Petra. And maybe Patagonia."

"Wait, you never visited Peru?" He asked.

"Of course, a few times when I was a kid. But only Lima and only to visit family. I want to see it all."

He smiled. "Well, it sounds like we have mutual plans of interest."

"Sounds like it. Not for nothing, but if I'm pretentious," I added. "It's only because I grew up watching your DVD collection."

He blinked, head turning to the side as he tried to make sense of what I was saying. "Wait… when I moved. Wait. You watched those?"

I nodded.

"Which was your favorite?"

"*Mermaids*."

He nodded, soft and slow. "That was my mom's favorite."

I swallowed hard, my eyes glistening. We stared at each other for a beat, our chests rising and falling in unison. Isaac was the first to break.

"Okay, fine! I surrender. I am pretentious with my film camera, and my van, and my Jack Kerouac collection and—"

"I'm not judging you," I said. "Well, maybe a little bit. A collection? The man only— never mind. I am judging. It's a little chilly out, isn't it?"

"Yeah," he nodded, eyes defeated. "It is. A bit. But not if you walk close to me."

"That wouldn't be very appropriate, would it?" I countered, but he didn't say a word. He just smiled, patiently waiting for me to drive off or join him. "Alright. Fine. I know a place."

IV

We agreed to drive separately for the sake of being appropriate.

I chose the location while Isaac followed close behind. Over the years, I memorized every speckled marking of life within a 10-mile radius of my house. I knew these streets, these sidewalks, and the gum-stained cracks along the path that only children waste time mapping out. And even though I tried to be mysterious and kept our rendezvous point a surprise, I had a feeling Isaac knew exactly where we were going.

The parking lot was bigger than I remembered it, but then again, Mami didn't take me to the park often enough to form a consistent picture.

I unbuckled my seat belt, scanning through the tree line and empty rows of parking spots as Isaac's black Mazda shifted into park beside mine. He hopped out of his car with urgency, jogging toward the driver's side of my car before I had time to put together what he was doing. He held the door open for me, guiding me out with an open-faced palm. I didn't take his hand, but I did take a moment to wipe excess sweat off my palm onto the back of my jeans in case of any future offers. Isaac shivered as he closed the door behind me, eyes adjusting to the grand nothingness surrounding us. To get to the park, you had to pass beneath an overpass that connected the highway to our small beach town. During the day, it appeared harmless, but at night, it was a pit of black tar five car lanes long and just as wide.

"This looks like the opening of a *Law and Order: SVU* episode." He joked, pressing his shoulder toward mine, gently knocking me off my axis. "One where the runner goes for a jog through Central Park, never to be seen again." I swatted at his shirt pocket, enjoying the scent of the aftershave radiating off his neck. Fresh laundry mixed with tobacco and wine.

My arms wrapped tight around my torso, holding myself steady like a flag in the wind. On the way over to the park, I found myself taking deep breaths at every intersection, reminding myself that if things went south, I could always drive back home. I was in full control of where the evening led. There was no need to worry because there was no danger. I repeated that mantra every day since the frat party to soothe my aching soul. Sometimes, I was able to manage the trauma, but often, I ended up fighting battles with my body that no one else saw.

I could have stayed home that night, but I had the right to go out, I had the right to drink, and I had the right to trust strangers just like every other college kid. But I was never angry at James, even when I wanted to be. I always found a reason to be angry with myself. I couldn't look in the mirror without seeing what he saw. I couldn't smile without questioning what kind of invitation I might be sending. And when I dressed in the mornings, I added an extra layer just for safety. My blood must have thinned from all the added coverage because even in the summertime, I found myself shivering.

I used to live in constant worry, but for some reason, none of that caution felt as present standing beside Isaac. I took that as a sign that I was on the right path. I was not afraid of getting hurt; I was afraid that one day, I'd wake up with bitterness so burned in my heart that I wouldn't be able to recognize myself in the mirror. I was afraid that I'd grow to build walls out of brick and mortar and concrete where no one could find me. But, just for tonight, I wanted to see what might happen if I loosened the chains of the drawbridge and welcomed someone in.

I leaned one hand on the car frame, cocking my hip to the side as I faced him, closing the gap between us with a single step. "Did it ever occur to you that maybe there are things in this world that are more afraid of you than you are of them?"

He sighed, a handheld over his heart as his smile carved dimples into his left cheek. "Whoa. I'm swooning."

"It was smooth, right?"

"If something bad went down, I know you'd step up to protect us." He laughed, dropping his head back to smile at the stars glittering above us. "See, this is why I need you on my trips. Who's going to give me the confidence boost I need to do something stupid?"

"Oh, don't worry." I stepped up in front of him, adjusting the lapels of his denim jacket like a mom getting her son ready for school. I could feel his stomach rising and falling against mine, but I tried not to notice the way he froze at my touch. His lips still and eyes soft as my hands flattened against his chest. "I think you'll do just fine."

I shook the nervous laughter from my hands, chewing on my cheek. His eyes skated across my lips. "To be fair, it's very pretty on the other side," I promised, stepping back with my palms held up in defense.

"Fine," he sighed, stretching out the kinks in his neck and joints in his hands as if he were a boxer heading into the ring. He bounced from shoe to shoe as if he were about to take off running, but instead, he grabbed his camera and snapped a photo of me before I had a chance to pose. The flash blinded us both in the process.

"What was that for?" I asked, blue dots clouding my vision.

He gestured to the camera with the flick of his fingers, eyebrows raised, the picture of innocence. "Oh, it's for when you murder me, and the police want evidence of my killer—"

He barely finished the sentence before he broke off into a sprint, pulling me along by the sleeve and laughing into the wind. Isaac's long limbs carried him past me. I never liked gym class growing up, but I practically ran for the Olympic qualifiers trying to beat him. He turned back halfway beneath the bridge the moment he realized I'd fallen behind.

"Samaya?" He called out to me.

"Are you insane?!" I gasped at the sound of my name ricocheting off the walls. He was trying to wake the dead. Grabbing his sleeve, I pulled him along with me to the other side, and it didn't escape my notice that his body weight settled into place beneath my touch. An anchor on a fishing boat drifting off at sea.

Isaac scanned the playground that once belonged to him. Not much had changed in the fifteen years since we shared our last play date. The swings still rusted in a way that begged for tetanus shots, the oversized plane remained fixed and buried beneath the earth, and Isaac fit just as easily into the cracks he left behind in the pavement when he moved away. He stretched his arms out wide, taking in the night air and spouting propeller noises that needed a bit of tuning. I unzipped my jacket, slipping it off my shoulders to carry it in my arms as I led us to the park bench our parents once occupied. Only now, there was a metal armrest dividing the bench into two equal halves, and we both settled into the curves, comfortable with the distance.

I cleared my throat, trying to find the right words to say, "So, I know I reacted a bit… intensely before, but… could we… maybe?" He nodded, already understanding my meaning without me having to blatantly ask to smoke his weed.

"Of course, but first answer me this," He placed an arm on the back of the bench, leaning his spine on the opposite end to face me. "Do you want to smoke because you want to, or because you think *I* want to and you're being kind. Or because you think it would be easier to hang out with me if we were both high?"

"You're very earnest." My eyes glanced over him as if he were a puzzle, and I finally filled the edges of the sky.

His head cocked to the side, casual and already used to people using that word to describe him. "Lying is a mortal sin."

"Sin, sin, sin. I never pegged you for churchy. But fair. The first one. I want to smoke. In fact, I'd like to roll as well, if that's alright with you. I'm quite good at it, I promise." I asked, extending my hands.

He undid his backpack straps and dug around until he found what he was looking for. "Oh, I believe you. No need to add the disclaimer." He passed the pineapple to me with a smile as we fell easily into companionable silence. I felt so at peace grinding away at the green flower he kept wrapped up in a plastic sandwich bag with the sliding zip lock. I licked the corners of the wrapper and rolled the bud up tight in its makeshift blanket, handing it to Isaac, who inspected my work like a pawnshop jeweler. He was pleased.

Isaac and I had one major difference: I spoke before I thought. He thought before he convinced himself not to speak. He fiddled with the joint between his fingers, weighing the merit of his thoughts versus the comfort of our silence. The words won out and I was grateful for it.

"My dad used to bring me and my buddies here every weekend. No exception. I still have the scar on my chin from falling off my skateboard and hitting the sidewalk. Right here." He leaned into me, pointing at the side of his jaw. "See, you weren't the only casualty of improper playground flooring of the late '90s."

"Oh, to have friends to play with." I turned to face him before he could interject with something polite or pitying, I wanted neither.

"Very rude of you, by the way. Not inviting me to your going away party." He mirrored me, and I didn't fight the laugh that bubbled from my chest, warm and fuzzy, at the sight of my indignant face mimicked on his.

His eyes rolled to the back of his head. "As you if you'd even come. You hated me."

"I did not," I lied.

"Samaya!" He sat up, hands pressed to his thighs and his jaw gaping open. "I value honesty. Please, don't lie. It's impolite to lie."

"Well, maybe I wouldn't have hated you if you invited me!" I hollered back like a child.

He lit up the joint and lifted it between his lips. "Now, that's the kind of friendship I need. Someone who can be easily bought with extravagant parties. There was a bounce house. It was huge. It was dope." He coughed out smoke and passed the joint back to me.

I let it burn between my fingers, and he didn't push me to hurry up. "What was Connecticut like?" I asked, but really, all I could do was think about the electric shock that ran through my hands when he touched me. I wanted him to do it again. "You don't speak very highly of it. In fact, I think tonight might be the only time I haven't heard you disparage the state of Connecticut. If I were the governor, I would sue you for defamation."

He laughed, shaking his head and selecting his words carefully as he fiddled with the joint as I might fiddle with my precious pens. "Wow," he said, blowing a raspberry into the night air in disbelief. "That's just rich coming from you."

"Are you laughing at me?" He hunched over, holding his stomach in a fit of ugly hysterics. I held in the smoke and let it out on a soft gust of air. "Just say whatever is on your mind, Isaac. I'd rather hear you disrespect me than imagine what you're thinking."

He reached out to me, taking my hands easily in his as his eyes begged me to understand him. "It's sweet, okay? So, please don't change anything about yourself, and please don't think I'm judging you. But Samaya. You talk about growing up in Florida all the time. It's like the only bit of information I can get on you. Are you getting a cut from the tourism fund? Because if not, we need to lawyer up. Fast."

I turned my nose to the sky and ignored him. But I couldn't fight the smile pulling at my lips. "What do you want to know?"

His nose scrunched as the blue, bitter smoke evaporated off his tongue and into the starry sky. "The usual. Your hopes, your dreams, your plans for the future."

"So, just the light, easy conversation topics?"

"Precisely."

"Honestly, no one's ever asked me before." Isaac was a boy filled with nothing but hopes, dreams, and plans for the future. Even as he sat beside me, I felt we were on borrowed time. He wasn't here. He was already planning out his next step in the great cosmic plan of his life. "My hope is to finish the year strong," I swallowed, and it's not like I didn't feel comfortable speaking with Isaac, but I never voiced my wants out loud before.

"And then?" His voice was soft, like a treat on the floor trying to lure out a kitten hiding beneath the bed.

My palms pressed firmly against my knees, cuddling my legs up close to my chest. "I want to work at the women's shelter. I think I could be good at that." My eyes started to water, and my throat constricted off emotion I didn't understand. "Wow, I don't know where that came from."

"What about the women's shelter inspires you?" Isaac moved us along with diplomatic self-assurance, clearing his throat as he leaned his body weight on the armrest.

"Oh, Isaac, it's not very smoke-in-the-park conversation…" I laughed, but he didn't match me. He didn't cut me off. He didn't change the subject, and he didn't look away. Isaac just waited for me to finish what I had to say on my own timeline. He didn't make the silence something scary or unintelligent. He just sat there, watching me, waiting for me to go on. "I'd like to live a life I can be proud of. Money is important, of course. But beyond that… I want to be able to do for others what I wished my mom, and I had growing up. I'd like to be there… for someone… other than myself."

Isaac nodded. "You're too young to be so altruistic."

"That's so funny. Because I feel like I should've started a long time ago." I laughed, wiping my eyes. "What about you? What are your hopes, your dreams?"

"Travel," he said.

"Photography," I overlapped him, confused when we didn't meet up in the middle.

"Photography is a means for travel. I want to see as much of everything as I possibly can before I can't any longer."

"Well," I cleared my throat, sizing up the rusting swing set that wouldn't stop moving. My elbow pressed to the back, and his in the front. I could feel the hair on his arms brush against mine, and the mere breath of him so close to me sent a blissful shiver through my chest. "What about money? Family?"

"Money will always be there wherever I go." He slipped the joint from my hands, inhaling deep. And though I waited for him to go on, he never spoke about family. "Did you come here often growing up? This feels like the place teenagers hang out when they're trying to get away with something they shouldn't be doing."

"You know, you don't talk about your life all that much," I shot back. He smiled, but it didn't reach his eyes. We sat in silence for a moment, both of us letting the joint sizzle in his fingertips. I broke away first, trying to mask the shudder under the crackling glow of outdated streetlamps in need of replacements. "It was, for sure. Though you have a very skewed image of my childhood. Honestly, I'm kind of surprised we're the only ones smoking out here. This used to be a huge spot for that. Or so I was told. I never did. I smoked in public once when I was like… thirteen at a movie theater, and it freaked me out so much that I never did it again. The public part. Not the smoking, obviously."

He let out a low whistle, absorbing my story as if he could picture it in his mind. "Thirteen. Oh, my Lord on High, I don't think I have a 'skewed' image. It's crystal clear. I was still playing with Legos when I was thirteen." We fell into an effortless pattern of puff, puff, pass. "What else did you do for fun?"

"I don't know. What did you do for fun?" I scooched closer to him, closing one knee over the other as if I were a talk show host and he was my guest. He smiled, nudging his shoulder against mine, patiently waiting for me to continue. "What happened to Mr. Honesty?"

"We'll get to me, but I want to hear about you."

"I don't believe you," I leaned in close, shaking my nose from side to side. He smiled down at me like a flower too sweet for picking.

"I'm an open book, Samaya."

"That's not true—"

"Pardon." He held a hand over his heart, teeth gleaming as he smiled. "That was a lie. I'm not. But you have my word, I'll be an open book for you. For tonight. So, what did you do for fun?"

"Pretty much whatever anybody else wanted to do… and I had read-a-thons. It's stupid, I know, but it was fun to me."

"It's not stupid." His words were gentle and affirming. "What kind of books did you read?"

"I can't tell you," I mumbled through the sweaty palms I pressed onto my lips.

"Why? Is it bad? Was it *smut?* Was it—" he gasped, pressing away from me like a vaudeville character in mock disgust. His lips brushed the side of my neck as he whispered, "the *Satanic Bible?*"

"What? No. Why—never mind. You're going to call me basic," I whined, shutting my eyes and shaking my head.

He laughed and reached out to pull my hands away from my face. "Samaya, relax, everyone goes through a Satanic phase. It's part of growing up." We fell into another fit of laughter, but neither of us pulled our hands away.

"It was *Twilight*—" But the word was barely out of my mouth before Isaac gasped so loudly that I feared something was behind me. He pulled away, arms tucked tight by his sides, shaking his head at me in disappointment.

"I'll pray for you," he promised, head nodding and hand pressed close to his chest.

We simmered, giggling softly and not really pushing the conversation further. We sat and listened to the vibration of our laughter rolling through the rickety old bench beneath our bodies.

"I actually love to read," he added. "Have you ever heard of Mary Pope Osborne?"

My eyebrows furrowed as I tried to place the name but couldn't. "No? Should I have?"

His brown eyes bugged out of his head in shock. "My God, yes. She's only the most prolific novelist of the fantasy genre."

He gave me a minute to look her up on my phone, but he was already laughing before I could glare at him. "The *Magic Tree House* series?"

"Look in my eyes and tell me honestly those books aren't amazing." His head hung low, eyes melting at the corners.

"You're high."

"Samaya, of course I'm high. But I could lend you one of my copies sometime. If you want." He grew very serious suddenly, reaching out to grab my shoulder as he added. "But only if you promise to give it back. They're first editions."

If you want, he offered, words soft like a breath caressing my cheeks, the tender tone dropping in octave as his nose nearly grazed mine and his eyelids fluttered with the sleepy sigh of unrequited desire. My smile faltered, and I couldn't speak. It should be illegal to look at someone like that.

He was supposed to kiss me. It was written all over his face, and I knew that if I looked down at his hands, I would catch him inching toward mine beneath the armrest. But I disagreed with the timing. *Not here,* I thought, *he would kiss me, but it shouldn't be here.* This park was the past, and I wanted a future with Isaac Haas.

I planted my palm firmly on the bench and pushed back against the green paint-chipped metal until my spine pressed back up against the other side. Again, he mirrored me, but it wasn't in jest as before. I did not take my eyes off him, and neither did he for me. I wrapped my arms around my chest, head tilted up and jaw locked as I regained control of where the evening led.

"So, come on. Tell me about you. Did you party a lot as a teen? Did you rob the local bodega, have your face plastered all over street corners, and get a nickname like 'local hooligan'?" He giggled, and so I kept going. "Did you get blitzed in back alleys and wake up covered in tattoos?"

"What does 'blitzed' mean?" he chuckled, scratching at the back of his neck, shaking off my rejection and trying not to let it sour his confidence.

"I don't know. I've never said it before in my life, but it felt right in the moment."

He smiled, and the silence that followed bubbled into the warmest laughter. Our bodies trembled, floating back and forth on an axis I never wanted to end. I didn't realize how at peace I was in the moment until something came by to disrupt it.

I didn't hear the wheels scraping across the asphalt until I saw the boy in my peripheral vision. My fight or flight took over, and I dove into Isaac's shoulder, clinging to him as three teenagers skated past us on boards decked out in neon stickers. They didn't seem to care about us if we didn't care about them. We were older, casually smoking a joint in a public park, and these kids looked at us to figure out what to do next. It was harmless fun.

"Jesus, Mary, and Joseph," I cursed. And for some reason, he lit up at that.

"Are you Catholic?" His voice cracked with childlike curiosity as if I'd quoted his favorite cartoon that he was too embarrassed to talk about but deeply wanted to. We were still clutching each other's sleeves, and he didn't seem to be in a rush to let go of me.

I slouched into the cold metal and ignored the chipped paint surely ruining my clothes. "In the way all Latinos are Catholic, yes. But not really, no. But you are?"

"Ooof, what a question." He shook his head and slowly released me from his clutches. "You want to get out of here?" I nodded, accepting his hands as we stepped off the bench. But just as easily as his fingers slipped between mine, did they fall away, hovering between the comfort of his pockets and the danger of being near me. My hand flexed at the ghost of his warmth, and I curled them into fists, filling the gaps by myself.

He took the joint back from me but didn't smoke it. Instead, we found ourselves drawn down a cobblestone path toward the playground equipment. Isaac sank into the vacant swing set, but I did not match him. I didn't like the nostalgia of that place or the gray afterglow the moon cast over it. It felt like a dream I wanted no part in. Confused, he looked up at me, puffing smoke into the air before handing me the jay.

I shook my head, declining the offer. I hugged the metal frame between my arms to see if that would help the anxiety fluttering in my chest pass. But I couldn't shake the feeling that if I looked hard enough, I would find the ripped-up flower petals buried beneath the sand. He rubbed the joint onto the back of his heel, snuffing out the flame before returning it wordlessly back into the pineapple.

"Samaya?" He asked.

"Yes?"

"May I ask you a question? And it might pry, but you must be honest with me." He was so casual on his swing, but it didn't match the heat crawling up my neck.

"Only if it's reciprocated," I countered. He took a moment before he nodded in agreement.

"What is it about these swings that makes you so uncomfortable?" He asked.

"They don't—" But I cut myself off at his eyes zeroing in on my face. I could hear his voice scolding me with the simple use of my name and caved. I rocked on my heels; hands pressed against the iron structure while he sat below me. His torso was so long that even at this angle, I was only a slight bit taller than him.

"I don't really know," I whispered. "I'm being honest."

"I know you are," he whispered back, nodding for me to continue.

I sighed, shaking out my thoughts. "It's multiple things. I can't stand the sound of chains clanking together. It... I can't explain it. I just don't. Maybe I have vertigo? I don't know. It's the smell. It's the germs, maybe, but..." It was not a lie, but it was not the whole truth. I couldn't stand the memory of sitting on those swings.

Tell him, the voice in my brain begged me. *Speak.*

"I was a very lonely child. And I feel like these swings bore witness to that in a way I don't want to remember." My words were barely a breath on the wind, but he heard me. I knew he did. His owl eyes scanned mine, and I think he was searching for something I couldn't give him.

He stood up, wiped his hands off his jeans, and planted himself so he was facing me straight on. His shoulders were easy, hands hanging loose at his sides, and backpack comfortable between his bones. The bags beneath his brown eyes were more pronounced in this patch of streetlight. I looked up at him, lips parted, and asked him something I wanted to know.

"Are you close with your parents?" It was not an icebreaker, but I did not feel the desire to break ice with him. Everything was warm. Everything was soft. But the silence was too charged and longed for actions I wasn't ready to take.

He did not recoil from the question, he just simply answered, "no."

"Why not?"

"You know why I like to hear you speak—"

"You like to hear me speak?" I cut in, blushing, and as I tried to add levity to a night that turned too serious to bear.

He smirked, but he didn't correct the phrasing. "I do like to hear you speak. But I ask about your mom and your life and why you would *choose* to move back in with her… because I find it fascinating. I've never met anyone who has that kind of safety net. You're lucky to have that."

You're lucky your father fought for you. I wanted to say. *You're someone worth fighting for.*

He could see the water bubbling at the corners of my eyes as he looked down at me. He took my hands in his, but it didn't feel romantic. He needed my hands to hold him steady as he forced the words out, and it sobered me.

"You're lucky to have your family, Samaya." He looked like he'd coveted this from afar for some time.

"What's your family like?

"If I told you, it would sound like I was complaining. I'd ramble—"

"Isaac Haas, you promised me honesty."

After a moment, he cleared his throat, focused on the sidewalk, and tried to paint the picture. "My mom… used to love to travel. So did my father. That's how they met. They met while she was backpacking Europe, and he was still living in Amsterdam, right? And at the time… she was very free-spirited. She planned on going to college… and then she got pregnant with me. But… I think my mother needed more than that to be happy?" He wiped his nose, and I pretended not to notice.

He cleared his throat, pressing on as if it were a class assigned speech and not his life story. "But my father did not. So, she couldn't go back to India because of… reasons I don't really know, but I imagine were serious enough to move to a different continent. So, she moved to America where she had somewhat distant… cousins, I'll call them. And she divorced my dad because they really were not compatible, but yeah. She remarried to an older man, who already had kids, a good job, a nice house, and happened to be heavily involved in a religious sect of the Catholic church. Fun for me." He shook out his hands like a jazz singer. "Very formal. Not necessarily a supporter of the arts. Not necessarily a fan of me." He nearly choked on the truth of that. "I don't have a problem with Connecticut. I just don't want to go back. Like, you find freedom in this place, right? I assume?" He gestured to the town around us. "That's why you stayed, right?" I nodded, and he mirrored my movements subconsciously. Tears filled the corners of his eyes, and I wanted nothing more than to kiss the memories away.

"You find safety in your home. I've never once known that. It's very rare, Samaya. You need to know that. Every choice I've made since my mom won custody of me was in the pursuit of getting as much distance between me and her house as I can."

"I'm sorry," I whispered. The wind picked up and sent a shiver down my spine. His hand reached out, and in one grip of his palm, the chains stopped shaking, and the sounds croaked into deafening silence. *Thank you,* I wanted to say, but I was still reeling from the gesture.

"I don't speak to my father." The words slipped out before I could stop them.

He nodded. "That's probably for the best."

My neck jerked back at his words. "No? I don't agree. I would prefer to have a relationship with my dad than not have one."

"Why?"

"You wouldn't get it."

"Why? Because I still speak to mine?" I didn't say anything. He continued. "I love my dad. But what does that change? He's not here. He's his own person. Having one good parent who cares about you is better than having two who sort of pay attention to your life."

"I'm sorry."

He cleared his throat. "Thank you, that's kind, but I'm not. I've never been happier. I built my life, and I'm proud of it. I can't wait to continue living it for as long as God lets me. Or whatever is out there, I don't know. I don't know why I told you all that." He rubbed his hands into his eyes as if trying to blur the memory of this night. I did not like seeing him second-guess himself all the time. I hated seeing him shrink. "I'm just high."

I shrugged, "I have one of those faces. People tell me things. Hence the therapy track."

He shook his head, "I don't think that's it." It's silent for a moment, and then, "May I take your picture?" The camera dangling from his neck was already positioned within his fingertips.

I snort in confusion. "Now you ask me?"

"I take it back. That sounded creepy." He stashed the camera immediately behind his back, shaking his head.

"No, now stop that. Just, why?"

"I'll tell you after," he promised.

"Now that sounds creepy!" I cackled.

"That's what I just said! Look, I was going to take it without asking, but I figured that was so pretentious and weird—"

"Just do it!"

He took my photo. The flash blinded me.

"Of course, you would. You're such a rom-com. And on film, no less," I wiped my brow, trying to believe this boy standing before me was real and not an amalgamation of everything I ever prayed for.

"Yes, Samaya, I am a very pretentious person, with a pretentious old-fashioned camera that uses grossly expensive film. And I only hang out with other people who watch pretentious movies and let me take their pictures. Which is why I only went out tonight because my ex begged me to be there because she felt bad I dropped out of the society after we broke up." He barreled through the truth as if it were a burden he needed to unload.

Red flag. Red flag red flag red flag.

"You're still friends with your ex?" I asked.

He cleared his throat, realizing his slip-up.

"Well, yes. No, not really. We were never that serious. Puppy love, if that? That's not right, either. She's the president, right? And we met at a party. She recruited me, but I don't really show up anymore on account of a lot of… reasons."

"Ah, reasons."

"And they need the numbers for recruits to think they're still relevant—"

I held up my hand, lips soft and eyes bleached of judgment.

He cleared his throat, hands buried in his pockets. "It's a very incestuous organization."

"Ahh…" I hummed, hoping it didn't sound too condescending.

"And it was freshman year. A long, long time ago." He coughed, scanning the sidewalk for… what? Salvation? "It's not getting better, is it?"

"Shh, it's okay," I whispered, patting him on the shoulder like an old buddy. "Let's just enjoy right now."

He moved closer to me, a smile carving into his cheek and hands pressed together in prayer. "But I'm happy she begged me because—"

"So, tell me about your internship," I suggested, waving the white flag of smoke. "You're planning a big trip, right? That's what you said?"

"Yes, but I didn't mention it was an internship?"

"Lila told me."

"And she told you why?"

"Because I asked."

"You asked," he blushed, his voice was soft and airy like he'd found the holy grail but didn't want to touch in case it was a mirage messing with his head.

"I was curious," I blushed back.

"You were curious. Samaya, can I ask you an invasive question?" I nodded at him, but he took a minute to work up the nerve to ask me what he was curious about. "When was the last time you were in a relationship?"

He might have just knocked the wind out of me with that one. But I was a cool girl. A cool girl who didn't get flustered by stupid boys with stupid cameras and pretty ex-girlfriends who probably would've been my friend in high school, actually, fuck. She seemed cool. But that's not the point. So, I chose honesty.

"High school. Why?"

"Good. I mean… cool. I was just curious," he danced on his toes. "Yeah… I, um, I reached out to this photographer on Instagram about that. Well no. I reached out to him over ten times until he finally responded. He works for National Geographic, and I've always been a big fan of his. I knew he was planning this big trip around the country soon, trying to cover all the US national parks, and I basically said, 'hi, I'll do whatever you need as long as I get the fuck out of Connecticut' for the summer. And he said yes."

"Damn, that's cool," I smiled, soft and slow like a child in wonder.

"Yeah, it is." His eyes glimmered with pride.

"What would happen if you went back to Connecticut?"

"Ugh," he sighed, licking his lips and biting the inside of his cheek. "I'd be stuck with my mom. She's not awful. I love her. I don't know why I said that. She just…" he took a moment to process his thoughts, choosing his next words carefully. "My mom cares a lot about what happens to us, to our souls, when we die. Which leads her to live a life that – she feels – will grant her eternal salvation. But in the meantime, that lifestyle mandates every inch of our lives, and it can sometimes feel… cumbersome? I don't know how to say what I'm trying to say politely. I'll just be honest. Have you seen the movie *Carrie*?" I nodded. "It's like that."

I let out a low whistle, eyes wide and lips bitten between my teeth as I tried to think of the right thing to say. "I'm sorry."

"It's okay," he sniffed, plucking invisible lint off his pants. He shrank again, wrapping his arms around himself, but he didn't back away from it. It was like he needed to get this off his chest. "It wasn't all bad. Yeah, sure, our idea of a family outing was protesting Planned Parenthood facilities, which, please don't hold that against me. I was seven, and it wasn't exactly up for debate. But I liked church sometimes. I liked the music and the quiet. It's pretty when it's all stripped down and easy. I think religion is supposed to be easy. But that's just me."

"I think so, too. My favorite part of Catholic school was the choir. I was a soprano before I hit puberty, and my career was over before it even started. What was yours?"

He placed a hand on his chest. "I played guitar for the church band. But more than anything, I liked the quiet of the adoration chapel. My mom used to make us spend every Wednesday and Saturday night there. So, no, I didn't get 'blitzed' with my friends. I think the craziest thing I did was break out of my house to go to Denny's one night when I was fourteen and ended up with pierced ears. But that is a story for another night." He joked, rocking on his heels.

"Shit... I'm sorry, but what is that?"

"Denny's? Oh, it's a twenty-four-hour diner with the best pancakes you can imagine—"

"Isaac," I rolled my eyes. We both laughed. He loosened up again.

"Adoration chapel is a place of twenty-four-hour prayer," he said.

"And you liked this place?" He nodded, a smile curving up his cheeks and into the corners of his eyes.

"Oh, I loved it. It was my favorite place to go in Connecticut. I used to specifically choose that as my 'designated volunteer' hours." He emphasized with finger quotations.

"Designated—?"

"Please, don't ask." He laughed.

I nodded, considering our next step and if it was the right choice. "Can we go?"

"Are you high?"

"A little," I smiled. "Is there one nearby?"

"Why? Please don't think I'm trying to indoctrinate you. I meant what I said: everyone goes through a satanic phase, and I wouldn't judge you if you currently were."

I waved him off with a flick of my fingers. "I haven't been to church since high school. And it never felt easy. This sounds peaceful. Maybe sitting beside you would make it easy."

We smiled at each other, neither one wanting to leave the park. But I could feel it. That look in his eye, the pit in my stomach, and the breath of life floating between us. I led our way back through the bridge, only this time, when we walked, our hands brushed together with increased frequency.

V

WE TOOK ONE CAR this time, making the quickest of stops to drop off my car before Mami woke up and realized the lateness of the hour. It was 3 am, and we parked in a painfully ordinary lot. The adoration chapel was a long structure ordained with flowers, pointed ceilings of moderate height, and red trimming with a simple plain sign out front to announce upcoming events for the congregation of the Sacred Heart Church. There were no stained-glass windows nor high vaulted ceilings like I imagined. I didn't know what I imagined, but something about this place felt stolen.

"Hey, Isaac," I cleared my throat but did not open the door. I unbuckled my seatbelt, and he did the same. He was less mystified by our surroundings and more enamored with my reaction. "Are you sure we're allowed to be here?"

"Yes. In fact, it would be encouraged." He leaned in close, but his hands remained deep in his pockets. "Church is for everyone and anyone who wants to be there. Even for the people who don't. Especially for the people who don't. But if you don't want to be here, we can go. Maybe drive-thru McDonald's and pick up McFlurries—?"

I hopped out of the car, running across the courtyard to avoid the security cameras lining the sides. Isaac ambled after me. His laughter followed me as I climbed the steps that led away from the main chapel two at a time. A canopy of string lights illuminated hand-drawn children's cartoons of their favorite patron saints taped along the walls.

"It's just so quiet," I noted.

Isaac mouthed back, "That's the point."

We turned a corner and nearly got spooked out of our skin by a man sitting on a bar stool blocking access to the door. He was middle-aged and balding beneath the protection of a New York Yankees beanie. He sat high up from the earth, knees bent close to his stomach, hands clasped in his lap, and head sagging as he fought sleep.

Without asking us a single thing, the gentleman stepped off his seat to type a numeric code into the doorknob, making it the only updated item of security on the property. A buzzer went off, and he wordlessly held open the painted metal door frame for us to enter. The gentleman walked in after us, settling into a new stool pressed to the back wall as if he were waiting for us to arrive, and now, he could finally rest. The room appeared more like a recreational hall than a place of worship. Apart from the baby Jesus statue suspended from the ceiling, there was very little to capture the eye. I mirrored Isaac as he dipped his fingers into the holy water and genuflected upon entering.

Mami and I performed the sign of the cross whenever we passed funeral homes, or watched scary movies, or merely heard stories that were too sad to bear. But it never had a religious connection in my eyes. It was always a symbol of my mother. Doing it now brought her picture into my mind, and I wondered if she'd still be mad about me sneaking around late at night with a boy and if she knew where Isaac had taken us.

I imagined gossiping with her over freshly brewed coffee in the early morning. It would be the first time in months that I openly offered up information about my personal life. I hugged the walls, watching the scene around us as if I were a ghost lording over the parishioners.

There were three other people in the room besides Isaac and me.

There was a woman with salt and pepper hair and ragged clothing snoring softly as she slept in the pew directly beneath the crucifix. It was odd watching someone sleep without their permission, but I wasn't sure what else I was expecting at this hour of the evening. The only man who seemed conscious enough to utilize the facility was a broad-shouldered gentleman with a thick, wrinkled neck and a green jacket covered in very important-looking military patches. Between his hands was a scrap of blue fabric, soft and sweet, that kept twisting in his oversized grip. His eyes were closed as he muttered to himself, but I turned away from him before he noticed I was watching.

I turned toward the crucifix hanging above us, locking eyes with the figure of Jesus. It had been years since the last time I willingly reconnected with that face, and it took everything inside of me not to spit at his feet. Blood boiled in my chest. I was angry, resentful, and ignorant, and there was nothing to be done about it. I felt empty and not even in a profound way. It was average, bleak, and I was embarrassed at the nothingness I kept locked up inside me. I desired purpose, but all that I felt was an insatiable want for more. I thought maybe if I came back to this place as an adult, I'd find comfort in the iconography, but the more I stared up at the crucifix, the sillier I felt for coming back.

Isaac roamed the room, focusing his attention on a rather large book that reminded me of the kind of bricks we used to lug around in high school. He scribbled something on the inside, but I couldn't take my eyes off the crucifix. I wanted to weed in my system to trigger the dormant sector of my brain that scientists always warn drug users about. This was the part of the movie where the main character confronts God for all the reasons why he let her suffer. This is the section of the story where I was supposed to rage at the ceiling, howling for salvation in return for a wise monologue about life, free will, and injustice delivered by the great Morgan Freeman. But I didn't get any of that. It was a cold, beige room, and whatever energy that seemed to fill the military man to the point of tears left me dry. Praying to a plastic doll purchased back in the 1970s would not rewrite the course of my life.

Isaac wandered over toward my section, taking up a seat in the row in front of me. His neck was long, and his knees spread just wide enough to place folded hands at the center. He was at peace in the silence. He asked for nothing more than a solid seat to bear his weight.

I tried to mirror him, but in the silence of the evening, my thoughts kept coming back to me in heinous waves of self-reflection. They were not wise or shocking. They were just loud and beat against my temples until I could do nothing else but listen. I had to witness myself. I had to submit to my own mind, and I feared the pressure of that honesty would leave me shaking on the linoleum floor.

I hate myself.

I tried to shake the thought away, but it wouldn't budge. It never did, and I didn't know why I expected it now to be any different. The voice sang, traipsing around the hollows of my mind with spray paint, tagging curses across garage doors, and leaving me to clean up the mess.

I hate myself.

The room was far too cold for my liking, and it seemed like Isaac was in tune with my shivers. The chair in front of me scraped as Isaac stood up. He tried to be discreet and not interrupt me, but I felt the fabric of his denim jacket rub against my arm as he sat close beside me. I was grateful to share in his warmth. I kept my eyes closed, syncing my breath with his.

Breathe in, he seemed to instruct, and so I followed. *Breathe out. Breathe in, breathe out.*

Breathe in —

I stared at the red spray paint burning behind my eyelids when suddenly soap suds came crashing down around me. Knocking me off my metaphoric feet, I tread through the current of bubbles, soap, and disinfectant filling my brain. I took another breath, and the words faded under the weight of the bubbles. I let myself drown in the water. I opened my eyes and did not fear the sting of chemicals.

I hate myself.

In my mind's eyes, I was a child sitting on a swing set on a sunny day. My hair was braided thick and pretty. I was floating on a breeze that bore the distinct rhythm of Isaac's breath. Circling my body were a million tiny wildflowers. There was no voice here nor paint. Only chalk-lined squares waiting for me to jump through them. Only the tiny creaks of a swing set kept me anchored in the daylight. The cracks along the sidewalk promised to carry me home.

I shivered, gasping as I felt Isaac's hand close around mine. I opened my eyes and let him brush away my tears with his fingers.

"What did you write in the book?" I asked.

We stood outside the chapel, shivering in the night as the sky blurred into shades of blue. I checked the car to make sure it wasn't a pumpkin just yet. I didn't want to leave this silence. I hadn't shivered since Isaac sat down next to me, but he was practically shaking. I asked again.

"What did you write in the book?"

His breath was hot, sighing little puffs of chimney smoke... He didn't turn toward me but focused a shy grin on his mud-stained converse. I stared at him, wanting him to speak to me. Willing him to confide in me, to trust me, and with every passing second that he didn't, I choked on the wanting. I wanted to know his every thought, every memory, and every story he cared to share.

He opened his mouth to speak but was interrupted by the sound of a door hinge cracking open, and the veteran walked out of the chapel. We tried to step out of his way, backing up against the wall. Isaac subconsciously moved in front of me, and I let him, tucking myself slightly behind his shoulder. It was subtle and felt so natural, but inside, I was burning. This was a new feeling. This was a strange feeling. Why did this small gesture make me want to cry?

Instead of walking by us, the man stopped and appraised our stance with a smile. He was two heads taller than Isaac and built like a tank engine in disarray. His eyes glistened with fresh tears.

"Evening," he said.

"Evening, sir," Isaac and I whispered back.

"You two alright?"

We nodded back.

"Marital problems?"

My cheeks burned hot at the thought. My forehead touched Isaac's shoulder, and he sagged toward me. We found a new form of gravity that night, though neither one of us knew how to say it.

Isaac replied, "No, sir."

The man nodded, but he didn't walk away. He wanted to say something to us. At least, that's how it felt. He rubbed at the white beard curling off his face as if searching for some wisdom, but he chuckled to himself when he realized he had none.

"Well, good. Stay safe tonight," he nodded.

"Thank you," I mumbled. We watched him walk away for a solid beat of time, not speaking as we pieced together the fabric of his life solely by the motorcycle he drove and the blue cloth he kept hidden in his hands. But I saw it. I saw it all.

Once he was out of the lot, Isaac turned back to me smiling, a hairline away from my nose. "Are you going to stay here? After graduation?"

"I guess it depends on whether I go to grad school. Or straight into a job. There's this program Professor Irma leads over at the grad school that I have my eye on. It's only for graduate students, but I practically live outside her office when I'm on campus so I think I have a pretty good chance at getting in. It's at the women's shelter in Miami. Close enough that I can stay at home. Save up money for… whatever comes next. I don't know. I'm not rushing to leave is what I'm trying to say. There is something beautiful about knowing where you are."

He coughed. "Well, good. That's… that's cool. Um, I mean, you don't… you could go anywhere if you wanted. You could… it's cool. I'm sorry, I'm not making sense." He rubbed at his face, covering his eyes with sweaty palms. "I'm tired."

"It's okay. Hey." I placed my hands on his shoulders and waited for him to look up at me. He was shrinking. It felt safe to tell him I was safe. *There is no danger here*, I wished to say, but I couldn't. "Isaac, look at me."

"I'm not really good with my words when I want to be."

"Conversation is easy." I told him. "But it is difficult to find someone you can be quiet with. I want to be quiet with you, Isaac. I just need you to teach me how."

He nodded at me, and when I moved to take my hands away, he held them in place with his palms. His fingers mindlessly interlocked with mine as we trembled, pressed close to the chest.

"What do you think about… when you're quiet? What's on your mind right now?" He whispered.

I took a deep breath and shivered as wave after wave of thoughts crashed through my brain.

I can't leave this town because I don't know what will happen once I'm alone with my thoughts.

I hate myself. I hate myself. I hate myself. I love myself. I hate myself. I hate myself. I hate myself. I love myself. I hate myself. I'm trying… It's like a never-ending loop. That's who I am. But right now…. all is quiet.

I want to say all these things to Isaac and more. I want to confess all my darkest secrets, and I want to pretend that I'm perfect even when I'm not. But I don't want to lie.

"Can I hold you?" I choked, sobs wracking through my body. I let out the thickest breath, and I didn't care if I looked crazy. He didn't seem to mind. There were tears in his eyes just the same. His lips parted in the most heart-breaking scar across his plump cheeks.

"Yes," he sighed, wrapping me in his arms. All the bones in my body evaporated as they touched his. My palms lay flat against his back, and I could feel him untangling. It was kind. It was quiet. We could have held each other for eternity, but a new day was upon us, thick with promise. He pulled away from me, and I looked into his brown eyes as if I'd known him all my life. It made me laugh, knowing that somehow, in some form, Isaac had followed me everywhere I went.

He didn't hesitate to ask, "Can I kiss you?"

I nodded. "Thank you for asking."

I closed my eyes, and he kissed me. But he didn't know that I secretly opened my eyes just to steal a peak at how we looked pressed so closely. I wanted to remember that moment forever. He'd never know that this felt like the first real kiss I'd had in my whole life.

He pulled away with something sad lodged in his eyes. "I don't know if I'm coming back to school next fall," he admitted. But I already knew that.

I nodded. "I know. Lila told me."

He shook his head, breath coming out in shivers as he tried to piece together all the ways we lost out on time. "I should've called you sooner—"

My lips pressed together as I tried to smile, but it came out all wobbly, chin trembling. "But you didn't, and that's okay."

"If I had known this is how it would feel… I would've—I would've—"

"But we didn't," I held his hands in mine, "and that's okay."

Deep down, I knew it wasn't. Feeling his skin pressed close to me made me wish I could wipe away the memory of every kiss, every touch, and every boy that ever entered my life and replace it with him. But I couldn't. That's not how life works. I could have wasted the rest of my life wishing I had more time with Isaac, or I could be grateful for this night and the awakening it blessed me with.

He held my hand all the way back to the car. He held my hand like a sacred text, toying with my fingertips as he drove me home, and he held my hand while I unlocked my house door, effectively ending the night. Isaac's car idled in the driveway. We stood on my front porch with our foreheads pressed together. This was what the chapel was supposed to feel like. Holy ground.

"Thanks for bringing me home," I whispered. I hadn't stopped crying. My eyelids were swollen and uncomfortably heavy. I didn't care. Neither did he.

"Anytime," he replied, and he meant it.

He drifted down the steps and out the front gate.

"Hey," I hollered because I couldn't resist it. He turned back to me, hand on the car door handle, and halfway out of my life when I smiled. "Have a beautiful life."

He nodded and disappeared into the neighborhood.

I stood outside my house, waiting to see if he'd turn around.

He didn't.

THE SIXTH KISS

I

Isaac's phone calls became as ritualistic to me as a warm cup of coffee. His updates, pictures, and stories of life on the road coexisted seamlessly between my sessions at the women's center, nights out with friends, and touring potential graduate programs that would determine the next chapter of my life. We were living parallel lives, and it hurt to consider that the lines were curving in opposite directions, where the only point of contact was a truth that was easier to express than experience.

He missed me, and I missed him too.

"Mami, please breathe. You're freaking me out." I flipped down the sun visor, checking to make sure my no-makeup-makeup looked casual enough to be mistaken for just-rolled-out-of-bed. I was about to spend three days in the Arizona Red Rocks with a group of run-and-gun photographers. I wanted to feel like 'one of the guys' while also being extremely aware of the fact that I hadn't seen Isaac since the end of sophomore year, and I'd been planning my hiking outfits for the last month.

Isaac's internship with National Geographic blossomed into a full-fledged assistantship that kept him exploring landscapes across the continental United States. He invited me to spend the weekend with the team, and I jumped at the opportunity. My flight left for Phoenix on Friday night, and a return flight was booked for Sunday morning.

"Samaya, stop it with the lip gloss. You're going to stick to the seat." Mami pulled into park outside the departures gate, clutching the steering wheel like an anxious child clutched the over-the-shoulder restraints of a rollercoaster before it shot off into space.

"You yell at me all the time to put makeup on—"

"*No te hagas,*" she warned, unbuckling her seatbelt to better look at me. "There's makeup, and then there's…" She waved her hands in my general direction, at a loss for words, seeing me in a cropped, loose-fitting tap tank and form-fitting yoga pants that showed off my suntanned skin. It was a bit sexy, I had to admit, especially coming from the girl who confidently wore sweatshirts three times my size in the summertime. The gesture was so ridiculous I curled up in a ball. She pulled me in close and pressed her chin to the top of my head as we laughed in each other's warmth. *Te ves hermosa*.

"But in a casual way, right? Like I'm not trying?"

"Exacto," Mami nodded, hopping out of the car to grab my suitcases. "Casual but also… very pretty."

There was too much energy bundled up in my veins. I jumped up and down the moment I got out of the car. My cheeks hurt from smiling all day. *"Gracias, Mami."* I reached out for my suitcase, but she pulled back.

"Pobre de ti si—"

"Nothing is going to happen!"

Mami covered her face with her hands as I pulled my suitcase free from her clutches. *"Aye,* I can't believe I'm doing this."

"Mami, everything is okay. You know Isaac. Nothing—"

"I know," she sighed, smiling at me. Her fingers twisted around the curls I had finally learned to maintain. My suitcase was mainly filled with mouse and gel and everything I needed to feel confident in the thick brown curls Mami passed down to me. "You look so much like me when you wear your hair down."

"Gracias, Mami."

She knew I needed to see him. It had been almost two years of phone calls, postcards, and stalking each other's Instagram accounts for little slivers of secrets as if we didn't already share everything with each other. The five-hour flight to Phoenix flew by in the blink of an eye.

Isaac waited for me in the pickup area with a homemade sign that read SAMAYA XIMENA in giant permanent marker. His clothing was washer-worn and cut in places that must have snagged while hiking. His hair reached well past his earlobes, held back with a black head-band, to keep it all off his face. He'd forgone a razor many months ago, and from the way he tried to discreetly check his body odor as I walked over to him, showers clearly weren't readily available at the campsite either. But I didn't care, I thought he looked handsome at his most uncensored. I held a single chocolate cupcake in my hand. I bought it at the airport when I arrived, but figured he'd appreciate the gesture.

"Happy Birthday," I chewed on my bottom lip as I handed the dessert over to him.

He took it from my hands, tucking the sign beneath his arm. "Thank you," he swallowed but didn't hug me. We couldn't move. I scanned every inch of his face, arms, and the tan lines forming along his copper skin, trying to pair any new markings with the stories he shared. I knew he did the same with me, but I didn't mind when his eyes skated over me because it never felt crass when Isaac did so. He took my bags, and I walked beside him, loving how his shoulder brushed against mine and how our arms sank into the gravitational pull of being near each other, like nothing had changed.

The car ride back to camp was filled with music we wanted to show each other and stupid jokes that served no purpose other than to hear each other's voices. Isaac cleared his throat and gestured to his appearance with his free hand. "Sorry, I meant to do something about all this, but there wasn't any time."

"It's okay. You look cute. Like a Billy Goat." I giggled, and he gasped, feigning offense but laughed all the same. "Has Jacques warmed up to the idea of me hanging around?"

Isaac swiveled his head back and forth, searching for the words somewhere out on the horizon. "He's hard to read. His emotions are very upbeat and exciting one minute, and then the next, he's just—"

"He's French," I finished for him, and he nodded, smiling at me in glimpses. I sat with my back pressed as close to the door as possible to look at him. "Just, please, navigate me so I don't say or do something stupid—"

"You're joining a campsite full of forty-something-year-old guys whose idea of a good time is stalking a bird for hours on end. They're over the moon to have you join us."

I bit my lip. "You don't seem very happy about that?"

"Well, you're pretty, and they're horny and lonely. So, yeah, my guard is a little up. But it's okay. They're harmless. And experienced so you won't have to do a thing all weekend. You're going to love the stars. And the sunrise. It's insane." Isaac told me he felt lonely with Jacques and their tiny crew, and I insisted my presence would change the energy. He agreed, and the date was set. I shifted in my seat, trying to play off how much I enjoyed Isaac's protective side.

"Where am I sleeping?" I asked. My backpack sank into my lap with the weight of everything I deemed essential for a weekend visiting… a friend.

Isaac gestured to the open road, hands lying limp on the steering wheel as he sighed. "I was thinking maybe you could bunk with me. If you're comfortable with that." He asked, but it came out in chokes and awkward pauses. "Separate sleeping bags, of course, but I figured it would be nice to… catch up."

I turned to him with lips pursed in a side smile. We had very little to 'catch up' on, but I didn't need to embarrass him by reading between his lines. "That sounds perfect."

The campsite was simple but nowhere near rudimentary. Four navy blue tents covered in thick black tarps formed a semicircle around a picnic bench where a rather buff yet compact, middle-aged man with thick dreadlocks reviewed stills beneath a microscope. He jumped up at the sight of us, kissing me on both cheeks and introducing himself as the famed Jacques who served as the starring role in Isaac's best and worst stories.

"The rest of the team are taking some time off at a swimming hole," he explained, gesturing to the empty tents and discarded cooking materials as he offered to take my backpack from me before I accepted. His thick Parisian accent created connections between letters that weren't meant to exist. "I thought it was, uh, maybe, better? For you two?" He winked at us, patting Isaac on the shoulder as if he were involved in a secret I didn't know they shared. Isaac blushed heavily, eyes wide as his mentor shoved him under a bus.

"Unless I understood wrong?" Neither of us corrected him, and he took the silence as a social faux pas. "Are you two not sleeping together?"

Isaac jumped back, clutching the back of his neck as his dark brown skin flushed with embarrassment. "Whoa, um. No. I wouldn't say that." I stared at him with my eyebrows raised to the ceiling, but he didn't look at me.

"Oh, I'm sorry. Are you two staying together, or should I empty my tent?" Jacques looked between us, trying to navigate his relationship with Isaac as his camp mate and his responsibility to me as the older man in power.

"Oh, well—" I started.

"Well, yeah, we don't have to—" Isaac interrupted.

"Have to—? I don't wanna impose—" I countered, confused by his change in persona. Just a moment ago, Isaac stood tall and confident, but now he could barely look at me. He stared anywhere but me, placing my suitcase on the floor in neutral territory like he couldn't care where I slept.

Jacques emptied his tent and offered it to me for privacy. It was a kind gesture, and one I tried to decline twice, but Jacques was already moving his things into Isaac's tent before I had a chance to stop him. Isaac was mute on the subject, but he stared at me with his mouth hanging open. No words came out to fill the confusion between us.

The team was kind to me but tired from all the months on the road. Their chatter was nonexistent, the simple jokes of men who'd known each other over decades of travel, and I found myself the center of attention as the shiny new toy. They didn't ask me much about my life but took my presence as an opportunity to tell the stories of their life from new perspectives. I awed respectfully, fully aware that Isaac quietly stared at me over the flames of the campfire. I went to bed early but stayed awake, considering my options. The night felt too unremarkable to merit the flight out here.

I could sneak over to Isaac's tent, confess my feelings, and plaster a big kiss on his lips… but what would that do? Surely flying to see him was a sign that I still had all the same feelings for him as I did during sophomore year. I needed to sleep, I needed to stop chasing, and I needed Isaac to make a move before I questioned us into oblivion.

The next day, we woke up early to shoot Cathedral Rock. I slipped out of my tent to find Isaac, fresh-faced and shaved.

"Good morning," we said, bowing our heads in unison. He held an aluminum cup filled with coffee, and it was easy to taste the instant powder in the mixture, but I appreciated the kindness.

He gestured to his face in a bashful way. "I was going to do this yesterday before you arrived, but I had errands all morning and… yeah. Did I smell? Would you tell me if I smelled?"

I shook my head, a heavy laugh bursting through my chest in a single huff. "No, Isaac. You don't smell. But you did look like a Billy goat," I giggled, and he instinctively covered his chin with his hands. I shrugged, chewing on my bottom lip. "You look good."

His shoulders loosened, pleased by this new fact. "Can I hug you?"

I responded by wrapping him tight in my arms. We held each other until the zippers of the other tents started to undo the binds of our arms, but the touch lingered on my skin all day.

Jacques saddled Isaac with the equipment like a pack mule while he hiked alongside me, pairing compliments of my physical beauty with obscure questions about the meaning of life. He liked that I studied psychology and that I dissected the human mind even though that's not how I viewed the profession, but more than anything, he loved how much he could talk at me, and I was forced to listen.

What a pretentious prick, I thought.

The day ended with fire, eating beans, and sitting in tired silence. Jacques went to sleep first, leaving us alone together. It was a small kindness; I was leaving the following morning, but he snored too loudly for the stars hanging overhead to have any romantic effect. I smiled at Isaac over the fire, and he smiled back.

"This weekend went by flying, didn't it?" He laughed it off, but the sadness of that fact shivered in his words.

"Isaac," I put down my plate of food. "I want you to visit me for graduation."

He put his plate of food down on the bench beside him, his palms rubbing rough against the back of his neck and thighs. "I know. I thought about that. I want that, too. I've mentioned it to Jacques."

"I think you're due time off." My hands interlaced as I tried to keep my wants casual, but Isaac was already playing defense.

"I'm trying to get him to recommend me for a new project opening in South America—"

"Oh," The word sounded more wounded than astounded. "For how long?"

"It would have me in Patagonia, which would be… amazing, Samaya, a dream come true."

"I know that."

"And I really want it, but I'm new. I'm at the bottom of the barrel, and a recommendation from him could really make a difference. Yes, yes, I will ask him if I can have time off to visit you in Florida."

"It's in two months, Isaac." My eyes bore into his, daring him to make a promise.

"Has anyone ever told you that you have cat eyes? Sharp at the corners, a little sleepy, but also like you're about to scratch me if I say or do the wrong thing?"

"Isaac."

"I'll make it happen," he reached for my hand along the picnic bench with his fingertips.

"When would you need to be in Patagonia?" I asked. He shrugged, and I guess I had to accept that as my only answer.

I scanned the lines of his palms with both of my own, feeling the rough callouses that developed while he was away from me. He did the same with the freckles on my cheeks, running his nails across my skin until my spine jolted off the wood. We nestled close together, heads hung low and foreheads pressed.

"Did you have a good birthday?" My voice horse and lips craving his.

"Yes," he whispered, his nose nudging mine.

But he did not get a chance to do much else as one of the crew members got a horrible stomach bug, and the entire campsite was aware of it within the hour. The mood died as quickly as it ignited, but we laughed it off. My face trembled in the crook of his neck, laughing as my hands weaved through his hair and his fingertips rubbed circles in my back.

I went back to my tent, and Isaac looked like he wanted to slam his head against the wall. *Of course, this would happen to us.*

Jacques drove back to the airport with us.

Isaac held me before the flight but nothing more. It did not feel right. None of it did. It felt like time was leaching away from us, and I was powerless to stop it. I wanted to keep him with me, but he was driving out the next morning, which would be too selfish. It wasn't our time. I was beginning to fear it never would be.

II

Gabriela opened the door for me with a gap-toothed smile that made my cheeks hurt. The four-year-old thrust her arms into the air and demanded I carry her on my hip. I charged toward her like a velociraptor and roared as we bounced up and down, brown curls tussling up in the butterfly barrettes her mother, Rapha, must have put in her hair earlier that morning.

"*Gabriela, deja en paz a la señorita.*" I waved over at Rapha on the couch, crocheting what looked like a doll's sweater or a very bad beanie baby, as she watched over her daughter and the off-brand dolls she left scattered in her wake.

"It's okay, no bother. *¿Quieres mostrarme lo que estás dibujando?*" I smiled wide but Gabriela shook her head. "*¿Porque no?*"

The Hialeah Women & Family Treatment Center flowed like a newborn baby trying to crawl. Professor Irma opened the center as a haven for women escaping abusive situations at home. We ran entirely off donations and the help of students looking for a gateway toward clinical and family psychology.

Rapha came to the center in the middle of the night with bruises around her wrists. Both she and her daughter were wearing pajamas when the night guard let them in. Apparently, she read about the shelter in a local paper at the grocery store, and she read that ad as a sign that she needed to leave her husband. What was supposed to be a single night became a month's long stay, and now Rapha was part of the family.

From what we could tell, Gabriela didn't have much of a memory of what happened before they came to our door. I held her close while I grabbed a piece of stale coffee cake. It was hard for me to be near

Gabriela and not think about how young she was. It was hard not to examine her features and wonder which parts of her would one day remind her of her father. It was hard not to think that she was lying when she claimed to remember nothing but loud screaming. Because I was younger than Gabriela when Mami and I left Papi, and though I did not say it at the time, I remembered everything.

Gabriela knotted stray strands of my hair in her fist, bringing me in close to whisper a secret in my ear. "*Hay chicos en la oficina!*"

"Boys?!" I gasped, dropping my jaw down low as she giggled. But I was already aware of the Perez family.

The shelter received a call that morning from a local priest about a Cuban mother and her two sons needing a safe house for the week before a family member could provide something more permanent. Professor Irma asked me to come in to bridge the language barrier with the boys while she conducted an initial assessment of their situation.

I set Gabriela down with two wobbly knees and prayed I didn't develop back problems at twenty-two years old. I knocked twice before entering the office, but it was always slightly cracked open, ready to push my way inside to introduce myself to the patients as the person who'd be watching over the children during their stay.

"You're late," Professor Irma yawned, handing over the family's file in the form of hello.

I narrowed my eyes as I snatched the file out of her hands. "I'm twenty minutes early," I corrected, but I knew she already knew that. Teasing was her way of showing affection, and I received a lot of affection. Irma waved me off, already returning to her patient.

Vanessa Perez had long blond hair, pale skin, and a face too young for her blue eyes to look so dull. I saw no noticeable bruising, but I knew most men hid the worst wounds where the public could never see them. Graduate school was the gateway to earning me a seat in the room, giving me the tools to help women like Vanessa secure some form of justice in a system set up to ignore her. But for now, my job was to stay with the children, making sure their transition out of their home went as seamlessly as possible. I just needed to make sure I chose the right institution to commit to.

My classmate and co-worker Marianne was already in the media room watching *SpongeBob* with Nico and Sebas Perez when I arrived. The boys were quiet, but I was used to that in the beginning stages.

She mouthed a greeting over at me as I settled into the room, tucking my backpack in its designated cubby.

"*¿Tienen hambre?* We have every cereal on the market." The cabinets unfolded like an accordion revealing rows and rows of colorful neon dishware to match the green, yellow, and orange painted walls of the kids' room. "Personally? *Hago los mejores* peanut butter and jelly sandwiches you've ever tasted."

The younger brother Nico wanted a bowl of cereal, while Sebas ignored my question in favor of *SpongeBob*.

I handed the fruit loops to Nico, already thanking me before the bowl even hit the table and sat a distance away from Sebas. He was about nine years old and watched *SpongeBob* make Krabby Patties with the focus of a Wimbledon match.

"*¿Cual es tu personaje favorito?*" I asked twice, and on the second try, he muttered, "Squidward." He liked his nose and sour-sounding voice. I agreed, and after another episode, he accepted a bowl of cereal. Marianne and I spent the day showing the boys how to use watercolor paints, discussing which *Power Ranger* was the strongest based on the color of their suit, and when they were comfortable, we showed them to their bedroom for the weekend with a bedtime story.

I gave Professor Irma a ride back north, so she didn't have to wait for the Tri-Rail.

She wasn't subtle when she asked me, "Well, don't keep me guessing. What's the verdict?"

I cleared my throat. "I accepted my spot at the University of Miami."

Irma smiled. "That's wonderful."

I turned to her. "You're not upset?"

Her eyebrows bunched in a way that made me self-conscious about worrying so much about her opinion of my decision. I put off telling her for weeks because I didn't want any outside interference trying to force me out of Florida because they thought it was the right decision for me. "I want all my students to dream bigger than their comfort zone. But if you're choosing between Boston and Miami, I can't see a bad choice either way. Miami has a great Childhood and Development program. You're going to flourish there. Plus, honey, you weren't born for winters in Massachusetts. And it's close to home," she finished for me.

And it's close to home, I nodded back.

"It would just mean a lot of student loan debt. Like, I'm already going to take on debt, but I thought the point of graduate school was to get a competitive degree and network around the area you'd like to live in. I don't see myself up north. At all."

"You've also never allowed yourself to call anywhere else home."

I didn't say anything after that because it sounded pathetic when I heard her say it.

"Samaya, life is both very long and very short. It's long when you hate it and short when you finally learn to appreciate it. I wrote your recommendation letters because I believe you will do well wherever you allow yourself to go. But I don't want you playing safe when life only gets better with the scent of risk in the air. As your advisor, I have to say that you should go wherever you will have a better chance in life. As your friend, I would miss you if you left."

I'd been waiting for an organic opening all day, and now seemed like the perfect moment to ask Irma about this summer. I sat up straight and cleared my throat as I tried to sound as professional as I could. "Actually, I wanted to ask—"

"Absolutely not." She cut me off, smiling softly without an ounce of apology laced in her eyes. "Go be selfish for a few years. Get your degree. Party it up in Miami and head to nightclubs at three in the morning. Because one day you'll have a bad back, kids, and people won't be so supportive of you wearing crop tops and miniskirts. Trust me. Go make money. Date. And when you're done, we can talk about a permanent position at the center. But not before."

The speech I prepared all morning died on my lips, but I didn't take her words as a rejection. It was a much-needed redirection, the kind I was too scared to give myself.

"Thank you, Professor Irma." But what I really wanted to say was, *that's all I ever wanted.*

It was well into the afternoon when we pulled up to the psych department parking lot. I still needed to drive by the grocery store for liquor and snacks for tonight. It would be a small graduation party, and the lack of a certain name on that guest list itched at my ego every time I gave it a moment of attention. I climbed out of the car just as Professor Irma called out to me.

"Wait, I almost forgot." She leaped out of the car, running over to the 2012 Lincoln that was one flat tire away from heading to the junkyard. From the trunk, she pulled out a thick pink envelope with my name written out in bubble letters. When I opened it, multiple sheets of children's drawings fell out, all of them bidding me farewell. "The kids wanted to do something special," Irma added, hands pressed to her hips as if it were all no big deal.

I gave her a big hug, knowing full well that she wouldn't return it.

III

Isaac kept calling no matter how often I told him not to. I was in the shower during the latest call and missed it by a few chimes of my ringtone. It felt like he had installed surveillance cameras in my bedroom because the second I walked back inside the phone charging on my desk began to chime yet again. It felt like it was screaming at me through the towel wrapped around my wet hair and ears. But that would mean Isaac had stepped foot in my room, which was a ridiculous impossibility only found in my sweetest dreams.

I used to wake up excited to read his name every morning as it popped up on my phone screen. Now, the letters blended in a red wave of resentment and stupidity. It made me feel stupid caring so much about Isaac Haas.

ISAAC: Samaya, please pick up.

ISAAC: I'm not going to stop calling so the least you could do is not leave me on read.

ISAAC: Did my package arrive? The tracking link says it did. Could you check?

ISAAC: Please, Samaya.

ISAAC: I'm sorry.

ISAAC: I don't know how many times you need me to say it.

I threw the phone against my pillowcase as I slipped into a fuzzy, yellow bathrobe fresh from the dryer. *Need me to say it,* I thought, scowling at the flowers printed across my bed sheets. I bit my lip, running heat protectant through my wet strands before flipping it into a claw clip.

The cardboard box he referred to lay tucked beneath my bed, hidden out of view if not for the rough texture rubbing against my ankles. I was aware of how ridiculous I was acting, but that didn't make me want to take his calls. I had nothing kind to say, and I'd run out of excuses for him. The last thing I needed was another phone call where Isaac did all the talking, and I did too good of a job playing the adoring best friend.

The phone rang again, and the sound was so grating that I vowed to change it as soon as possible. I plopped onto my pillows with fingers scratching at the corners of my eyes.

SAMAYA: I'm a bit busy.

The text barely slipped my fingers before he started typing his reply. My stomach clenched at the sight of the gray vibrating dots in the corner of the screen, and it made me mad to think Isaac could make me feel so unsatisfied. He sent me another series of texts begging for my understanding, and each time he hit send, another series of gray dots vibrated in the corner, showing me, he wouldn't go away until he got what he wanted, and I was sick of feeling sick over Isaac Haas.

He answered on the first ring, but there was a pregnant pause before we spoke.

"Hello?" There was a palpable irritation in my voice. I wanted him to know I did not call him back out of desire but out of resignation. This must be how mothers felt once they realized their beloved children were growing into spoiled brats who got their toys not out of love but obligation.

"Hi," he croaked, breathing out the word as if I might go away in a blink. I thought about doing it just to make him feel as raw as his absence left me. But I took a breath and forced myself to take the high road.

"What's up, Isaac? You wanted to talk, and because that's what *you* wanted, that's what we're going to do. So, let's talk. I got your package. It was kind of you to send a graduation gift, but unnecessary." My words were so clipped and formal that they were downright rude.

"Please, Samaya, lower your swords. Don't be hostile with me—"

I snorted, "I'm not being hostile. I'm being polite. What's overwhelmingly hostile is when a boy *promised* he would show up for me when I specifically asked him to but didn't. And instead of just leaving me alone to move on, he calls me seventeen times to say… what? That's hostile. This is me being civil. What do you want?" My fingernails scratched at the back of my head.

"Samaya," his voice cracked in a way that could have been caused by a poor connection, but I suspected it was due to fear or frustration. A strong knock at the door cut him off mid-sentence, privately wiping away a tear that I hoped Isaac could not hear in my breathing.

"Samaya! *Ya, pues.*" Mami forced her way into the room on the hunt for something she didn't feel the need to ask permission to use. Instead, she opened drawers, fished through hangers in the mess I made of my closet, all before realizing I was on the phone, hoping she'd leave quickly. "What's the point of throwing a party if I'm the only one getting ready? *¿Estas llorando?*"

Her eyes hardened at the sight of the red splotches taking control of my complexion. I tried to cover my face with the palms of my hands, but that just made it worse. I did not want to shrink. I was past shrinking, and today was a day to celebrate that fact. I didn't need this; I needed to hang up, but for some juvenile reason, I felt like I needed Isaac's permission to leave him in the past. I mouthed a denial rather aggressively, but she wouldn't back away so easily. I showed Mami the contact on my phone screen and she sat down beside me, taking the phone away before I had a chance to argue. She held a soft finger to her lips as she put on her most diplomatic facade.

"*Hola, mi amor.* It's Rebeca! How are you? How's Peru? When do you leave for Chile? You better come back with perfect Spanish after a year down there." Her voice was cheery and kind. I crumbled into a ball, turning my back on her while my breathing steadied. I could feel my chest thumping through my fingertips as I tried to focus on solid objects in the room, but it didn't seem to work. "Be careful with the pisco! It's stronger than you think. Oh, that's good, honey. That's wonderful. You deserve a nice hotel room. Samaya told me all about the camping, and *ay,* no, I could never!" She laughed, and I held out my hand, trying to take the phone back, but she pushed me away with a single finger, her smile sharpening into a shield.

"*Por supuesto, mi amor. Pero,* you know Samaya must get ready for her party, yes? I know, my love, I know. Of course you do. You're a sweet boy and I know you want her to have a fun night, yes? Beautiful.

So, let's try to wrap this up in five minutes, okay? Samaya—" She directed her words at me so that Isaac could listen. "Your friends are starting to show up so, please, honey, don't be late. Okay, *ciao,* Isaac. It's so sad you couldn't make it; I got the guest room ready for you and everything. Bye bye, my love." She ended with a big smacking kiss at the phone before handing it back to me. But the expression she gave me was less warm than the performance she'd put on for his sake.

Mami pantomimed, wiping off my tears as if it were bird poop before she mouthed a promise to cut off his balls if he made me cry again. I waited for her to exit, and from his silence, I figured he did the same.

"How's your mom doing?" He asked.

"She's good," I answered.

"That's good. Is that her music playing in the background?" His voice was light, a hint of helium slithering through his intention and falling flat like a balloon pumped with stale air. "Robert's not a very good singer, is he?"

"Yeah, but he's kind and put a lot of effort into making tonight special for me so he can sing as loud as he wants," I commanded. I wanted to run outside and join them. I had a party in less than an hour and could be outside jamming to Latin music with people filling my cup, but instead, I was stuck in here waiting for Isaac to hang up.

He cleared his throat, and I could hear the creak of a chair as he did so. "Did you open the package yet?"

"No, I didn't. I promised I wouldn't open it until I was with you. Remember?" He paused, and I sat up straight against the wall. "Want me to open it now?"

"Yes, that would be kind," he sniffed, his words soft and gravely with emotion.

"Give me a second. I just got out of the shower," I don't know why I gave that disclaimer. I don't know why some girlish part of me wanted to tease Isaac with the idea of me walking about my room fresh from the shower and all that imagery would entail.

"Samaya, please. Have some decorum," he joked, blushing at the raunchiness of my comment. "People might get the wrong idea about us."

I got the wrong idea about us, I thought.

"Ha ha." I rolled my eyes as I pulled out the package with the word 'fragile' taped across every surface. But a slight flush was rushing through my skin no matter how much I wanted to deny it.

I closed my eyes and undid the wrapping. Inside were three luxurious framed photographs, each individually wrapped in thick bubble wrap. It was a bundle of black and white portraits from our time together in Sedona. There were shots of us sitting on boulders, hiking through marble canyons, and a few blurry loose pictures of us laughing he threw in at the bottom just because.

"This is beautiful," I whispered.

"Thank you for coming to see me," he sniffed, choking on the words. It sounded as if he'd been crying. "It was my favorite birthday. You made me feel special. I hope those make you feel special, too… because you're very special to me, Samaya."

I spent many years of my life dreaming about the type of man I would marry. I saw him in glimpses as I tucked myself in at night, imagining how he would rub circles in my back until sleep finally found me. Pretty lips, nice eyes, and a laugh that made my heart twist out of shape until all I could think about was ripping it out of my chest to present it to him.

Isaac was my first close male friend, and I never knew what to think about our relationship. We did not have much in common, but all the things that made us different created a balance I thought only occurred a few times in nature. I used to think we were yin and yang, but I realized now that ideology was for the benefit of my daydreaming. Isaac hadn't earned the laurels I bestowed upon him. He didn't deserve my heart, and yet I stupidly wondered why he wasn't dying to take it from me when I laid it flat for his grasp.

"Samaya, if I hurt you, that was not my intention. I swear. I never want to hurt you, and I'm sorry if you feel hurt by me right now. But what was I supposed to do?" He was begging, but his form of begging redacted the conversations we had that led us to my silence.

"You were supposed to tell me you took the job a month ago. Not one week before you promised me you'd fly out here. You were supposed to cut me off when I rambled about all the plans I had for the weekend and how excited I was to see you—"

"You were so happy I didn't want to ruin anything. It never felt like the right time. I was always on the road, and I couldn't talk, or you had a stressful day at the center, and I didn't want to top it by telling you I couldn't come. It was immature, and I'm sorry." His words were faster now, more desperate, and I trembled at the pressure of them. "But cutting me out isn't fair, Samaya! You're getting mad at me as if…"

I set the pictures aside and cleared my throat. "As if… what? As if we've talked nonstop for two fucking years. As if I didn't pathetically spend money on plane tickets to see you when I'm still in school and working a volunteer job? Say it, Isaac, say it." I sat up, legs crossed, as I waited for him to finish the sentence.

End this, I begged. *Please just say it so I can move on.*

"I need to focus on my career right now—"

I cut him off, jumping out of my desk chair as I paced about the room, searching for a fight and finding only him. "I have never stepped between you and your career—"

"You kind of are, Samaya. You should be happy for me! I worked hard to get this promotion, and I wanted to tell you about it, and when I did, you just got so cold with me. So, angry—" his voice was getting whiny, and I couldn't handle a second of it.

"Listen to yourself!" I shrieked, rubbing a hand across my face. "What do you think I wanted? I wanted one weekend, Isaac. I wanted one time where you thought of *me* and not you. One time where you surprised me. Like I wasn't crazy…. like this wasn't one-sided and you kept lying about it—"

"I did not lie." His voice hardened as his battle axes blocked my blow.

"Isaac, I asked you, multiple times, did you get your tickets yet? Should I reserve an extra seat at graduation? What fucking snacks do you like? And every time you said… 'Not yet, but I'm making it happen.' How is that not a lie? How is that not as mean as telling me you just can't come? I would've preferred you didn't constantly lead me on, Isaac! So, tell me, Isaac, what are we? What's going on here?" My throat throbbed, and I wanted to swallow the tears, but they just kept coming. "I'm getting mad at you as if… what?"

He swallowed; a bit nervous about where this might lead. "You're my best friend, Samaya."

"Oh," I shivered, lips wobbling between my teeth. "I don't treat my friends like I treat you."

"Samaya, I just like talking to you. I thought we were on the same page. I can't take anything on right now—"

"What page? The one where you used me as a security blanket—"

He raised his voice ever so slightly. "That is so evil. I did not do that. I care about you, Samaya. You know that I do."

"You care enough to invite me into your tent but not enough to show up for me?" I was gripping the wooden desk chair, staring at myself in the vanity mirror. I refused to cry. "You know what? It's fine, Isaac. I need to get ready for my party if that's all right with you?"

"Samaya," he hissed. His words came out as a whisper, a spell. "I am begging you. It's just bad timing."

"There's no such thing as 'good timing', Isaac. You either make time or you don't. You gave me your word, Isaac. You said, 'I will make it happen' and you didn't. What kind of friend would I be to myself if I let that slide? Would you?"

"I'd forgive you a thousand times over," he trembled. "You know that—"

"Of course, you would because I show up when I promise."

"There's so much about that weekend in Sedona that didn't sit well with me, and so much I wish I could've done differently, but I think we just need to… wait? I want to be your boyfriend, Samaya, but I can't be right now. Ya know? Doesn't that make sense? It's just…"

I smiled at the room that witnessed all my greatest falls, and I silently apologized for adding one more to the list. "But we're friends."

The word dug a dagger deep into my chest, but I nodded all the same, ripping out the weapon to let every piece of Isaac I kept hidden in my soul bleed out on the bedroom floor. It had been two years since our kiss outside the church. There was chemistry between us, but there wasn't timing. Nothing was lining up, and everything was lining up. Maybe all the loneliness haunting me led me to believe Isaac was more than a passing encounter.

"Samaya, we were eating beans and wiping ourselves with wet wipes…" he laughed, trailing off. "It wasn't right."

"I get it," I agreed, combing out my hair to blow dry. "I waited for you every night. I thought maybe you'd tap on my tent or come see me or…"

"Samaya, I am so sorry." He said it over and over until I finally cut him off.

"You don't have to be sorry we're just friends." I shook off the words, a little more resigned to the idea each time I said it. "I don't want to be that girl, Isaac. I think I deserve better. I think I'm going to have a lifetime of better. But… this is hurting me. Thank you for the present, but… stop calling me. I'm happy that things are working out so well for you. I just kind of wish that one of your many flights might have been to see me." I gasped, the type of tearless sob that came with choking. "But I get it. You're traveling the mountains, interviewing monks on the meaning of life, and it's just too busy to come back—" I pressed my hands against my trembling lips, willing them into stillness.

"Samaya!" Mami screamed through the door. "Lila's here!"

I ran toward the entrance to block her from barging in. "Just a second! I promise!"

"Samaya—" he spoke, but it was too late.

"I hope you have a great time in Peru." I moved to hang up but couldn't bring myself to do it.

"You deserve better than to be my lighthouse. You deserve a home as beautiful as—"

I hung up before I could hear what he said next. It wasn't until I heard the click of a dead phone line that I realized my room hadn't been this ghostly silent in days. I ran into my closet, shaking my head as if I could erase the last ten minutes from my memories. But I couldn't. That's not how life worked, and I refused to let it break me. I blew out my hair and spoke as many lovely things into my reflection as my stomach could handle because I deserved it.

"Fuck this," I muttered, brushing concealer and bronzer where I needed it. I pointed at my reflection in the mirror. "You are going to go outside, drink delicious punch, eat crap tons of chips, and you are *not* checking your phone for the rest of the night!" I brushed my hair until it sat the way I wanted it, and the redness in my eyes faded away.

By tomorrow, I would forget this ever happened. Because I would pretend Isaac was nothing more than a pretty boy, with pretty brown eyes, filling pretty memories of my childhood. I put on a long-sleeved black top and matching black jeans but left the shoes in the closet. The beauty of having a party at your own house was the pleasure of getting drunk wearing socks.

I found Mami finishing her makeup in her bedroom with the door open. I gave her a big bright smile, joining her in the doorway as if I wasn't just making a fool of myself with a boy living a dream I was too scared to attempt. I wanted to see the world. I wanted to be adventurous and untethered. But every time I walked out my front door, I couldn't shake the overwhelming feeling that whatever was out there couldn't top the love and joy I felt within these walls.

"What happened?" She prompted, dropping her makeup on the surface of her vanity. "Wait. No! No more. *Cojudo. Ya no lo hables con el.* Okay? It's done."

"Yeah, no, we're on the same page," I shivered off the last remnants of the phone call, shaking off the adrenalin.

Mami waved the idea of Isaac off as she ran back into her room for the second earring she clearly could not find. She wore high heels, leggings, and a blouse that cut deep down the front in a way that showed off her cleavage. "*No vale la pena que se te hinchen los ojos.* You're going to wake up tomorrow with puffy eyes, and why? To be miserable? *Ya pues.* There are too many beautiful things in life to smile about. *Oye,* are you wearing that?"

"The clothing on my body? Yes."

"Color, Samaya! Wear color!"

"Where's Lila?" I asked.

"She's not here yet. What? Don't look at me like that. He was never going to leave you alone without a push!" Mami exclaimed, confused as to why I wasn't applauding her quick thinking. As if she were summoned from the heavens, the doorbell rang, and I knew just the girl who wouldn't stop pressing it.

"Hey, can somebody get that?" Robert cried out from the backyard, his voice strained and breath heavy.

"There she is," Mami said as if she found the keys for the car right on the hook where she left them.

"Coming!" I hollered back, running over to the doorway to cut off the annoying number of chimes from our new visitor. I opened the door mid-button press — again — to see Lila standing outside like a raccoon caught in the headlights. "Stop it. Or I'll call the men with butterfly nets to take you away."

"Ooo, flexing your connections, aren't you." She laughed, handing me a bottle of my favorite prosecco and a plastic container with a strip of scotch tape pasted to the top that read 'Congratulations!' in black permanent marker.

I popped it open and gasped at the fresh, strawberry-glazed donuts staring back at me. "Are these homemade?"

"Yeah, George got into baking after his clinicals. He's exhausted, but… whatever, it's nice. It makes him happy. It makes me happy. Very domestic. If he ever quit medicine, I wouldn't mind dating a baker." Lila's words were kind, but her eyes held this jaded tint I hadn't seen in years. Her car was missing from the driveway, and there was no sign of George. "I Ubered," she said, noticing me scanning the foliage. "Also, I'm sleeping over. And… what's Robert doing in the backyard?"

I turned around to see the commotion that caught her attention.

It wasn't until this year that Robert was invited to one of my parties. Mami had a strict code of conduct when it came to dating. No boys in the house, no sleepovers, and no getting too close to her daughter. Then, one day, Mami came home from work and asked — after three years— if I wanted to meet him.

He was a nice man. Fifth generation Floridian and proud of it. He had kids who were all grown up and all very much married. He asked me if he could get me anything for my birthday, but I didn't need any-thing. So, instead, he asked if he could come up with a special surprise for the party. The only catch was that I had to say yes and couldn't ask any questions. Robert paced in the backyard with measuring tape, trying to line up a row of flags while a butterfly-shaped piñata hung from a palm tree. I liked him a great deal.

"Eh… I don't know. But he gives me *Hallmark* channel vibes. Right?" I asked over my shoulder, carrying the donuts to the kitchen with Lila on my heels, but her attention set on the mysterious backyard.

"Absolutely. Wait, am I the first one here? Ew." She grimaced.

"It's okay," I laughed. I pulled a platter from the cabinet in the kitchen and started plating the donuts. Robert and Mami covered the kitchen table with so many platters of pizza, bowls of chips and buffalo dip, and trays of sliders that I feared we'd be eating the leftovers until August. "I can't come up with a proper icebreaker, so I'm just going to ask. No George?"

Lila's jaw jutted out a bit. "I can go places without him. It's normal."

"Yeah, of course." *Only I haven't seen you alone in over three years.* "The same way a dog can bark its ABCs, but ya don't see it every day."

"Don't compare me to a dog," she snapped, eyes like glass, and I took a step back before I got cut.

"I'm sorry. I thought it would make you laugh," I muttered, talking too quickly and worried that I might have shoved my foot too far into my own mouth.

"Were you crying?" She asked.

I shook my head and thought of a better lie. "Well, yeah, kind of. I just finished this book, and it turns out the couple didn't stay together in the end—"

"Hmm," she nodded, eyes searching my face as if to say, *I don't believe you, but I'm not going to push.*

The doorbell rang. Mami answered it and screamed out. "*Hola, girls! Samaya!*"

"Coming," I hollered back. "I am very popular today." I joked with Lila, leaning in close and chewing on the donut I saved special for myself.

"I noticed." Her voice was soft, pensive, and I could see the slight hint of a smile curving at her cheeks when she looked at me.

My eyes rolled to the back of my skull as I slapped a hand down on the counter. "My word, these donuts are Godly."

"I know." Lila rolled her eyes. "Okay. Introduce me to people. Immediately. I feel weird just hovering beside you." Lila sighed, shaking her shoulders. She wore faded blue jeans and a *Pink Floyd* T-shirt. I'm positive she'd been living in it all week. "Why are you laughing?"

"Because I've never seen you so flustered before. Who is this person?" I reached over to check her temperature, her limbs, and to see if the birthmark on her shoulder was still visible. She swatted me away as I pulled at her sleeve. "Lila doesn't get socially awkward. Who are you, and what have you done with my best friend?" I gently shook her by the arms, making my best impression of a southern mother in a sci-fi alien invasion flick.

"I'm not," Lila sneered, and then she gave me a wet willy a beat later.

"Ow! How old are you?!"

IV

"His name was Milo Rojas, and he was a gorgeous dancer," Mami gushed, clearly a little drunk if her rosy cheeks were any indication. "He had big, stiff hair from all the hair gel. He played basket, he sang— Oh. He was wonderful!"

"And *abuela* hated him," I roared, overenunciating the H in hate for dramatic effect. I laid back in my chair while my friends became Mami's new fans. We surrounded the dining room table, sharing edges of seats and leaning on chairbacks to gaze at her as she told stories of her high school escapades. They were like moths enchanted by her flame, and she lived for it.

Our living room was filled to the brim with friends I had met through the psychology department and clubs Mami forced me to join back in sophomore year. I never thanked her for pushing me out of my depression. I needed it, like an IV dripping straight to my heart, but I was too afraid to ask someone to connect it. I was dying so privately, and if it weren't for Rebeca Ximena, I wouldn't be sipping on watered-down margaritas as a never-ending stream of college students flooded through our living room.

"She didn't hate him!" Mami argued.

"Then what do you call bullying your child's boyfriend?!" I hollered into the ether while the girls around the table cheered with me.

"No, no. She did not bully," Mami laughed. "She just made jokes that… he could never know."

"She nicknamed him 'Thriller' because she thought he looked like the zombies in the Michael Jackson music video." I sipped my drink as the girls around the table gasped.

I'd heard the story many times before but didn't care. I loved her stories and the way her eyes lit up as if they happened just a moment ago. I couldn't see Robert anywhere nearby, but I knew he also liked the spark in her eyes. I knew he did, but I wanted to hear him agree.

"She played the song every time he picked me up from the house." Mami laughed so hard she had tears streaming down her face. We turned toward each other at the table, heads titled back to the ceiling as we cried out the lyrics to Michael Jackson's *Thriller*. Including all the *hee hees* and clapping with the beat.

Mami wiped a bit of vodka off her bottom lip, nodding as if to finish the sentences she was itching to tell. *"A su cara!* To his face! *Ay,* no. I'm embarrassing you all, no?"

"No!" I howled in unison with the rest of her posse. I slipped away from the group just to pour myself another drink but ended up making a margarita pitcher instead. Obviously, it was well received. I dipped low to set the pitcher on the coffee table, grabbing my phone to blast Michael Jackson's greatest hits at the highest volume I could.

The rest of my cinema friends were hanging around the TV playing *Guitar Hero* and painfully losing, one after the other, to Ms. Lila Park. She looked so happy. Seeing her roast a bunch of dudes who worshipped her over a video game tugged at a piece of nostalgia I thought I had lost at thirteen. I never thought I would miss that feeling. But the moment was cut short when I saw a guy who was not George place his hand on the small of her back, and she didn't push him away.

His name was Preston (maybe, I couldn't remember), and we hadn't spoken much, but I kind of made my graduation party open-ended. He had a smug smile, black hair, and reached just an inch above Lila's natural height. I took a sip of my drink, and when I saw the pair of them slip onto the couch, ankles crossed over the other, I made my move. I danced over to the gaming area and hauled two of my guy friends off their feet and over to the dancing, screaming women. Happily enough, they didn't protest. Lila, on the other hand, did not budge. She sat on the couch with Preston, too close for my liking.

"Hey!" They looked up at me as if to say, *can we help you?* "Join us. Mami is telling us the story of her first love." I said it a bit more emphatically than necessary.

Lila laughed, tilting her head into the cushions, her chin scraping the side of her new friend's shoulder. "Ugh, the guy with the hair?"

"The guy with the hair," I nodded back but then focused on this stranger and the arm he lingered on the back of Lila's seat. "I don't believe we've met. Samaya. Preston, right? Jacob's friend?" I offered up my hand for him to shake, and he accepted, looking utterly elated.

"Yeah, thanks for inviting me. Cool house."

"Of course, the more the merrier." I kept my eyes on Lila, who eyeballed the table with the ladies, as if I were offering her a plate of broccoli when she was in the mood for chocolate.

"We'll come by in a second," Lila responded. *We.*

"Of course, do your thing. Do you guys need anything?" They shook their heads at my offer, and I accepted it. "Just let me know if that… changes."

I danced my way back into the hands flailing, feet stomping, joy of the group. Somewhere in the chaos, I found Mami. We held hands, screaming the lyrics at each other.

"Oye," she yelled over the music. "You're lucky I was nice and didn't make up any names for Keenan—"

"Ah!" I hollered, covering my ears with my hands and shutting my eyes tight. "I was only sixteen!"

I used to think about Keenan all the time. Before we were together, I wondered if he liked me, and while we were together, I worried if all he wanted from me was sex. In the years after we ended, I feared that was the only form of relationship I'd ever be able to have. I often wished we just stayed friends. But maybe I deserved better than friends with ulterior motives.

"So was I!" She screamed right back, shaking me until we collapsed into a tight ball of folded limbs cradling each other.

Robert came barreling through the sliding glass doors connecting to the backyard with a megaphone and the brightest smile I'd ever seen. His baseball cap nearly fell off his head from running so fast.

"Attention, please!" He let loose a whistle that could've rounded up every cow in the county. Everyone physically recoiled. "I need everyone in the backyard immediately! We are in a state of emergency! Grab your shoes unless they're heels. Honey, that was aimed at you." Mami drunkenly fell into his embrace as he held her close. Seeing him in his dad-core attire was so pure, they felt like an odd couple ripped directly from *Modern Family.* "You'll be better off barefoot than wearing those needles."

Mami shook her head with a sly smile curling around her cheekbone. She had sleepy eyes that seemed at peace. I don't think I ever saw her so physically relaxed around a man.

Outside awaited a full-fledged obstacle course. The winner got to crack open a butterfly-shaped piñata. I told him once that I really liked butterflies and he never forgot. I guess that's what dads did.

There was a corn hole and a three-legged race with old pillowcases he found around the house. What made it even better was how drunk we all were, shamelessly falling on our asses. I cackled into the night air, not caring that I was covered in grass stains and bruises because I knew those would fade, but the memory of this act of kindness would live with me forever. It was wholesome. It was kind. Robert would never understand how healing this gesture was for my inner child.

"Oye," Mami pulled me aside while my friends lined up to hit the piñata. To no one's surprise, Marianne and her drunken mojo wiped all our asses in the obstacle course. "Do you mind if Robert sleeps over?" Mami asked me.

I smiled, not because I was over the moon about the idea of a man sleeping in our house, but for the tender look on her face when she asked me. My mother had me young. Every day, someone asked if she was my sister, and every time I'd answer, yes, because she felt like my sister. She was the greatest gift the universe ever gave me. I knew she'd put him in a cab and send him on his way if I said no. But I didn't.

"He's drunk. There's no way he can drive home."

"Okay…," she nodded, but she still didn't look sure. "It's just… weird… no?"

"I know…" I grimaced, partially for the show but partially not.

"Ewwww boyssss." We whined in unison, melting into laughter. She hugged me and nodded over at a very drunk Robert, nearly falling asleep on the side of the dock.

I took my place in the piñata lineup when I noticed one person who hadn't gone yet. "Where's Lila?" I asked the air around me, not expecting a response.

At first, I felt kind of bad about it. I was having so much fun I didn't notice she was missing. But then I saw Preston walking out of the living room, and my guilt morphed into dread very quickly. I dropped the papier mache-coated plastic rod onto the grass and ran back inside, looking for Lila.

She was sitting by the kitchen counter, just as she was when the party first started.

"I kissed a guy tonight," Lila said. I sat down on the stool beside her.

"Did you want to?"

"Yes," Lila quickly responded.

"Were you drunk?"

Lila shook her head.

"Did something happen with George?"

Lila swished her head from side to side as if to say, *more or less.*

"Was it fun?" I asked.

Lila nodded once but then changed her mind, shaking her head 'no'. "That's the problem."

"Damn. Is this a weed in the park kind of problem or ice cream on 5th, kind of problem?"

Lila chewed on her lips, trying to keep from laughing.

"Both it is." I got up, but Lila looked confused. "What?"

"We can't go. We didn't even blow out your candles?" She asked it like a question, but I don't think that's what she meant to ask. It sounded like Lila was trying to say, *why would you leave your own party for this?*

"Lila, it's my party. I can do whatever I want. Plus, I ate so many donuts how could I even look at cake?"

"But you'll eat ice cream?" she sniffed, laughing lightly as if nothing were wrong.

I smiled. "I'll always have ice cream with you."

V

We locked up the house and walked down to the local ice cream shop. They were closing in an hour, but the same attendant who had worked there since we were little girls gave us the okay to take over the sidewalk while she locked up. I texted Mami to let her know I was okay, but I didn't give too many details about what was going on. Lila had chocolate fudge while I ate strawberry ice cream with cookie dough chunks. Lila paid.

"So, we can eat ice cream in silence or…"

"I don't feel bad about it." Lila admitted, pushing around the rest of her ice cream until it melted before her eyes.

"I would never judge you—"

"But I do… kind of. I met his parents last weekend." The way she said it felt more like she was telling me about a girl who wore Crocs to the prom.

"Mhm, I hate when that happens," I sighed.

"Samaya," Lila snapped.

I held my hands up in defense. "Sorry, not funny."

"I met his parents last weekend, and they were nice. I spent the week prior cleaning the apartment, which is dumb because I am organized while George has frat house behavior ingrained in his stupid, handsome brain."

"I thought you said he was, and I quote, 'oddly clean,'" I sucked the strawberry ice cream off the spoon, squatting down on the curb as Lila did the same.

"Just let me talk shit. Please. Whatever. The point is that *his* parents came into town, but *I* cleaned. I asked him questions to make sure I said nothing stupid. They're separated, right? Like, did they prefer Mr.

210

& Mrs. Carmen, or do they go by their first names?"

"Does George call your dad by his first name?" I gasped, my hand landing flat on her shoulder.

"No, never! He doesn't want to get smacked in the face. The point is… I was nervous."

"You were nervous? Lila Park. You are about to graduate with your bachelor's degree in biology, you got a spot at a top med school with your name on it next year, and you are the most beautiful girl this town has ever seen." My eyes welled up as a nervous form of earnest laughter trickled out of my chest. "What do you have to be nervous about?"

"It's dumb, I know." She swallowed, shaking her head, and filling her mouth with a big spoon of ice cream.

"Utterly moronic." I nodded, and she repeated the movement back to me. Her shoulders were pinched, and there was this permanent crease between her eyebrows that I couldn't stand the sight of. I reached across the space between our shoulders and lightly tapped a finger where the tension was, just to bring her awareness to it, and she immediately softened. A car passed by, and once the taillights disappeared down the corner, she continued.

"And I wore that blue dress my mom got me… back in high school," Lila added, but I understood the meaning. *Back when she was alive.* Lila puffed the dab pen she brought with us on our walk. It was strong, and I could only take a hit or two. "The problem was… I knew about his parents coming in for graduation over a month. Over a month, he told me about them. Over a month, he watched me clean the house and act… weird. I couldn't *fucking* sleep, Maya."

"Why?" I asked, my voice soft and shoulders leaning over the table.

"Because I wanted them to like me. I wanted his mom—" she held a hand over her mouth to stop shaking. I held her other hand over my lap, and she didn't pull away. After a moment, Lila looked me straight in the eyes while tears built up in the corner of hers.

"They didn't know anything about me, Samaya. I picked them up from the airport, and the first thing out of his mom's mouth was, 'So you're Georgie's girl?' Samaya. She didn't mean to be mean. She was just curious, I know that, but. We've been dating for three years. She asked me what I was studying, which was fine, but… she didn't know anything about me other that I'm allergic to shellfish."

"Some people aren't close with their families like that," I countered, but she was already shaking her head.

"Not them. Not him. He talks to his brother every day. They have a family reunion every summer with matching shirts and cookouts and—" she stammered.

"He never invited you?"

Lila waved me off with a flick of her wrist as if this was a topic that was long since dead and buried. "They have an agreement that no one brings a plus one unless there's a ring. And I'm not saying I want that. But I thought…" Lila cried in earnest, and I held her hand tighter.

"Lila, you deserve the ring. Do you want to leave him?" I asked her. My voice was soft, and words spread out so that each left their mark.

"That's the thing…," she huffed, but there was no humor in it. "I love him. I just feel stupid—"

"You're not stupid—"

She held up a hand to cut me off. Her face was serious, and she slowly crossed her arms.

"You can talk to me." I insisted, leaning in closer.

She nodded back but kept her eyes focused on the pavement. The roads were empty at that time of night. Behind us sat at a small metal table on busted-up plastic chairs that had seen better days, but this felt like the type of conversation held on solid ground. The ice cream shop was just about to close when we showed up, which was the only reason we felt comfortable smoking so openly in public. It was hot and mucky outside, but that didn't stop Lila from shivering as she pressed on.

"I feel stupid for settling down with a guy at nineteen, who probably doesn't feel the same way for me. And it's my fault. It's my fault because I never wanted anything. We never talked about it. Ever. And it's his fault because he's always so… tired. Oh, fuck. That's shitty. He's busy. He's in med school. He's going to be a doctor, and I'm fucking complaining, but. Fuck. Samaya, he doesn't touch me anymore. He makes fucking donuts all of a sudden, but we never have sex. He's too tired! I'm tired, but… we had sex one-time last month, and he fell asleep. We just… lived like we were married, and so I just assumed…" she trailed off, wiping the tip of her nose. "And now he's like imprinted on me."

She giggled and I laughed along with her as we both realized the *Twilight* reference.

"And I just wanted to make out with some douche. And it felt like shit! Ugh. I hated it. Because I couldn't stop thinking about stupid fucking George! And I hate him. What if I settled too early like my parents, and he dies, and it's all I've ever had? What if I'm never meant to be happy? Because what if… what if…" Lila was full-blown sobbing. "What if he breaks up with me, and I won't be able to move on?"

"Lila, what happened to your mom was a tragedy, and there is nothing I can ever say to make that better for you." I tried not to cry, but I couldn't help it. "That's not going to happen. But, if he ever, *ever,* ended things with you, he would be an idiot. But if you, Lila Park chose not to wait for him to show up for you… you will survive it. Lila, if someone loves you, they'll let you know. It'll hurt at the start, for sure. And yeah, you'll compare people to him. That's human. Though no one likes to admit it. But if George Carmen, who I truly, deeply think is kicking the earth at the thought of losing you… if he breaks your heart then he wasn't the one. I swear. He's not the one that got away. You are." I pointed at her in a menacing way, and she laughed just like I hoped she would.

"I've really missed you, Maya." She choked.

I smiled. "Me too, Lila."

"I don't think I've been a very good friend to you," she whispered.

"Well, I've been an absolutely trash friend to you. So, I think we can let it go."

"No. Damn it, Samaya." Lila's trembling hands pressed on my knee. I watched her form words I never thought she'd say. She looked up at me, and I swallowed all the pain leaching color from her face. "I'm sorry."

"Please," my voice went dry, shoulders locked as I knew which direction she was trying to force this conversation toward. "Don't."

"I should have never left you that night."

I knew the night she was talking about, and I wanted to speak, but I couldn't.

"You deserved a better friend. You were drunk, and I was sensitive. I'm sorry—"

"Lila, I made you leave," I whispered, lips smacking together with saliva. I swear I thought I was drowning in the memory. I never wanted to live it again. "It was my fault—"

"No, it wasn't, Samaya. It was not your fault. It was his. It was mine."

"Lila—"

"I wasn't drunk that night, Samaya. I wasn't. I was just upset. I smoked, yeah. But I was just so angry with you, and I wanted to leave you there because I couldn't look at you. Samaya, you've always been my sister, and that night, you looked at me like I was trash. But I turned right back. I swear I did. I dropped Danielle home, and I turned around, and you were gone." Snot came out of her nose, but she didn't wipe it away. "And I'm never going to forgive myself."

"There's nothing to forgive. There is nothing you can do because it's already done. We were both wrong." I gripped her hands with both of mine. "I shouldn't have gotten so drunk—"

"Samaya, you were nineteen." The words died on her tongue, and I watched her swallow them just like I had for the past three years. "It's not your fault that you drank. It was his fault for taking advantage of you. It was *him,* not you. It's your fucking *right* to drink too much and dress how you want and be where you want without worrying about a fucking predator. Do you think guys talk like this? Do you think they call themselves sluts? No! Because there's no such thing! But women talk about this all the fucking time. Dude, we're talking about it at a goddamn ice cream shop. And I tell you all of that because I wish… I wish someone had said that to me."

Our foreheads pressed tight, whisps of hair falling loose from her bun, and the earth trembling off the weight of our sobs. Our sweaty palms interlocked all twenty fingers into one solid mass. An unbreakable bond. We sat in the silence of years we let pass because we feared being uncomfortable.

I kissed her fingertips, and she did the same for me. Snot covered her face, but we just looked at each other with so much kindness.

"You're too good for this world, Lila. And if George is smart, he'll fight until you see it. And if he's not, then there will be so many more for you—"

Lila snorted. "That is so rich. You took the words right out of my mouth." She laughed, shaking her head as if thinking better of what she was about to say.

"What is it?"

"No, nothing."

"Just say it."

"I— I don't mean this in a bitchy way—"

"Which probably means it will be, but okay. Continue."

"He's not coming out for graduation," Lila said, already knowing I knew about Isaac's travel plans. "And… that might not be a bad thing."

I shook my head in contemplation. "That's subjective."

"When's the last time you two spoke?" She asked. "Correction, when's the last time you two saw each other and you left thinking… yeah, this guy is someone I can depend on?"

My smile slipped, and my words came out quietly like I hoped she couldn't hear them. "I really thought he was."

"Isaac Haas isn't the 'one'. He's the one right now! He's sexy and mysterious and blah blah blah, but he's not… it." She sighed. "At least, I don't think so."

"What makes you say that?" I wanted someone to save me from this crush.

"Because you're the kind of girl who gets a stable job, gets married to someone who wears glasses, and wants to have a bunch of kids right away. He's just not that. Isaac is going to sleep in bunkers and fool around with random people he'll never remember, and maybe one day, he'll be ready. When he's fifty. And he'll compare everyone to you because he's got unresolved mommy issues and a Madonna complex—"

"Whoa."

"But you don't deserve to wait around for *his* timeline."

"But what if I want to travel? What if I want to make stupid choices and sleep with people I'm never going to remember—"

"Well, then, yeah. You should do those things. Go for it. But you can't do that with a long-distance boyfriend holding you back." She was confused as to why I wasn't connecting the dots that all this rejection was for my protection.

"I think we're always going to think the other deserves better than what they get," I sniffed and then dove in to wrap Lila in a bear hug that had us tumbling onto the sidewalk. She pushed away from me, laughing into my arms as I covered her head in kisses, and she did the same for me.

Headlights came down the road, glaring so high and bright I had to block them out with a handheld over my eyes. Lila's mouth dropped open slightly, untangling herself from my body to get a better view but holding firm to my hand. I wrapped my arm around the small of her back as the jeep pulled up to park along the curb beside us. The headlights went out. But Lila was already on the defense as George hopped out of the driver's seat with a bouquet, lilies to be precise.

"Hi, Samaya," he sighed, keeping his distance and focus on Lila. Lila stared off down the road like a petulant child.

"Hey, George." I waved a limp hand over to him, squeezing Lila's shoulder.

He nodded over to his girlfriend. His eyebrows creased as he tried to bring me over onto his side of the battle. "Can we talk?"

"I'm hanging out with my friend, George." Lila didn't turn to face him as she clutched me closer to her side like a shield.

He nodded. "I know… but can we talk? And you can come right back?"

I sat on the curb, the ice cream shop officially closed, and the tables and chairs stowed away inside for the following morning. Lila and Goerge chatted rather peacefully inside the car. From what I could see, Lila fumbled with the air freshener dangling off the rearview mirror while George caressed her cheek.

The store signs slowly shut off up and down the block. A cold chill swept through my shoulders, and there was no moon overhead to keep me company as I waited to see where the night would lead. I dusted the dirt off my pants and jogged to Lila's side of the car. I knocked lightly, trying not to kill the mood, but there was no way to break up the way they stared at each other. I cleared my throat and knocked again. Lila jumped in her seat and lowered the window.

"Hey, I'm just going to head back."

"I'll go with you." Lila pushed open the door, but I shook my head.

"It's okay. It's a pretty night for a walk."

"But what about our sleepover?"

George leaned forward. "I can drop you both off. No problem."

"It's okay. I got it."

I walked off down the sidewalk, hands buried in my pockets as I counted the cracks in the sidewalk I hadn't noticed before. The quiet creep of their car followed close behind me. I huffed, turning toward Lila and George with crossed arms. "I can literally see you following me."

Lila leaned out the window. "Don't be a baby and get in!"

Lila slept over that night. I told her to grab a pair of pajamas out of my closet, completely forgetting what I had stashed inside.

"Samaya?" She asked, holding up the package filled with black and white portraits of Isaac and me in Sedona, Arizona. I didn't take them out of her hands. I just crawled into bed and looked at them with a soft smile.

"They're nice, right? He developed them for me."

She looked at the photos and then back at me. "They're really nice."

"Yeah, well…"

She climbed into bed beside me, and I handed her the pillow I knew she loved most.

"I can't believe you still remember that," she huffed. "Apparently, George's mom wants to go to the spa with me after graduation. Just us."

"That's beautiful. Hey, Lila?"

"Yeah," she mumbled, her back pressed to mine.

"Wanna stay over tomorrow and hang out?" I asked.

"Yeah. I'd really like that. Thanks for asking."

I snuggled deeper into the bedding, eyes focused on the window above my head and how lucky it was to have a full moon to stare at.

"Samaya?" Lila asked, head turning slightly toward me.

"Yeah?"

"You deserve better than Isaac Haas."

She didn't know it, or maybe she suspected it, but her words made me cry. I was boy crazy. It consumed me.

I checked to see if he was stalking my posts online, and I read meaning into every like, every message, and every nugget of hope that maybe, just maybe, my crush was reciprocated. I prayed I wouldn't be this way forever, but maybe that was normal. Because though it hurt to think he didn't feel the same way back, it was still so much *fun* to have feelings for someone. It made me excited to go on my phone, to see his name on my screen, and I didn't think that was a bad thing.

Yes, Lila, I still cried over boys but there was nothing wrong with it. I wasn't wasting my life; this was my life. I'm going to go to grad school, and I'm going to travel. I'm going to get a job, move, and do whatever else people believe to be a worthwhile way of living.

It was so easy for Lila to mock because she was just as boy-crazy as I was until she found a boy who was crazy about her. She found her person. I'm happy for her. But being boy-crazy did not make me any less of a woman. It did not make me any less feminist or smart or strong or independent than anyone else. It just made me human.

THE SEVENTH KISS

I

Our fourth date went well enough for me to invite him back to my apartment. He lingered on my bed, his clothes scattered somewhere in the living room, resting as if he knew this space better than the glimpses he consumed from the entryway of my front door.

"What's with the look?" I pushed open the bathroom door, towel-drying my hair as I looked over at him in the reflection of the mirror. His hands rested behind his head as he tried to appear casual, but it didn't suit him.

Carson Grant had never known a casual day in his life. He was a lawyer, fresh out of Georgetown Law and doing well for himself by the look of it. He was one of the rare ones who did good things for people who couldn't afford his hours yet still found a way to earn a proper living in Miami. He was ways away from having steady clients, which meant every encounter held meaning, every conversation was an opportunity to prove himself, and every night that I agreed to see him again meant he succeeded in yet another area of his life.

He pushed himself up on the palm of his hands, veins protruding along the forearm muscles earned from long hours on a golf course. He wore a navy-blue jacket and a matching set of chinos for our date. We went to a sushi place down by Wynwood that was heinously expensive but so delicious it made me angry to know I couldn't eat it every minute of every day. "It's just… I don't know what I'm supposed to do. Which is strange for me because I'm very rarely at a loss for choice." His Virginia accent hidden thick beneath his Princeton-bred speech patterns.

"Well, what do you usually do at this time of night?" My combed, wet hair dripped down my bare shoulders as I turned to face him. The cool granite solid at my spine as Carson took in his surroundings.

The duvet was light blue with ruffled trim, and my furnishings were modern, with slight touches of pastel colors in the artwork and framed photographs I kept along every wall.

His hands folded on his stomach, slight abs poking through his thin frame. "Well, that's the thing… this would be my place, typically. Not…" He pointed at me, a tiny smirk forming at the corner of his lips.

I laughed at his timid way of explaining his nightly escapades as if I hadn't clocked him when my coworker Lisa first introduced me to her cousin. "You usually sleep with women at your place. Got it. Well, sorry to disappoint you, but I'm not exactly running a brothel. There are no gift bags to hand out."

"Do brothels give out gift bags?"

"If you open the top drawer of my nightstand, you'll find small chocolates to take with you." I walked over to him, opening the drawer when he wrapped me in his arms, pulling me off the floor and pinning me on the bed. I couldn't stop laughing.

"That's not what I meant," he murmured, brushing my wet hair off my forehead. He had pale skin with birthmarks scattered across his cheeks in ways that made me want to trace constellations around them. His silky blond hair fell easily along his scalp, just short enough not to be mistaken for a *Princess Bride* cosplay. He had blue eyes that crinkled when he smiled at me. When I smiled at him, it never reached my eyes. "Why can't I sleep over?"

"Because it would be inappropriate." I smiled, but he didn't get the joke.

Carson rolled his eyes. "I think we did plenty of inappropriate activities—" I cut him off with a hand to his lips.

"You're not my boyfriend. You're not sleeping over."

"Well… we could talk about that." He leaned in to kiss me, soft and sweet, but I rolled away before he could.

"Seriously, I do have to be up early tomorrow morning. You know this. And I've been told I kick in my sleep—"

"Told by who?"

"Tell me. How does this usually go? Pretend I'm you, and I want to kick someone out."

His eyebrows raised, neck pulling back as he scanned my body. "Are you kicking me out?"

I shrugged, my bottom lip slipping between my teeth as his hands pressed lightly upon my shoulders. "I'm following your lead."

"Well, depending on the day of the week," he trailed off, the words forming and disappearing from his lips multiple times. "I try to keep a routine and wake up early—"

I gasped. "You're that guy?"

"What's wrong with that guy?" He asked, laughing as I rolled out from under him, clutching my towel like a string of pearls. "There's coffee and pastries. I'm polite about it."

"Do you leave a note?" He said nothing. His smile screamed. "Oh, Carson, please."

He gave me a once over, knees bent on my duvet and hands limp in his lap. "You're not exactly promising to make me breakfast in the morning."

I shook my head. "My eggs always come out too runny or too burnt."

He ran his hands through his hair and hopped off the bed in a fluid stride. "In that case, I better start going." He smiled, and I didn't discourage him. I've never had a boy sleepover before, and I didn't want to start now.

"Are you getting married?" He stared down at the invitation I kept propped up on display on my nightstand as he buttoned his white collared shirt.

"Kind of," I joked, rubbing lotion onto my legs while I watched him gather his belongings. "My best friend is getting married to her college sweetheart."

"Huh, are you going with anyone?" He stared down at his buttons as he asked, even though he already finished buttoning them up to the neck.

"No. My mom and her boyfriend are coming with me. I won't be alone."

"Ahh, so your ex is going," he sighed, meeting my surprised gaze from the doorway.

"That's not true."

"Relax, it's okay. Just know that… I love weddings."

"Do you?" I murmured, hands folded behind my back, mirroring his body language from earlier. He laughed, grabbing his keys off my dresser.

"You know the polite thing to do would be to walk me to the door," he said over his shoulder, heading out into the living room of my one-bedroom apartment.

"But then I wouldn't be able to enjoy watching you go," I giggled, and he shook his head, hiding the blush creeping over his creamy skin.

"Hey, wait," I stopped him in the hallway of my apartment building, bare legs beneath an oversized band t-shirt. "What are you doing Thursday night?"

II

WE SAT AT A restaurant on South Beach, waiting for the bill and idly scanning the room for our fourth dinner guest to return from the bathroom. I couldn't stand the silence, mainly because it came from Mami, who pointedly dissected what type of crystal the restaurant used for their wine glasses instead of making conversation. That was my first sign that the night would not end with an invitation for a second double date.

"Okay, please. Speak. The silence is killing me." I leaned forward, hands folded on the table as if waiting to sign a contract.

Robert spoke first. "He's nice." He smiled, but it did not reach his eyes.

"You're a horrible liar, Robert," I grumbled, running a hand through my hair.

"*Aye,* no. He is! He is a very… nice boy, Samaya," Mami spoke as if *nice* were a slur.

"So, what's the problem?"

Robert opened his mouth, but a firm hand on his knee from Mami had him close it again. "You don't have to bring a plus one to the wedding." As if that had anything to do with my question.

"No one has to, but I want to. Lila wants me to! George was already asking if Carson wanted to go out with the guys after the reception—"

"Darling, do you think that's a good idea? All things considered?" Robert tiptoed around it, but I knew who he was referring to.

"Why should it matter? It's not like Isaac was my boyfriend. If he has a problem with me bringing a date, he probably should have said something. And even if he did, which he didn't, it doesn't matter."

"*¿Porque?*" Mami asked.

I sipped my glass of chardonnay, averting my eyes as I added.

"Because he's bringing a date."

That bit of information made Robert let out a low whistle, patting an invisible sweat off his forehead.

"Good, Lord almighty, darling… you sure know how to throw down," Robert huffed, clearly uncomfortable at the idea of the drama that was about to ensue come Saturday night.

"I could go alone to the wedding. It's not a big deal," I said, arms crossed over my chest.

"Samaya. You can take a date. But I have to ask, are you going alone because you *want* to go alone or because you're leaving the door open for Isaac?"

"Can we please change the subject? He's coming back any minute, and I don't want—"

"Okay," Mami said. But her face said something else entirely. *Okay* was code word for *we'll speak about this later.*

A moment later, Carson joined the table. "Sorry about that, there was a long line." He didn't sit down. Instead, Carson collected his sports jacket from the back of his chair. "Ready to go?"

Mami sat up straight, guiding him back to the table. "Oh, we're still waiting on the check."

"That's alright, I already paid." He smiled, and it was easy. "Let's go."

Robert and Mami gave me a pointed look that I tried to ignore. Carson kissed Mami on both cheeks as we left the restaurant. He shook Robert's hand and asked to play golf with him sometime.

"Thank you for dinner, my love. That was very kind. Your mother raised you well," Mami gushed, clasping his hand in hers. But Carson waved them off. He was humble.

On the car ride back to my apartment, I stared out the window while he played soft music in the background. He liked listening to soothing music, the kind you'd hear in coffee shops on early mornings. If I checked his phone, it would probably be a playlist entitled 'coffee shop'. He was an easy companion.

"Tonight was really wonderful," I stared out along the Miami skyline.

"Well, you talk about your family so much. I'm honored to finally meet them." He reached over to me and placed a warm palm on my knee.

This was our fifth date. Each was lovely and easy. He was dependable, kind, and friendly. He wasn't much for movies, but he did like to read. Non-fiction, mostly. He liked to golf and go on morning runs. He took supplements and knew which protein powders were better than others. I had a funny feeling in my belly that if I let go and let the current pull me downstream, I'd have a happy life with Carson Grant.

He'd propose in two years, and in three, we'd move into a starter house. He'd take care of us, and he'd make certain that that starter house flourished into a home. I'd have kids. I'd grow old. And I needed so desperately to get out of that car immediately.

He held the door open for me, but I didn't go up to my apartment just yet.

"Hey, Carson, are you doing anything this weekend?"

He smiled, hands digging into his pockets in an easy way. He was always so comfortable I was envious of it.

"Nothing in particular," he murmured.

"Would you like to attend a wedding with me? It's nearby. An hour north, on Saturday. It's by the beach, so you don't need to wear a tux—"

"Stop," he held up a hand and brought it down on my shoulder, squeezing tight. "I'd love to."

"Great." He moved in to kiss me just as I moved in for a hug. It was weird, but we settled on the hug.

III

THE WEDDING TOOK PLACE on the beach outside Mami's hotel. She hooked the future Mr. and Mrs. Carmen up with so many discounts it would have been ridiculous to do it anywhere else. The bridesmaids gathered in Lila's hotel room three hours before the ceremony. I walked in carrying a bottle of prosecco, kissing cheeks and beelining toward the woman of the hour.

Lila sat beneath a blow dryer wearing a white satin robe with the word 'bride' etched across the back. Each of the bridesmaids had pink satin robes to match. George's mother perched on a chair across from her, patting her cheeks dry as she held Lila's hand while the makeup artist applied the last bit of lipstick. In her hand sat a nearly empty glass of prosecco. I popped open a new bottle, splashing a little on the carpet in the process, and filled her cup with a theatrical bow. A photographer snapped pictures of us as I leaned in to hug her.

"You look so happy," I whispered, hand clutching hers.

Her smile burned so bright it would live in my memories for the rest of time. "I'm getting married."

A laugh bubbled out of my chest to match the one escaping from hers. "Yeah, you are."

She smiled and stumbled as she stood to address her posse. "Pour one out, ladies! I'm getting married!"

All the ladies in the room cheered. I moved my glass away to avoid the mess.

"Never mind, you're officially cut off!" I scolded her, taking her glass away. No one contested the decision.

We lined up against the hallway wall leading out to the beach. Wedding guests walked by us toward the ceremony while a wedding planner in a sharp gray pantsuit barked orders into her headset. "Anyone got eyes on the groom? Spray some cologne on him before coming in. No one wants to smell a tobacco farm as he walks down the aisle!"

George still looked like a punk college kid to me. He entered the hall leading the pack of tuxedo-clad, overgrown fraternity brothers, beaming with happiness. At the sight of me, he ran over, and scooped me into a big hug. He was clearly wasted as he howled, "I'M GETTING MARRIED!"

"There really is a lid for every pot," I muttered, patting him on the shoulder until he put me down.

The wedding planner, Joyce, I believe her name was, snapped her fingers. "George, up front!" He complied, running over. "Maid of Honor and Best Man?"

I stepped forward, my shoulders pressed back with a bit more pride than I anticipated. Joyce handed me a bouquet, then refocused on the empty spot beside me. George was already making excuses for his missing friend.

"I just got off the phone with him, and he should—"

The door behind us swung open, but I refused to turn around. I adjusted my bangs; they were new, but they were not the result of finding out Isaac had been invited to the wedding. I needed a change and hoped the movement looked casual as Isaac stepped up beside me.

"Here," he breathed, hugging George with a single arm and facing his attention toward a rather irritated Joyce.

Isaac looked down at me, only an inch away from touching my shoulder. "Samaya."

I looked up at him, meeting his brown eyes with empty lungs and chattering teeth. All I could say was, "You shaved your beard."

He laughed. "Yeah, someone told me I looked like a Billy goat."

I nodded, considering the comment and the truth behind it. "That's rude."

His lip quirked to the side. His smile was the sweetest thing I'd ever seen. "Agreed."

The church doors burst open.

George nudged Isaac with an elbow and mouthed, "I'm getting fucking married!"

"Has he been doing that all day?" Isaac whispered, leaning close enough to my ear that his nose sent a shiver down my spine.

I cleared my throat, shaking him off. "Yes. They both have."

The wedding march started to play. I wrapped my hand around Isaac's elbow and tried to ignore how easy it felt to fall into step beside him. Carson stood with Robert and Mami. He waved at me, and I knew it was rude, but I kept looking forward as if I did not see him. I tried to breathe, but I could not ignore the shiver running down the side of my body touching Isaac.

I hadn't seen him in three years, yet here he was, standing beside me like nothing had changed. I stared at the floor instead of catching his eyes as we separated at the top of the aisle. But I could feel him staring.

George cried as Lila walked down the aisle. So did she. The ceremony flashed in a blur of promises and silver bands, and George choked down sobs as he stomped on cloth-covered glass. The bride and groom shared an infamous kiss. It was finally okay for me to cry, but I tried to smile as I did.

IV

THE RECEPTION WAS HELD at a cozy bungalow by the beach. Candles and string lights illuminated the stone path to the shoreline. Children in miniature suits and gowns grooved to a live jazz band while their parents enjoyed the open bar. Mami shimmied in the center of the dance floor with Mr. Park. I sipped whiskey on ice in the corner, pretending to watch Mami dance the night away, when I felt Carson shift in his seat.

"So." Carson leaned close to my ear, startling me. I sat up straight and let him cup the back of my neck with his palm. He pulled his chair up close and tracked my view toward Isaac. "It's the Best Man, right?"

Isaac Haas sat at an empty table, smoking a cigarette, and sipping on a water bottle. He shaved his beard but kept his thick brown hair hanging around his shoulders, pulled back by a loose ponytail. Our eyes locked, and I felt a cold sweat creep across my brow.

"What?" I huffed out a laugh, shaking my head. "No."

"Okay, then kiss me."

My eyebrows creased, and the idea of him ordering me around made my stomach turn. "No."

He shook his head, tossing back the rest of his drink. He was onto his second cocktail. "Fair. Okay, that was forward. But I'm not judging you. I get it. We all have exes."

"He's not my ex."

Carson stood up and extended his palm for me to take. "Care to make him jealous?"

My eyebrows flared up as I slipped my hand in his. "You dance?"

His smile deepened, and he did a little spin. "Oh, I've got moves."

That he did.

The party erupted once the DJ started playing the YMCA. We screamed the lyrics while Carson twirled me around on the dance floor. Lila grabbed my hands, spinning me in circles, howling drunkenly. Mami bumped hips with Mr. Park, clearly a bit comfortable with the years. George's father and doppelganger started a conga line, while Robert accidentally stomped on my feet multiple times, forcing me to bow out. I held onto Carson's shoulder to catch my breath. "I'm going to go powder my nose."

George kneeled before Lila, sitting on a chair at the center of the dance floor. He pushed her dress up one leg and removed the garter belt from her thigh with his teeth. The crowd cheered but Mr. Park looked like he might vomit right on the beach. George threw the belt into the crowd, and it fell directly on Robert's lap, which made me grimace to the point of sickness. Lila stole the microphone from the band, tapping it to make sure it worked, and then ran into the center of the crowd.

The audience gasped at her use of language as she called all the single ladies to the dance floor. Mr. Park shouted something in Korean that made one-half of the reception laugh into their sleeves while the other half pretended, they were included in the joke.

I shoved my way through the crowd until I found the ladies' room. It was blissfully empty and the only place at the wedding where I could catch my breath. I laid my hands on the lip of the sink, taking stock of how crazy I looked after all the dancing and champagne. Luckily, I used so much hair spray that everything stayed in place. I took a deep breath, splashed water on my face, and when I opened the bathroom door again, I saw Isaac standing outside.

"Hi." He bit his lips between his teeth, bouncing in his shoes like an impatient child.

"Could I have one of those?" I gestured to the cigarettes in his hand and thanked him as I bent down low for him to light it. His knuckles brushed my lips accidentally, and the jolt made me take a small step back.

"Sorry," he muttered, but I brushed him off with the flick of my fingers. "Lila did a good job with the cupcake-to-human ratio," he gestured toward my dress. It was a satin fabric that wrapped around my neck and plunged low on the back. I had to pinch the sides to walk comfortably down the aisle, a fact Isaac must have noticed because we marched slower than I could have imagined down that path.

I did a little twirl, letting the dress swirl along my shoes. Isaac blushed at the sight of my bare skin, but I pretended not to notice. "She has good taste."

"I agree, you look good." We stood in companionable silence, blowing smoke into the air around us as he leaned beside me on the wall. I could feel every centimeter of space he left empty between us. Up the stairs and across the lawn, we watched Lila wobble up onto a chair, groomsmen surrounded her, so she didn't fall. I took a step forward, clutching Isaac's sleeve on instinct.

His hand settled on mine, holding me in place. "She's okay."

I nodded, watching Lila settle onto her feet as George grabbed her waist to keep her in place. She gestured for the girls on the dance floor to gather around as she tossed the bouquet blindly into the crowd. There were cheers of joy as the music came back on, and I didn't move a muscle. My hand stayed firmly planted on Isaac's suit jacket.

"Would you want to go for a walk?" Isaac stared down at me, and somehow, the distance between us evaporated into thin air. I tilted my neck back, cigarette burning idly in my fingertips while the other traced the shape of his tie. He cupped my cheek in his hands, and I nuzzled my nose into the scent of cologne lingering on his wrists. Fresh tobacco. I lifted the cigarette to my lips, inhaling deep as I took a single step back, my hand planted firmly on his chest as if to keep him at bay.

"Not really," I exhaled, smoke billowing around us.

"Samaya—"

"Where's your date?" I asked, already moving back toward the party.

That question confused him. He stepped closer and pointed at a rather burly man wearing a khaki suit dancing like wild. "My 'date' works with me. We've been in town all week shooting a new episode of our show. Which you would know if you answered any of my calls."

"Hmm." I clicked my tongue at the new fact. "I didn't get any calls."

"Well, I made them." His eyes pierced mine making it impossible to move.

I stopped on the steps, halfway from the privacy of the dark hall and back toward my family, my friends, and my date. "I have nothing to say."

He scoffed, scrubbing his chin. "So, that's how it is, huh? You choose when to walk away. Samaya, you know how mean it is for someone you care about to hang up on you and never even give you a chance to explain?"

"I understood your explanation—"

"I'm not talking about why I couldn't come to Florida *three years ago*. You know that. Don't run away from this." He begged me. It hurt to look at him.

I said nothing, but I didn't move either.

"Your date seems nice."

"Will everyone stop saying that?" The use of the word 'nice' set me off. I sighed, looking him up and down with the shake of my head. "You look good in that suit." I snubbed the cigarette on the bottom of my shoe, avoiding his eyes as the compliment settled into the air between us.

He laughed, rubbing at his jawline. His owl eyes glistened when he looked back at me. "I haven't stopped thinking about you." He exhaled heavily.

I swallowed, looking back at the party. "Where have you been?"

"Honestly... I haven't really had a solid 'residence' for the past eight months." He placed quotation marks around the idea of a home as if it were a dated experience he only read about in history books.

"Are you homeless?" I already knew the answer.

"Voluntarily?"

"Hmmm." I nodded. "That suits you."

We both laughed, and it was sweet.

"I have something for you." He stepped closer with a small manila envelope. But I didn't want it.

"You know you really missed your calling as a private investigator—" I joked, but Isaac wasn't looking at me. Behind us stood Carson, arms crossed and listening to everything. He wasn't angry. He just seemed a bit hurt.

"This doesn't look like nothing to me." His voice coated thick in discomfort.

"He's not—"

Carson cut me off. "We're adults. Don't insult me."

Isaac stepped forward, and for the first time in our time together, I saw him look angry. "Don't cut her off."

I held my hand up. "Not your life, not your place." He stepped back like a puppy who'd been swatted at with a newspaper.

Carson looked him up and down before ignoring him altogether. "Everyone has a past. But if we're going to date, I need to know it's behind you. Mine is behind me. I really like you, and I think you like me too."

"It is behind me." Frustration made me want to yell, but there were too many witnesses.

"It doesn't look like that." Carson stared directly at Isaac as he said it.

I nodded. "Yeah, fine. This is my life; I don't need the macho boyfriend act. I'm sorry, Carson. This is happening way too fast. There are no hard feelings if you leave now."

"Look, I get it. I do. I… look, let's agree to this. If you want to try again, and all this is really done, call me next week." He looked so sincere, so understanding, and it made my smile ache.

"That sounds perfect." I cleared my throat, trying to readjust my dress discreetly beneath his gaze. Carson blushed, but it didn't meet his eyes. He was getting rejected. This was just the nicest way of delaying it. This time, I didn't love watching him walk away.

Isaac said nothing; he pretended not to be listening, but he was rather garbage at it. Before the silence could swallow me whole, the microphone reverbed as the crowd followed Lila and George out the front door. I ran after them.

A car with the words 'JUST MARRIED' painted on the back window waited in the driveway for Lila and George to hop in. I ran out in time to catch Lila, trying to shove the tule of her dress into the backseat. The car started up just as the crowd of wedding guests crowded around, cheering them on. Lila waved at her family out the window but paused when she saw me. She waved me over, and I ran straight for the open window. I was on the verge of tears as she pulled away, adjusting the hair that smashed into my face.

"Why are you leaving so early? We didn't even cut the cake." I whined.

"I'm drunk," Lila sniffed, laughing. "Appa will box it up."

"I had a speech planned for you, and you weren't even going to say bye?"

"Ugh, pass." She rolled her eyes, grossed out by the idea of such a public display of affection. Then, something in her wasted logic told her it was okay to smack my arm. "Why are you crying?"

I smacked her arm right back. "You're crying!"

"I'm getting married!"

"You *are* married!" I sobbed. "It feels like you're breaking up with me."

"Samaya."

"Yeah?"

"I love you."

"You're leaving," I sniffed, wiping my nose, but I couldn't stop smiling.

"I know." The corners of her lips curved down as she tried to smile through the tears bubbling up in her chest. She gripped my hand in hers. "Thank you for loving me."

"He's a great guy." I promised her, and the words snapped whatever cool girl facade she built up.

"I wouldn't accept anything less," she croaked. I wiped the tear that broke through her mascara before it could ruin the makeup.

"But he's the side hoe!"

She cupped my face, laughing. "He knows, babe."

The car pulled out of the driveway, leaving me in its wake. Mami came up behind me and collected me in her open arms.

I was full-on sobbing on her shoulder blade. "Don't look at me. I'm perfectly chill. I'm being totally, perfectly... cool. Fuck. *Bebí mucho.*"

"Ay! Para lo, Samaya. You're not a teenager anymore. Learn to hold your liquor."

"I'm trying," I breathed.

"Pareces un mapache." Mami shook her head at the embarrassing sight.

Mami was about to make another comment when Isaac ran outside to join the procession of partygoers leaving the venue. He was walking over to us, and I immediately turned to Mami, wiping the mascara from beneath my eyes as she waved over to him with the fakest smile plastered across her face.

"Do I look like I've been crying?" I whispered to Mami.

She pretended like I said a funny joke as she whispered back, "Yes, but it's too late now, so smile and laugh." We fake laughed at each other, playing off the mood as normal as possible. Isaac joined us, giving Mami a hug and kiss on both cheeks.

"Beautiful to see you again! How did you like Lima?" Mami, on the other hand, flawlessly took his hand as if he wasn't the cause of many sleepless nights in the Ximena household.

"Oh, I loved it. I wish I could've stayed there longer. But the schedule is crazy. We're never in the same place longer than a few days or weeks at most." He glanced at me as he said it.

"Ay por dios! Mi amor! That's incredible." Mami gasped, visibly melting like butter in the palm of Isaac's well-traveled hands. "You know Samaya is top of her class at UM and she's already accepted an offer at a psychiatric clinic. Did you tell him?"

"No, she hasn't told me." His eyes focused on me with a pleading smile.

"You two should exchange information or make plans while you're in town?"

I cut Mami off with a hand on the shoulder, "Mami. I'm sure Isaac is busy."

"Actually, I'm heading back down to Miami tonight." He admitted cautiously. "We fly out tomorrow afternoon for Cape Town."

I nodded. "Of course you are."

"I'll be there for a month. But I think I'm getting routed back to North America soon after. I applied for the United States, but I don't know yet. They kind of send me wherever and whenever they want to. I don't really have much of a choice. But I'm free now." He looked straight at me, and I shuddered under the weight of his eyes. His voice pitching up as if to say, *please?*

"That's funny, my love because Samaya lives in Miami now."

"Mami?" My neck snapped in her direction, confused by what she was doing.

Mami fake yawned and started her exit. "I have to find Robert before he chats Mr. Park's ear off. Isaac, please make sure she calls me once you're in the cab?" It was an order, and he understood that.

"Absolutely." He confirmed.

"Next time you're in the area, you must come by for a visit. I'll feed you my famous *lomo saltado!*" Mami walked back toward the venue, giving Isaac two thumbs up to know the invitation was serious.

He leaned back and hovered a hand over his belly. "Oof, okay. I'll never say no to that."

I pulled Mami to the side out of earshot. "You're seriously leaving me alone at night with a guy?"

She smirked; a knowing laugh spread out across her cheeks as she wiped hair out of my face. "You're an adult. I trust you. Have fun." She winked.

Isaac hailed a cab outside the venue. Mami hugged us both goodbye, got in the car with a rather inebriated Robert, and rode off down the street, leaving Isaac and me in loaded silence.

"You want to walk along the beach?" He asked.

"No," I replied, turning toward him with tired eyes as I pointed down the end of the shoreline. "I can walk to my mom's house from here... can you believe that? My entire life has consisted within walking distance."

"Are you happy?" He asked.

"Yes." I lied and wiped a tear off my cheek.

"You cry an awful lot for a happy person," he said softly.

"Can I ask you an inappropriate question?" I asked, and he nodded. "What did you write in the prayer book that night?"

"Ahh," he sniffed, meeting my gaze. From inside his pocket, he retrieved the manila envelope he had tried to give me earlier and handed it to me with a shy smile. "Your gift."

I slipped open the envelope to find the picture he had taken of me that night in the park. A tear fell on the portrait, and I wiped it away before it did any damage. "Do you have a stockpile of pictures of us hidden in a bunker somewhere?"

He laughed. "I think I wrote something along the lines of wishing you well. I was high so if you're asking for anything specific, I can't tell you that. But... I kept that picture with me everywhere I went. Always wishing you well."

"Why?" My voice was too breathy to hear over the sounds of the janitorial staff clearing out the party venue as if it never existed.

"Because you felt more like a home than a lighthouse."

"You keep saying that, and it makes no sense," I laughed.

He waved his hands over me, shooing away my judgmental tone. "Shh, it's poetic."

I closed my eyes, breathing deeply as I extended my hand towards him, and he clasped his fingers into mine. It felt so right being near him, and I hated him for it.

I hated how it didn't feel this comfortable with anyone else, and I wanted to erase him from my memories, but I couldn't. I pictured myself as a child sitting peacefully on the swing beside five-year-old Isaac. Isaac and Mami laughing in the kitchen, cooking dinner together. Isaac and I laying on the beach, smiling at each other as he took our picture.

"Lighthouses guide sailors onto shore on stormy nights or redirect them when they're lost at sea. I want to apologize to you, Samaya. Because you were right about the way I treated you in college. You were never my security blanket. You deserved better than being my lighthouse." He shivered, and it was so honest I hated him for it. "You're a home, not a lighthouse."

"It's okay. I think I misjudged your purpose in my life. I used to think that if I found you earlier, I could have saved myself so much pain, but I don't think that's the purpose of you." I whispered, and he leaned in closer to hear me better. He was practically laying his face on top of mine, hands cupping my cheeks, totally oblivious to the world at large.

"Tell me my purpose, Samaya." He ordered, his hands brushing my bangs out of my face.

"You're the guy who rolls into my life and makes me think… is something missing? Am I happy on my path, or should I change course? And it sucks because… obviously, something is missing. But I'm not ready to receive it yet. I like my life, and I like my plans. I want all the normal things. I'm not ashamed of wanting a normal life. But, over the years, I think I used you as this… character to fixate on. If I needed something sweet to fall asleep to, I'd think of you. And if things weren't going well with someone, I'd picture you and your gentleness, and I'd think 'things would be different with Isaac.' I built up a reality with you that doesn't exist, and I am mourning it." I felt tears streaming down my cheeks even as I tried to laugh it off. Isaac wiped them away with the pads of his fingers. He brushed his nose against mine, eyes closed, and lips parted into a smile.

"Likewise," he whispered, breath hot on my lips.

"Liar," I cackled, pushing him away, but he held me close. His elbows were on either side of my torso, and his eyes bore into mine. I didn't dare move. I leaned in, eyes drifting closed and lips parting as he pulled away.

"I'm not your goodbye kiss."

I looked genuinely hurt by the assumption. "I think you need to be."

"Samaya, I have loved you since the first day I saw you. And I hated you because you made me feel so inadequate. Like there was this social rule book I didn't get to read. And I never had problems with anybody else, but then I'd look at you, and you were so focused on… yourself. Not in a bad way. You were just consumed with your dolls and your alone time inside while everyone else was outside, and I just thought… what must it be like to be Samaya Ximena? I recognized you immediately at the party. I just didn't want to believe it. Because you hadn't changed a bit, but I had. You became more of yourself."

"So did you."

"Sure. But I'm afraid that the person I've become doesn't like to stay. And it's hard to love someone who doesn't sit still. I don't know why but I have looked for you in every girl I've ever met, and you weren't there. I thought about calling you, and every time I did, you wouldn't answer. I know what I said to you was hurtful. But I wasn't ready. I don't think I'll ever be ready or aligned just right to the path you're living, but I don't want to say goodbye to you. I just can't stay here. We are not like everyone else, Samaya Ximena. It's just you and me. I don't think we get a simple story, but isn't that better?" He begged me.

I backed up with my hands on my hips to fully illustrate how seriously I'd come to this conclusion. "I think we should have sex."

His eyes bugged out of his head, a laugh escaping his mouth that made me laugh through the pain of seeing his face. "Was that a question?"

I thought about it for a moment, then shook my head. "No, I know we should have sex."

"I'm pouring my heart out over here but, no, please continue telling me how you just want to use me for my body." He laughed, hands flaring out in melodrama.

I shrugged, taking in the coastline and the rising sun over the water. "I don't know. I just looked at you, and I thought… hmm, I'd like to have sex with him."

He laughed. "Samaya, what do you have to say?"

"This isn't a very good seduction, is it?" I admitted, hoping I was wrong.

"Why do I feel like this is the last time you're going to let me touch you?" I said nothing. I kept his stare level with mine, and though I could see the pain written across his lips, he did a good job of wiping it all away with the back of his hand. He crossed his arms, foot jutting out with sass written all over his face. "What makes you so sure I'll say yes?"

My eyes drifted shut just a tad, sleepy and honest. "Because I know you want to have sex with me, too."

He blushed, pulling an invisible robe tight across his chest. "I feel like a tramp."

"What can I say? I have a one-track mind." I joked, and he cackled on impact.

He bit his lip, sighing out all the stress from his shoulders. I'd never seen him so tall.

"Ask me," he instructed.

I took a deep breath and asked him. "Isaac Haas, would you have sex with me?"

He stepped up close, losing his hands in my hair. "I would've skipped the reception just to have a moment alone with you."

V

I NEEDED TO GET over Isaac Haas. I needed to stop thinking about his hands and how they brushed across my body as if I were too delicate to touch. I needed to make him human and say goodbye so I could finally be at peace, knowing I experienced every ounce of what our story had in store. I needed closure, and I needed to mourn our ending. But seeing him in my apartment left me so hollow. I braced myself along the walls to accept he was real, not an apparition, gone tomorrow like the breeze fluttering through the curtains. He was real, but he was temporary.

We finally arrived at my apartment at six in the morning. We held hands during the hour-long Uber ride back down to Miami, neither one of us inclined to breaking the silence. When I invited him into my bedroom, he stood quietly near the doorway, staring at the scene surrounding him like it was something precious he did not want to disrupt. I sat on the bed, thinking he would join me, but he didn't.

Instead, Isaac swept through the room, checking out my books, my closet, and the stuffed animals I kept stashed on the top shelf for no one to see. He pulled out the bear I had had since I was a little girl. It was missing an eye, but I loved it. He gently pet its purple fur like a holy relic. Instead of putting it back in the closet, he placed it right on the desk facing the wall.

"Don't want to rob it of its innocence," he whispered, covering the bear's eyes with a scarf off the top shelf of my closet. He stood by my vanity, back pressed against the surface as he undressed me with his eyes, lips parted, and tongue tracing the outline of his teeth. "Samaya, we don't have to do this."

"I know." I nodded as I unzipped the length of my dress, discarding it on the floor.

Isaac started pacing, lips trembling and his hands raging through his hair.

"Do you not want to?" I asked, and he stopped short.

"Of course I do," he trembled, his eyebrows threading as he held his hands in prayer. "I just don't want to leave this place, and you have a certain set of expectations from me that I can't fulfill. I want this. I want you to like us like this. But I can't risk you being angry with me again."

"I have no expectations of you." I shook my head slowly, voice an octave lower than normal.

"Please, Samaya, don't say it like that."

"I don't know what you want me to say, Isaac. You want me to be the girl waiting in the wings while you fly around the world."

"I don't want that."

"You want my time, Isaac. That's one expectation of me I will not give. It's just you and me. It's just now." I promised, my voice soft, but he was shaking his head.

He walked over to me, but I did not get up. He spread his legs on either side of my lap, towering over me with a soft expression. His hands wedged their way into my hair again, removing any clips so that it sat loose around my shoulders. He lifted my chin so that I stared up at him.

"No, I want more than now, Samaya. I want my flights to have you on them. I want to make this work." He settled onto the side of my bed, Adam's apple bobbing, and skin covered in goosebumps. "And I never want to see you at another wedding with someone who's not me."

I pulled him close beside me. His stubble scraped across the back of my fingertips, and he melted into my touch, pushing me to hold him closer.

"I'm nervous." He admitted, and I smiled, pressing my lips against his. His jacket slipped easily from his shoulders as his chest pressed tight against mine. This kiss wasn't kind; it was starving.

My hands explored the length of his body before he stopped me with a soft hand on the wrist. I pulled away with a start, a mischievous smile cutting across my face. He smirked, shaking his head, and came to kneel between my legs. I stripped off his shirt until there was nothing but his bare chest beneath my fingertips. He pulled me to my feet, and ever so slowly, his fingers found the clasp of my bra.

"May I?" He asked.

"Yes," I allowed.

He let it drop to the floor, pulled back, and stared at me in a way that made me feel like a painting. I wanted him to stare at me like that for the rest of time. But I knew I'd survive if he couldn't.

"You're so beautiful," he promised, his lips trembling as they hovered across my neck, my chest, and lower and lower until his head pressed firm against the soft skin of my belly. My head fell against the pillow, and it felt so easy to let him explore my body. My fingers twisted into the sides of the bedding as his twisted inside of me. I suppressed a moan pressed deep against my pillowcase.

I could die from this, I thought.

I had to pull him toward me, his eyes locking into mine as he stripped off his pants and pressed inside of me. Our lips parted at the same time, hips moving at a natural rhythm. He wiped a tear off my cheek, and I pressed a kiss to the inside of his palm. I moaned, smiling like the world was on fire. I had to cover my mouth against his chest to keep from crying out at the release.

Our hands intertwined on the bedding, holding each other in the aftermath of sweat and heavy breathing. He curled tight against my chest while I rubbed soothing circles on his back. It was then that his alarm clock went off. He grabbed it as if cutting it off would give him more time with me. I peered over his shoulder and saw the flight itinerary written across his phone screen. There were tears forming on the sides of his face.

"Time to go," I whispered, brushing his cheek with the back of my hand.

We waited outside my apartment building, him still in formal attire and me wearing a robe over my undergarments. We leaned against each other, foreheads anchoring our bodies into place. Our hands clasped between our stomachs as I ran my fingernails along the length of his arm.

"Question." He cleared his throat, not moving his head from mine. "Would you take me to the next wedding?"

"No. Why would I bring sand to the beach?" I joked, but it sounded more like a cry.

"Ow," he laughed. "I'm just hoping I have time to shower at the hotel before I have to catch this flight." The words came out gargled, his Adam's apple jumping in his throat.

Uber arrived quickly. But Isaac did not move. This was it. The proper goodbye.

"Plans for your day?"

"Chug water for my hangover," I joked. "What about you?"

He searched the air for dramatic effect. "Probably wait by the phone until you call."

"Hmm," I mused, "I have a strict belief that if you want something, you'll make it happen."

"I hope so," he whispered. We hugged. It was long, tight, and I could feel his nose digging into my hair.

"I don't like that frown, honey," he whispered.

I sniffed, shaking off the negative energy, and pulled back to get one last look at him.

"It's just funny," I said.

"What?"

"How people meet." I smiled.

He nodded as if he understood. "Yeah, it is."

I pushed him away, pulling my robe closer around my body.

"Okay, you can kiss me." My shoulders pulled back and my torso twisted in my hips in the same sassy manner he did last night. "Only once. But not on the lips, and never again."

Isaac tilted my head up, pulling me close to his chest as I closed my eyes. But he did not kiss me. Instead, he lowered down on one knee, his hands and nose trailing across every inch of my body until he landed flat on the earth. He looked at me, hands folded in front of him. My heart stopped at the sight of him.

"Samaya Ximena," he breathed, and I took a step back on instinct. But he stopped me with a hand placed at the curve of my thigh. He slid the fabric of my robe and pressed his lips against the scar on my knee. "Have a beautiful life."

He piled into the car, leaning out the window as the cab pulled out of my driveway.

But I didn't see that. Instead, I walked back into my apartment and never looked back.

Acknowledgements

The initial idea for Seven Little Kisses arose on a car ride with my then-boyfriend. We chatted about our past loves and the people we became in the aftermath. Every heartbreak physically, mentally, and spiritually changed me for the next. I am not the same girl writing these acknowledgments as I was sitting in that car all those years ago.

Thank you to the boy who held my hand in the car that day. I hope the sun shines brightly through your window every morning.

Gracias a mi Mami. It is impossible not to write about you. Thank you for liking me just as much as you love me. Thank you for your smile and support and for watching my TikToks across several devices because you want my books to go 'viral.' Thank you for gifting me your eyes and forgiving all my faults. Te amo, Mami.

Thank you to my mother's mother, Rebeca, for being a pillar of beauty, elegance, and femininity. You are the writer of this family, and I cannot wait until the world has your words in its grasp. You raised me to be your best friend, and I never want to imagine life without you by my side.

Thank you to my sister, Scheherazade, my sunshine and protector. You are the sun, and I am the moon. Whenever I feel myself slipping into shadows, you pull me out of the darkness, shining your light. The only person whose opinion of me I care about is yours. Always yours. Thank you for loving me.

Thank you to my DC family for setting time aside from their busy schedules to read through my work and marking it up with footnotes. FOOTNOTES!

"Isaac needs to kiss her knee," Beliz demanded.

Thank you to my dear friend, Beliz, for reading every single draft of *Seven Little Kisses* in all its forms. If the universe aligns and we get to make this story into a motion picture, there is no one I would embark on that journey with than you. So much of what makes Samaya and Lila special reminds me of our friendship. College classmates living together in Los Angeles and now co-owners of our production company, Heartbreaker Films. You are my other half. Isaac and Samaya's final kiss would have looked so different without you.

Thank you to Speedy for making our house a home and for sitting patiently in my bedroom as I read excerpts from this book. Thank you for being so lovely, funny, and supportive of all my secrets. You two are my family, and I am in love with you, ladies!

Sisterhood is looking your friend in the eye and telling her she deserves more, even if it means walking away from her dreams. Thank you to my New Jersey guardian angel, Dominique, for reading my contracts and rewriting emails when I did not know how to stand up for myself. Watching you marry the love of your life makes me believe in happy endings. You are so beautiful, funny, and warm. Thank you for moving to Florida, holding me on bathroom floors, and teaching me the true meaning of friendship.

Thank you to my Found Family, my sisters, and the girls that I genuinely think I manifested throughout my lifetime. Stacey, Maggie, Hannah, Kaven, and Amber. I love you. Deeply love you. When you hurt, I hurt, and when you succeed, I feel a rush of happiness I didn't know was possible. It just feels so right when we're together. To think we only met each other because we decided to download an app, read silly fairy books, and talk to this beautiful bombshell named Maggie about our upcoming novels. What a wild ride. I want to buy land and live near you all like a coven of witches straight out of *Practical Magic*. Thank you for making me feel so safe. I am most myself when I am with you. I can't wait to introduce you all to my future French babies.

Thank you, Selina, editor extraordinaire, for keeping this story in a single POV and supporting the ending. I almost changed it out of fear, but you understood this story better than me. Thank you to my editor, Paige, and formatter, Patrick, for making my dreams a reality.

And most importantly, I want to take a moment to thank BookTok and the entire #LiteraryLibraBookClub for transforming my life into what it is now. We met in 2020 when I felt my life falling apart with no idea how to fix it. You made me feel beautiful when I felt most uncomfortable in my skin. You became my friend when I read fantasy books in my bathtub and made me feel like my voice mattered when I felt most alone. But more than anything, BookTok held my hand when I spoke my greatest secret aloud.

"I want to write books," I said.

"We want to read them!" You responded.

No gratitude can equal the books I have received, the letters I have exchanged with readers across the globe, and the friendships I made along the way. Thank you. Please know that I count my blessings every night.

You, dear reader, are the greatest blessing yet.

Samantha Ferrand: Author Biography

Samantha Ferrand is a Peruvian American writer and filmmaker. In 2020, she turned to BookTok as a form of escape and found her life forever changed when she created the #literarylibrabookclub. Through her alter ego LiteraryLibra, Samantha was featured in Forbes, invited to speak at Barnes & Nobles, and had the privilege of interviewing New York Times best-selling authors such as Holly Black & VE Schwab. As a director, Samatha's films have won several awards in Directing, Cinematography, Production Design, and Performance and played in festivals worldwide, including the Vienna International Film Festival and Hollywood IWAA International Film Festival.

Seven Little Kisses is her debut novel.

www.ingramcontent.com/pod-product-compliance
Lightning Source LLC
Chambersburg PA
CBHW072107300726
48975CB00003B/744